R100

A percentage of the proceeds of this book will be
donated to the D'Kar Cultural Centre.

Copyright © 2000 Willemien le Roux c/o Kwela Books
28 Wale Street, Cape Town 8001;
P.O. Box 6525, Roggebaai 8012

The wax etching on the cover, *Storks Eating Corn Crickets*, by Gamnqoa Kukama,
and the details from *Woman, Bird and Worm*, by Coex'ae Bob, used inside the book,
are reproduced with the kind permission of the artists and
the Kuru Development Trust of Ghanzi, Botswana.

All rights reserved.
No part of this book may be reproduced or transmitted
in any form or by any means, electronic, electrostatic, magnetic tape or
mechanical, including photocopying, recording,
or by any information storage and retrieval system,
without written permission of the publisher.

Cover design and typography by Nazli Jacobs
Set in 10 on 13pt Photina
Printed and bound by Paarl Print
Drukkery Street, Cape Town, South Africa
First edition, second printing 2002

ISBN 0-7957-0108-X

This book is dedicated to my parents, Dirk and Pollie Jerling, who had walked this way ahead of me, in acknowledgement of their faith, perseverance, and unconditional love for all people.

Thank you to those who held my hand through the sometimes very painful process of writing this book: Braam, Sue Armstrong, James Suzman, Pierre and Avrille du Plessis, Magdalena Brörmann and Catharina Scheepers.

Thanks, too, to my publisher, Annari van der Merwe, who did not spare me and helped me grow.

# Contents

Guide to the pronunciation of the click
   symbols in Naro    8

ONE: Ja, Baas    9
TWO: D'Kar    19
THREE: Oom Jimmy    27
FOUR: Embers in the Milky Way    45
FIVE: A dog's life    54
SIX: Killer child    64
SEVEN: What's in a name?    77
EIGHT: Girls    85
NINE: Boys    91
TEN: Milk and money    105
ELEVEN: Red skin    118
TWELVE: Two letters    131
THIRTEEN: The teacher    144
FOURTEEN: Shadow bird    155
FIFTEEN: Dumbstruck    165
SIXTEEN: The plastic wreaths    172
SEVENTEEN: Someone's war    182

Note to my Ncoakhoe and other
   friends in Ghanzi    191

About the author    192

## GUIDE TO THE PRONUNCIATION OF THE CLICK SYMBOLS IN NARO[*]

c (/)   dental click: tip of the tongue is pressed against the front teeth and quickly withdrawn.

tc (≠)  alveolar-palatal click: tip of tongue is pressed against the alveolar ridge and adjacent palate, then released sharply downwards.

q (!)   palatal click: tongue is pressed against the upper palate and released sharply downwards, something like when a cork is pulled from a bottle.

x (//)  lateral click: click sound produced at the side of the tongue when tongue is held pressed against the palate.

The more commonly used IPA symbols are given in brackets.

[*] The orthography for the Naro language in Botswana has been developed by the Naro Language Team in D'Kar, under the leadership of Hessel and Coby Visser from the Christian Reformed Churches in the Netherlands.

ONE

# Ja, Baas

The snake is still inside the stove. I can hear its gliding movements from time to time. As long as I know it is there, things are under control. I am reassured by the sound of its scales scraping against the sides of the oven walls. As long as it does not escape. It is definitely a cobra. I saw it come in; as it slid next to the wall, the bands under its neck were clearly visible. It started to lift its head when it saw me, and then disappeared under the stove. It was huge, thick and brown.

At the moment I feel no fear. Mmapula is playing in the sand just outside the kitchen door. As long as she stays there and the snake remains in the stove, everything will be fine. Her chubby legs are covered in dust; she and her little friends from the village have been building roads and farms in the sand all day long. There is a dark ring of dirt around her mouth from nibbling on the titbits I have been feeding her since her friends left, to keep her from wandering out of my sight. Her blonde crop is ruffled at the back, a dry mass of tangles – the effect of the dust and dry Kalahari air on my children's fine hair. From my chair in the corner of the kitchen I keep my eyes on both her and the area around the stove, to see that the snake does not escape. The pile of toys, half-eaten apples and cookies, spoons and cups around her tell the tale of my efforts at managing the situation. Mmapula – Mother of the Rain, I say softly to myself. The name the villagers had given her, because on the day she was born at the health post in Ghanzi, there was a sudden rainstorm, an unusual occurrence in mid-winter in the desert.

She carefully tries to push a long, white acacia thorn into some dried donkey dung buns, as her friends had taught her earlier. Next to her, in a miniature kraal made with sticks stuck into the sand, a few of these black dung cows with their white acacia horns and legs are still standing.

Other signs of the farm they were building in the sand all afternoon are visible as well, but her clumsy movements have flattened the meticulously built stick-fences of most of the little paddocks, the fields carefully ploughed by tiny fingers and the little cardboard house ringed with wilted flowers. I have lost all sense of time. How long has it been? I refrain from thinking about it too deeply, to suppress the hysteria that I feel just below the surface of my mind.

From time to time Mmapula tires of what she is doing, gets up and waddles off in some direction. I have to yell after her and coax her back with something new from the kitchen. Something between a sob and a giggle escapes my throat when I try to talk to her: "Look here, love, scoop up some sand with this nice, red cup and pour it into the orange one. The sand will run through these holes, you see?"

The last thing I can allow to happen is that she wanders over to the people outside.

"The snake still there, Mommy? It will kill us, Mommy?" Her eyes are large with conspiracy and adventure. If only the older two were here I could have sent for help. At moments like these the pain of their absence and the guilt of having had to send them to boarding-school surface nauseatingly, sending shivers through me.

Each one of us are fighting snakes, my babies; each one in his or her own way. But we will conquer them all, you will see. I say these words softly, imagining the wind carrying my thoughts to our other children on the scrap of cloud floating in the sky outside the door.

It is getting dark quickly. I have my torch ready on my lap, but if I have to go out to fill the lamps with paraffin, the snake might slip deeper into the house and in the darkness we will not know where it is.

Why does Braam not come home! He will have to, eventually. When it gets too dark, they will disperse. Luckily there is no moon tonight. I can hear the voices, but I have to get up and stand at the kitchen door to see them. Before the snake came, I occasionally went closer, trying to catch what they were saying from a distance. They were just outside our yard fence, silhouetted against the afternoon light. Earlier, when Braam saw the fighting outside and went out to investigate, the sun was still high in the sky. When he did not return, I saw that he had ended up right in the middle of the wrestling and tugging group of people, his tall shape clearly towering above them. The young black guy with the Rastafarian hairstyle also stood out. His name is not known to me. The others are all villagers, all Bushmen. Some were squatting on the sand, others standing around. I smiled. They too had their little group of children, playing a few yards away in the sand, seemingly oblivious of the tension between the grown-ups.

Once I walked as far as the woodpile near the yard fence and watched, leaning against the big leadwood tree growing next to our house, an old farmhouse with a thatch roof. The highway to the north passes right in front of our house, but the road has been quiet all day. A few women and children were walking home with buckets of water on their heads, balancing them with one arm. In the late afternoon sun the round grass huts of the Bushmen, and the Herero and Tswana people's sturdier, rectangular clay structures with their flat, corrugated iron roofs, had become indistinguishable from each other. A dusty haze, tinted red by the retreating rays of the sun, enveloped every home. Because the land is so flat, I could see the horizon all around me. Between the huts the ground was more or less bare, but the last rows of huts seemed to melt into the bush behind them. Greenish, endless bush of even height, stretching as far as one could see over the dull red sand. Hardly any trees, just bush and shrub kilometre after kilometre.

Bushmen. I played with the name on my tongue. Or "red people", as they call themselves. Are they referring to the colour of their skin, or does the name indicate their closeness to the red soil on which they had lived before anyone else?

"I do not mind if they call me a Bushman," Komtsha had once said to us. "It shows that the bush belongs to us; it shows that we are the ones who truly come from here."

I stood there for quite a while. Vaguely aware of Mmapula and her friends building their little farm behind me. I did not want to aggravate the obviously tense situation by joining or distracting the group. There were no other women around anyway. I could hear Braam: "How dare you do this? We're trying to help these people make a living. You're not even part of the group! What have we done to you?"

"You!" the Rasta shouted. "How can you accuse me? What have you *not* done to my people? Who are you? You are an oppressor! You do not belong in Africa. Give me back the land you have stolen from my people!"

"What land? What have I done? Tell me."

"Your forefathers took the land from my ancestors! If it wasn't for *you*, the whole of Johannesburg would've been mine! Now you dare come here and pretend to help the poor Basarwa!"

"I don't understand how my forefathers could have taken your land. Apartheid and Johannesburg are in South Africa, not here. This is your land. You've always been in Botswana." Braam paused. "If I or anyone of my people have hurt you, I apologise, but I do not see what the problems of black people in another country have got to do with these people here, now, who are trying to do something for themselves."

The young man looked like he was going to go off his head. He lashed out hysterically at Braam who grabbed him by the wrists and held the kicking and wriggling young man in front of him. Some of the other men were hanging around the Rasta's waist, restraining him.

"You whites, I hate you! You think you know everything, but I'll kill you! You will see, I'll go for the weak ones, for the old people. I'll make them die slowly. I'll kill your wife. I'll rape her when you're away!"

Although he was breathless, the words shot out crystal clear. There was no mistaking what he said. I couldn't see his face, but I could imagine the bloodshot eyes and the saliva on his lips. I could feel his hatred, imagine his hot breath on Braam's face.

This is our third year here. We have just started to feel that we are beginning to understand what it means to live here, in this large, unstructured and mixed community of people who mostly have no other refuge. The majority of them, but the Bushmen in particular, are desperately clinging to life, despite the most shocking poverty we've ever seen. Since we started the income-generating projects, we have begun to feel that we may be able to make a difference.

And now this. While I tried to move away unseen, my heart was beating against my ribs. I could still hear Braam's calm, but now icy voice: "I am sorry that you hate me so. I apologise for what has happened in your life to make you so bitter. I do not know what my people have done to you, but still I am sorry. Can we not start over ..."

The trouble started yesterday afternoon. Although, to be honest, something has been brewing for a while now. The one or two projects we started after the first year we came are by now so well established that we have been able to organise working groups and allocate working space. The sewing group and the leather workers each have a storage room in the outbuildings of the old farmhouse, a place where they can store their materials and lock up their machines. Lately our own house is surrounded by the commotion all day, with everybody's children playing in our garden while their parents are occupied with making patchwork dresses, saddles, shoes and harnesses. The people working on the projects actually prefer to sit and work under the tall bluegum trees in our yard, but we felt that special working rooms would be a source of pride and give substance and visibility to their work.

In the beginning, when we first arrived at D'Kar, people used to come to the back door, where they would take off their hats and insist on calling Braam "Baas". Now, at least, the old farmyard is everybody's space. On the stoep, under the bronze bougainvillaea that crawls up the side of the house, pieces of cloth and sewing-pattern parts lie on the table, and in the one corner of the garden a huge old cast-iron pot is constantly brewing sweet, strong tea for everyone. On the kitchen floor my baby often falls asleep next to Dina's grandchild, while on the stoep she and I bend over long, colourful sheets of material, draped over the table to cut the patterns for the women sitting next to their hand sewing-machines on the floor.

We chose an inspiring name for the projects: Kuru, which in Naro means "to do". And after struggling at first to get the idea off the ground, we began to organise meetings of all the participants, to keep minutes, make weekly joint decisions. We were all in it together. Somehow the feeling that nothing could stop us had begun to grow.

Now, here on my snake watch, I think how naïve we have been. Others have tried before us – why did we believe that our efforts would succeed where theirs had failed? What made us think that this time it would be different, that the groups would not break up after a few months and start quarrelling about whom took what from whom? How many of the white farmers, who live around here on large cattle ranches, some for almost a century, had not warned us when we moved in: "These people just do not have it in them to adjust to a different lifestyle. They are not able to do anything for longer than three months at a stretch. You are wasting your time. They will all walk out on you and go back to the bush."

How well I remember the words of Oom Fanus, one of the oldest settlers, and our nearest white neighbour. Tanned and brown as a well-

13

used leather bag, he sat on our stoep one day, smoking his pipe and listening to all our excited plans. He was returning from his monthly visit to the bank and the post office in Ghanzi, and D'Kar was a good place to break the two-hour journey on the potholed gravel road with the more than twenty gates to open and close between Ghanzi and his farm. He drew on his pipe and shook his head. "They are not aggressive, but they are stubborn. You will be under the impression that they are doing what you agreed, but in the meantime they are digging the sand from under your feet, undermining you so slowly that you do not realise it, until you topple over ..."

Our first project, a communal garden, failed so miserably that the memories are still painful, even now. With so much enthusiasm we joined the group each late afternoon, Braam and I both digging away at our own patches, encouraging and explaining all the while: "This is how you take out the quick grass, otherwise it will strangle the roots of your vegetables. This is how you make mulch and spread it so the sun will not dry out the ground and your tomatoes will have moisture ..."

As the group that joined our first project slowly diminished, day by day, we tried to get to the bottom of the problem. Surely they could see the benefits? They had some food, and it must mean something because the veldkos on the farm was almost depleted. People were walking home in the evenings with peppers and carrots. Why then were they deserting their plots and leaving us to dig at ours like fools? Why did they keep on coming to our back door to ask for food while we were taking such pains to show them how to grow their own?

It was one of Oom Jimmy's sons who explained it to us. He often had to explain things to us, because his father is an Afrikaner and his mother a Bushman. Like all Oom Jimmy's children, Tshabu is tall and light-skinned and speaks all the languages of the area, and in the beginning he had to translate not only language but also the deeper meaning of events to us. "Don't you see?" he said. "They are all constantly stealing from each other's plots and they know there will be nothing to harvest in the end. That's why they do not want to continue."

"But they do not steal from our plots! We have plenty of vegetables."

Patiently: "Yes, they know you will find out and they think you will punish them. They are still afraid of the Boers."

Then, early one Sunday morning, there she was, the demented old woman who always came by for scraps and "brou" – leftover tea. She lived on her own, and as far as we could find out, had nobody in the village to care for her. Most days she would come around, so I got into the habit of keeping a plate of leftovers for her.

I looked up from where I was stirring some batter in the kitchen. Braam had gone off to church already to conduct Sunday school, and I was preparing a baked pudding for a Sunday treat. Old Agu was bending over in the garden. At first I thought she was picking vegetables. Intrigued, I took a closer look. I saw she had a knife and she was wildly slashing away at the watermelons, some still half-ripe! One by one she was ripping open our prize product, the biggest achievement yet of our work, disrespectfully stepping on the vines we had so carefully cultivated. The pink flesh of the watermelons lay exposed, the proud fruits ruined and soiled with sand.

We had planned to wait until more fruit had ripened, then to have a feast with all the gardeners. We wanted everyone to share the watermelons, which we knew would be the ultimate treat, while we discussed the future of the gardening project. It seemed like such a good idea, showing with the crop from our own plots that success *was* possible, even though we would be discussing the reasons for the failure of their crops.

I called out to Agu, but she ignored me. It was as if a door slammed in my mind. I flew out of the kitchen door, the wooden spoon still in my hand. With both hands I pressed down the barbed wires of the fence, catching and ripping my Sunday dress as I slid through. I dashed over and with the wooden spoon started beating the old woman as if she was a naughty child. As I pulled her away from the fruit, I brought the spoon down hard on her ample behind. "How dare you, Agu! Come away! It's not yours!" I cried, pushing the mumbling old woman out of the gate, leaving the broken pieces of fruit lying there.

When we came back after church, they were all gone.

Now, it is the workshops. Yesterday afternoon this Rasta guy came to the Kuru buildings next to the old farmhouse and, with his kierie, broke all the window-panes. People saw him doing it. He was drunk, they said; he usually is. He might even be drunk now, as he confronts Braam in the failing light, but he seems perfectly lucid. He must have known what he was doing, yesterday. He could not be stopped! One of the project people who passed in the road tried to pull him away. Others, too, tried to hold him back, but he kept breaking loose and dashing back, smashing the glass, shouting curses. They say he is a University of Gaborone drop-out who returned to D'Kar some months ago. What could he be thinking? What motivates him, makes him hate so much?

I know where he lives, although I have not had much to do with the small group of Kgalagadi people with whom he stays. These people, coming from a minor tribe of the Batswana, keep together and have built a little cluster of clay huts near the main road. They say the old woman, who is clearly the matriarch of the little clan, is the Rasta's mother. She has always been quite polite, even friendly to me when we come across each other in the village, but she never comes to church, neither has she ever attended any of our meetings with the villagers. She and her group seem to be self-contained. I was amazed at the size of their goat herd when one of the young herders opened the pen rather late one morning and the goats came trotting out to find grazing as I drove past.

Mmapula has finally fallen asleep on my lap. She is still unwashed; her limp body is getting cold. I have covered her with a kitchen towel and shield her body with my arms. It is dark now, save for the small candle I managed to find in a drawer. I dare not leave the room. Occasionally I still hear the snake, its scales making a lazy scraping sound on the metal. Every now and then I shine the torch along the skirting-board to make sure it hasn't abandoned the stove. If only I could light the gas oven and roast the creature to charcoal! But I dare not open the oven door. With an effort I suppress the tears, swallowing down the choking feeling in my throat. Be brave now, you knew you were not going to have it easy when you agreed to come to this far-flung part of Botswana, I tell myself.

But let's face it, I quietly add in defence of the threatening tears, very often things have been harder than you had ever imagined. Making sense of it all has in fact been the most difficult part of living here. Why do people say that they need you and yet keep you at a distance? Why do they co-operate as if they agree, only to let you find yourself alone later, without any explanation?

Footsteps outside. It is Braam, but he is being supported by Kelebetse and Komtsha, both of them church elders. Tears stream down his face, tracing little furrows in the dust on his cheeks. He covers his eyes with his one hand. Quietly I lay the sleeping child on the kitchen table and pull the hand from his face. By the light of the torch I see that his eyes are filled with sand which clogs around the edges and clings to the lashes. At my request the two elders shine the torch underneath the stove to find the snake, while I lead my stumbling, blinded husband through the dark house to the bathroom.

It is deep into the night. We are both awake, have been for hours. In the dim light I watch Braam looking at the bright Southern Cross that hangs low on the horizon, outside our window. Occasionally he reaches out and puts drops in his eyes. Earlier I placed a jar of ice-water next to him in which to soak cotton-wool swabs. He is to cover his eyes with these when the pain becomes too much. We have managed to wash out most of the sand, but both eyes were left red and swollen. The corneas might be scratched, if not worse. The nearest doctor who would be able to tell lives hours away.

An owl screeches. An eerie, almost human sound. I can see the bird's shadow against the night sky as it flits past the window. It is easy to imagine why this sound has been associated with a departing soul leaving earth.

Will the owl eat the snake in the acacia tree in the yard outside, I wonder. The broken body hangs draped over the lowest branch.

The first moments after the young man had shot two handfuls of sand into his face, Braam said earlier, were of utter darkness, pierced by sharp, white pain. He was crawling on all fours to get away from the circle of people until the two elders helped him up and brought him home. What had become of the young man he did not know.

At first, after the elders had left us, we were both quiet. We ate our supper in silence. Afterwards I concentrated on the evening chores, while Braam lay on the sofa with his eyes covered. Only after we had got into the bath together, revelling in the hot steam, did we start talking. We came to bed early and holding on to each other, we continued to talk until we were both exhausted.

No clarity, no relief came.

I fell asleep with my cheek against Braam's shoulder, listening to his heartbeat. We should have known, we had concluded earlier. What did we expect, we asked each other. That what we tried to do here would erase the rift of centuries between our kind and the other people of Africa? This continent was our only home, it was our mother as much as any one else's, but tonight it felt as if the true home-coming would elude us for ever.

Something must have woken me. What was that sound? Braam is also awake. He leans upon his elbows. There it is again, a shuffling noise outside. The dog starts barking. Someone is shaking our fence.
"Ja, Baas!"
A few moments of deadly silence. Then, louder, at the top of his voice, almost screeching: "Ja, Baas! Ja, Baas!" The fence rattles.
"Ja, Baaaaaaaas ...!"
We shiver with shock. We sit up, trying to see who it could be. We can make out a man's dark shape, leaning against the fence.
The dog goes mad.
"Just be very quiet," Braam says. "It is him."
We cling to each other, hearts beating in our ears. A century passes. He slowly moves away, staggering.
"Ja, Baas ...! Ja ... Baas!" The voice chokes and breaks off. As he leaves, he shouts it over his shoulder a few more times. Then the figure disappears in the darkness, the voice growing fainter and fainter in the night.

TWO
# D'Kar

Almost nothing has remained of her. As if her body has gone back to childhood again. As he looked down on the shrivelled little form curled up on the floor, he thought of the many children that were born from that same body, when it was still a full, lively figure with a round bottom and an air of challenge.

They had called him a couple of months ago, when she had first stopped eating. He and she had sat talking inside her half-dark hut, where she had withdrawn from the pressure of family and friends.

"I just don't feel like eating, Moruti," she had said. "You must just let me be."

It had continued for weeks. All they could get her to swallow was water and occasionally some milk. Together with her family, he had tried to find the root of her anger or resentment or what ever it was that had made her stop eating. After more than a month, he urged the clinic to do something. Afterwards they told him that she had cried bitterly when the psychiatric nurse came to fetch her. They had had to give her an injection to calm her down.

They would have to bury her fairly soon, he thought. The family had waited so long for her to die that they did not want to take her to the mortuary and thereby postpone the funeral. Her sons had already started digging the grave. In this heat, the corpse would go bad quickly.

He looked up in the sky. It was a typical September day. The sky was a dome of grey dust while the continuous gushing of the wind from the east had created little ridges, like miniature dunes, on the bare ground all around. When he closed his mouth sand gritted under his teeth. Every day was scorching hot, yet the landscape was still as barren as in midwinter. This was the one month when it was clear why this area was called a desert, he thought, even though it was usually completely covered with vegetation. The naked trees and thorn bushes were hanging on in the hot sand, barely surviving, waiting for the first rains which usually arrived only in midsummer.

They had all done what they could, but old Sophie did not want to live any longer. He understood her desire to die, yet as pastor he did what was expected of him. So when he had visited her in the mental hospital in Lobatse, some seven hundred kilometres away, he felt that he had betrayed her by asking the clinic in D'Kar to move her there. She was eating again, the staff in Lobatse told him. And she talked to him, but he was not sure that she recognised him. She was heavily sedated. With eyes looking beyond him, she spoke in an incoherent way. He could make out something about the veld and animals, however, and one sentence stayed with him afterwards since it came up a few times during his visit: "Our place. It is our place."

She did not mean the hospital. She could hardly have known that she was there. And she could not have referred to her shack in D'Kar either; it was too scraggy to evoke such passion. The settlement, D'Kar, too, was small and too overcrowded for her to want to lay claim to it. Which place was she referring to, then? In many ways, he thought, D'Kar could not even be called a place. To most passers-by it was just a loose collection of mud houses and scraggy Bushman huts that suddenly materialised alongside the main road. It had a temporary, unfinished look, and in a way it had always been exactly that. On his visits to the village, the thought often struck him that the place, the people and even its many dogs shared the same character – an air of insecurity and self-consciousness, as if they were ready to slink away at any moment. Yet the place, like its inhabitants, displayed a stubborn resilience and a surprising independence.

Throughout D'Kar's history its existence had been controversial, for it always seemed to be hanging in the balance of time, or of ownership. The government of Botswana did not want to acknowledge it, since a village on a farm contradicted all district development planning. Yet this overpopulated, unwanted little settlement in the middle of nowhere, surrounded by vast cattle ranches and the great sand-sea of the Kalahari, not only remained, but expanded.

Whose place was it really? Sophie and her people were not the only ones who lay claim to it. So many people had strong feelings as to why the place should be theirs, that it ended up not clearly belonging to anyone. Maybe that explained something of the uncomfortable and knotted human relationships, he mused. This place could not give an identity to its inhabitants because it was struggling to find its own.

In fact, the name of the place was shrouded in as much mystery as its ownership. Although the Bushmen had their own name for the area, Dtcoaga, the first settlers from the south had found four letters carved on a tree, which grew into the name adopted by most groups, each distorting it according to their own linguistic pattern: D'Kar, Dekar, Dikara. The origin of the name still had not been clarified. The four letters did not make sense in any language, nor were they recognisably the name of a particular person.

Who carved those letters and what did they mean? Were they the initials of an explorer, a hunter, an escaped convict? A word in a foreign language, the name of a slave trader perhaps? These random letters, devoid of apparent meaning, symbolised the ambiguity which had dogged the place for more than a hundred years. It was like a curse the place could not shake off.

The first white settlers who moved into the area chose pans and springs as watering points for their cattle, and as places suitable to build their first homes. D'Kar was such a place. These first settlers, a group of close to fifty families who had trekked for longer than a year from their native Marico country in the old Transvaal Republic, were looking for new grazing for their cattle, but they were also trying to find peace from interference. They moved away because the British had already established a strong presence in their neighbouring town of Mafikeng, and they were starting to feel the pinch of the government taxes. Here, across the border, they didn't need to fret about the rumours of yet another war, or about more trekkers approaching from the south, with whom they would soon have to share their land in the Marico.

And they thought the new land they moved into was empty. How much did old Sophie and her children know about what had happened to squeeze them into this undesirable little corner of an area they had had all to themselves before? They would not have known that Cecil John Rhodes, probably the most energetic of all British imperialists, had promised the Ghanzi area of the Kalahari to the Transvaal Boers, because he was nervous of the intentions of the German settlers in the

21

former German West Africa. The man obviously thought that if he put a barrier of rugged Boers between the Germans and his beloved South Rhodesia, the threat of expansion and war would be less. Any power wishing to expand to the east would move through Ghanzi, because unlike the rest of the arid Kalahari Desert, here water was trapped by the limestone ridges not far below the surface of the sand. The area was known to all the Bushmen, as well as foreign hunters and explorers alike, as a good place to linger and replenish yourself, sometimes for a few months.

Of the original group of white families who came in 1889, only one remained behind in D'Kar when the others became disillusioned and returned to the Marico. In what must have been a harsh wilderness, one man settled with his young wife and children. To reach other white people would have taken them more than thirty days by ox-wagon. Only small bands of Bushmen roamed the area, in their unpredictable sort of way. It might even have been Sophie's family who had lived at the D'Kar Pan when the small white family arrived and they suddenly had to share their land.

But he could also understand why the white farmers around D'Kar felt such a sense of ownership towards the place. Where once the voorhuis and kombuis had stood, the ruins of the first trekker homestead were still visible in the tumbled mounds of clay bricks. Of the stoep only three steps were left, leading nowhere. The neatly chiselled stones on which the farmer would once have stood watching the sun rise or set on the far horizons of his land, had been carried off one by one to the shacks of the people who had started to build more permanent homes in the village.

Slowly, the infrastructure of the farm, built up over more than ninety years, had crumbled away from lack of care. The once abundant orchards were reclaimed by the bush, some of the trees now just dry, goat-eaten stumps. The fences had collapsed and the outhouses had become derelict. A few exotic trees from the north, planted by the first settlers, still grew around the place, their survival a small triumph in the harsh climate: a mopane, a baobab, a marula and a cluster of date palms, the only surviving signs of former ownership by Afrikaner farmers who saw D'Kar as one of "their" places. That was, until the Namibian branch of the church many of them belonged to, bought the farm and handed it to the undeserving Bushmen. Many of them felt deeply betrayed. Imagine, now the place belonged to a Bushman church! And the irony was that when the Namibian Mission Church decided to withdraw, they built, as a parting gesture, a church in D'Kar that was bigger, stronger and more visible than anything the farmers had ever had themselves.

It could not have been the neglect of the old farmyards that troubled Sophie, he thought. The present inhabitants of D'Kar seemed unmoved by the decay. The only people who noticed seemed to be the white farmers who drove past with resentful stares, and who sometimes stopped at the house of the Kgosi, the local Tswana chief, to report their suspicions about possible cattle thieves hiding in the village. The Kgosi was a man from the south, posted here by the government.

Now, as he walked past the church building and the pump and followed the winding footpath through the huts, he thought that the further irony about this place, which so many people claimed as their own and still associated with their history, was that it wasn't attractive by anyone's standards. It had no features that would have stopped the first traveller in his tracks to exclaim: "Ah, this is where I would want to live."

Yet this small "farm" surrounded by the vast cattle ranches of northwestern Botswana is called home even by himself and his family. And the landscape was starting to grow on him, he had to admit. There were many beautiful spots on the limestone ridge running in the centre of the Kalahari where the farms were established. Lovely big leadwood trees grew at some of the pans which turned into shiny lakes during the rainy season; on others, rolling grassy plains reached as far as the eye could see. Because you knew that all the beauty would soon disappear, soaked up by the hot sand and the blinding sun, for months and months on end, and sometimes even years, until the rains came again, you treasured it more.

But D'Kar, especially the patch on which the settlement had developed, had no such spots. It was just an endless stretch of untidy shrubs. Thorny, unfriendly shrubs without distinctive leaves or shape, growing just high enough to prevent one from getting a proper perspective, a real sense of where the landscape began and ended. The ground was scattered with limestone, white blotches on the dull red sand.

He smiled at the irony of Sophie being willing to die for a place his family had had so much trouble accepting as theirs. In the beginning especially his wife had displayed a deep and irrational fear of the elements over which you had no control; the white sun that scorched you from above while its glare blinded and burnt you from below as it reflected on the limestone and sand. Pests which would suddenly appear and rule your life for an unknown period before they would make place for the next horror creature to penetrate your existence. In the rainy season it was impossible to read at night, or to have a light outside, because of the red-neck bugs which would crawl all over you and leave you with festering blisters.

Then, after the rains had turned the parched sand into a verdant greenness which you would never had believed possible, the corn crickets would appear in their millions, devouring every green blade, filling your footpaths, your garden, every bush in sight. Their heavy-set, prehistoric bodies not only pierced your skin with their thorny, tank-like armour, but they squirted a foul yellow liquid onto your hand if you dared try to move them away. The worst was that they devoured their own injured and dead mates, and would scream in annoyance if you attempted to scoop such a heap of wriggling, chewing cannibals and their dead brothers out of your way.

Then, when you were tired of walking on the hot sand and wanted to rest in the shade of a tree for a while, dull grey, blood-sucking tampan ticks would crawl from underneath the sand to find you and leave you with horribly itching bumps, and often a fever and headache that would last for days as well.

"Everything here attacks you!" a hitchhiker once exclaimed.

Yet, in the evenings, when the late afternoon light had softened the harsh lines of the bushes and the surprising coolness of the desert nights called you outside to watch the first stars appear in the pale sky, the daily realities softened and the sounds of pleasant chatter and laughter from the village made you forget the complexities of the day. Each evening was like a rebirth.

The same happened when it rained. Within days the whole place would be transformed into a soft, green landscape with a crazy assortment of wild flowers and strange insects coming as if from nowhere. On the wet sand, within minutes after a storm, the little red spider mites with their velvet skin stopped you in your tracks with their bold display of colour in an otherwise monotone landscape. Bright-eyed children collected them in matchboxes and held them walking on their palms. The pans filled up and created shiny lakes which contrasted pleasantly with the white cloud stacks building up to create another late afternoon thunderstorm that would fill the senses with awe and wonder. But even more fascinating were the inhabitants of these pans which seemed to have rained down with the water. Suddenly all kinds of water birds, even fish eagles from far away north, from the Okavango Swamps, would appear to peer down at this wonder.

Massive bullfrogs were suddenly there, appearing overnight, their bellowing voices filling the night and their croaking mouths displaying a dangerous-looking set of bony teeth that kept you at bay. Children sat next to puddles, poking with sticks to make the bullfrogs jump at them. Then, all at the same time, the mating calls of hundreds of these frogs would fill the night and the water would stir with the movement of their round bodies. The next morning, they would all be gone, without a trace.

He should not have interfered when Sophie decided that she no longer wanted to live. After she had returned from Lobatse, she continued eating for about a week before a deep despair gripped her again. Once again she stopped eating. Until her body finally gave up.

Sophie had made her own decision about living or dying. But for so many other people and animals, the land had been the ultimate arbiter of whether they would eat or not. The struggle for water, for survival, was written in the several wells, now dry, their mouths open to the sky; reminders of the terrible dry spells when no surface water could be found anywhere for man or beast. The wells told the story of days and months of chipping at solid limestone; of buckets heavy with chiselled rock heaved up by sweaty arms from a slowly deepening hole in the hard earth; of a desperate search for the elusive substance which had made humans stay here through all these years.

More recently, when boreholes sunk deep into the earth had solved the immediate water problem, D'Kar had become so overpopulated and overgrazed that the desert virtually reclaimed the land during the dry season. When the government tried to discourage the Bushmen from living on the commercial farms by providing alternative settlements on state land with schools, clinics and tapped water, a large number of them resisted going there, and moved to D'Kar instead.

Huts spread like a wild rash across the farm, and gradually a sense of uncaring and anarchy took hold. Garbage started filling the footpaths, plastic bags clung to the bushes and the dilapidated fences along the road; soft-drink and beer cans piled up, especially around the drinking places. On weekend nights gumba-gumba music would rock through the quiet till the early hours of the morning. The next morning senseless bodies could be found lying in the veld, flies buzzing around their half-open mouths. People walked past, knowing the revellers would wake when the heat from the sun penetrated the veil of alcohol.

D'Kar was but a farm and had never pretended to be anything else. The Bushmen Church Council, left in control after the departure of the Mission Church, had no way of dealing with the responsibilities it had inherited along with the land; no money for municipal services; no power to dictate who should be allowed to stay here and who not. The place had therefore become a refuge for people of all origins, individuals who for one reason or another had nowhere else to stay. Some came to D'Kar not to seek refuge but to start businesses, drawn by the opportunity to profit from the income stimulated by the Kuru projects. The many groups lured to the place by these benefits left the Bushmen owners in the awkward position of harbouring and hosting people who were mostly of higher social and economic status than they were. This caused resentment on both sides.

His wife would be relieved to hear that Sophie had at last closed her eyes one final time. Even though they never said so, he knew that Sophie's family shared their relief. While the old woman was alive, peace eluded her. All around her was poverty and disease; developments had come into her world too fast for her to keep up with them. D'Kar was the last piece of the land of her childhood on which she could still walk freely and which did not belong to someone else. But it had changed so much in front of her very eyes that it could no longer give her the refuge she needed.

As he enters his yard, he notices a few black birds circling high above the village on the air currents. As if they are also waiting for something to happen, he thinks. Tomorrow morning they will bury Sophie, and the same earth which had made her give up, will welcome her and embrace her sad little body. One of the many players on the complex but rich and sometimes frightening stage of D'Kar will have finished her role and bowed off. But his part and that of his family must still be played, and maybe it was better that they did not know the script.

THREE

# Oom Jimmy

Around him was light, everything shone white. He knew that he was lying in a bed, everything was soft and white. The light from above blinded him and he shut his eyes against it. But the light remained all around and a feeling of intense relief and joy filled him. So he had made it. It was not the solemn darkness and pain which he had somehow expected. No, he was in the place of light, as he was told when he was little. This was exactly how he had imagined it to be, then. Warm tears of gratitude welled up under his closed eyelids, trickled past his ears and moistened the pillow under his head. Maybe he would see his mother and father now, maybe they would welcome him and say everything was fine, everything was forgiven. He would play with his little sisters under the big tree next to their house again.

Yet something did not feel quite right. The harsh sound of clanging metal broke through his consciousness. He became aware of smells that did not fit here. But he saw no one else, only this bright light. It was as if a hood was gradually being pulled from his mind, as if he was slowly arriving from somewhere. Then, suddenly, everything made sense. He opened his eyes.

The brightness above him came from an electric bulb in a stained, plastic lampshade which hung from the ceiling. He was lying on an iron bed; the bedposts were white, but in places the paint was peeling off. Across the floor stood another bed, and on it lay a very thin black man with all kinds of machines connected to his body. The man was asleep. Oom Jimmy turned his head. Through the gauze frame of the door he could see black women in white dresses moving down the corridor outside the room.

This was not heaven.

It was, however, the first real bed he had slept in since his childhood. But it was not as soft and white as he had first thought it to be. The sheets were marked with the words *Ghanzi Hospital*; the covers were stained with old blood. Around the bed was a railing to keep him from falling out. After a while a nurse opened the door, looked at him and smiled. She called to someone outside.

He saw a little brown hand folded around the door frame and suddenly knew, with joy, who was coming. It was his Ntcisa, with their youngest child on her hip! So, she had been waiting for him. He felt the tears coming again and wiped them away irritably. Yes, it seemed he would have to carry on living.

"You slept a long time," she said simply. "Many days."

She lifted the little one onto the bed. The tiny round figure crawled up against him, its chubby little hands feeling his face. Smooth and somewhat moist, just like a bush-baby's, he thought. He folded his hand round the baby's bare bottom and tickled the child's belly with the other until the little chap chuckled and nestled into the curve of his arm. Ntcisa laughed. "Your other children are coming," she said. "We all waited here, but now they went to the shops to buy porridge and tea. The hospital people said we could camp outside under the tree."

The nurse called her and the child out again. He sighed, fell back on his pillow. He was dead tired. Ntcisa was his fifth wife. She was many years younger than he, a quiet woman in her early thirties. He was going home to her again, he thought, and it was fine. It would turn out all right.

Oom Jimmy stayed home with Ntcisa and their children most days now, because he did not go out to the veld as much as he used to. But he liked being at home, enjoyed watching her struggling to keep the fire burning, raking the yard or playing with the little ones.

These were the times when he liked thinking far back, losing himself on a journey into his own thoughts. His hands might be working on a donkey harness, carving thin leather strips from the tanned hide in his lap, but his mind would be wandering on routes which nobody else could see.

Sometimes he remembered Casa, the woman who opened the door of his life to follow the strange, different route it had taken. How soft and smooth her copper skin had been, how shiny and firm the thighs that shone under her springbok apron and hip cloth! She was always so shy, yet playful. She reminded him of the antelopes he hunted with the friends of his youth who taught him how to stalk the animals until you were so close you could see them blink. As long as you kept downwind. He smiled.

Her eyes were a clear, shiny brown, watching him impassively the way a duiker ewe would when she met his gaze above the tall grass she was chewing peacefully, unaware of the slight hunters with their bows and arrows hiding downwind, just beyond the first trees.

His life was so easy, then. The veld came right to the stoep of his parents' humble trekker house. From a distance you could hardly see the house because it blended in so well with the grassy plains and the leadwood trees. His father had built the house by himself with clay bricks baked in hollows in the ground. To make the bricks, his father looked for the few patches of good, red soil that could be found in this sandy area. Here the soil turned to clay when it rained, ideal stuff for making bricks. He helped his father form the bricks in a four-sided wooden frame and stack them in rows, layer upon layer in the shallow ditch they had dug. Then from a fire built for the purpose, they would take red-hot hardwood coals and distribute them evenly among the rows of bricks, before covering the hollow and leaving the coals to smoulder for many days until the bricks were hard and dried out.

His parents' four-roomed house had a thatched roof. Often he would be sent out to the plains with his friends to collect new grass to fix the leaks that developed every year during the short rainy season. His friends never entered the house but would lie in the shade outside, waiting for him. They seemed to care little about how long he had to stay inside, helping his mother churn the butter or cut strips of biltong from meat brought back from a hunt. His sisters were so small still and his father out on horseback so often, herding cattle which had wandered off to find water, that his mother depended on him for the house chores.

Their farm had no fixed borders. His father had come to some agreement with their one and only neighbour, the nearest white man, who lived more than half a day's journey on horseback from them. With the

Bushmen who had always lived in this area, he also had an arrangement. They did not have permanent homes and seemed to turn up out of the blue, you could never predict when, but you knew they would be back. They appeared to know every nook and cranny, every plant and animal in the area. To him as a young boy, the land seemed limitless.

The Bushmen sometimes helped with herding the cattle, and if he needed their assistance with branding, slaughtering or digging wells, his father would pay for their services with tobacco, sugar or cloth. As long as they tended his cattle, it was agreed, they had free access to the milk, which they loved. The Bushmen enjoyed working with his father's animals. He could remember how grown men would roll in the sand, laughing with each other because an angry cow had chased one of them up the wooden fence, outraged that he had had the nerve to try to separate her from her calf, span her or herd her into a kraal. Later, when he started hunting with his young friends, he realised what a tremendous thrill it must have given these men to get so close to these large animals without having to stalk them, or having to wait, sometimes for days, until they succumbed to the poison of their arrows.

There were few people of their own kind in the area. After the first few years most of the trekkers returned to the Marico. The promises of water, vast grassy plains and empty land were true, but the isolation was too frightening. It took weeks by ox-wagon on mere tracks to replenish stocks. And for more than nine months every year the rains stayed away. The occasional hunter who came through, mostly in search of ivory, would not have much with him and was often more of a burden to the settlers with their scarce supplies than a help. But at least he was a bearer of news from the outside world.

The Bushmen also made many white farmers turn back. What had looked like uninhabited land to them, turned out to be the home of bands of free-spirited hunters and gatherers over whom they had little control. The Boers could never tell where these half-naked little people were going to or when they would be back. The Bushmen at first didn't understand and later refused to believe that the farmers' big, red cattle were not to be hunted along with all the other animals. Furthermore they were not submissive; and although at times they were willing helpers, one could not rely on them. Yet the farmers were somehow at their mercy, because they knew much better how to survive in this dry veld than the farmers ever would. They had strange ways of storing water and also knew how to extract water from the moist earth of the sip-wells by sucking long and hard on hollow reeds. During the long, dry months they knew where to dig wells, which in some years were the only sources of water for months on end.

But what was most irritating to some of the farmers was the joyful spirit of these people, their irrepressible mirth and the endless games they played. With a smile Oom Jimmy remembered his embarrassment when he first discovered what fun a group of grown men were having trying to fit both their footprints into one of the huge, broad velskoen tracks of his father. They were falling about, shrieking with laughter. The only time they were serious was when they were stalking an animal. Then they were dead silent.

The Boers' fear of the Bushmen increased after Koos de Bruyn died in mysterious circumstances. De Bruyn was known as a hard man. Oom Jimmy remembered his parents talking in concerned voices about how harshly he treated both the people and the animals on his farm. Once his father told him how Koos de Bruyn had lost more cattle than anyone else on the trek north because he was too impatient to wait until nighttime to trek his animals, and many of them had perished from heat exhaustion and thirst on a particularly dry stretch.

One day, Koos de Bruyn had lashed a Bushman with his whip for some crime Oom Jimmy had now forgotten. The little band was outraged but powerless. Or so Koos thought. The next morning, his wife found his body cold and stiff, a blue ring around his mouth and eyes. When she ran out to call one of the Bushmen to get help, she found their huts deserted, the fires cold. They had left during the night; probably around the time her husband died. This particular group was never again seen around that area.

The few farmers who remained behind with their wives and children came to realise that an occasional pair of hands on the farm was better than none. In the great isolation that surrounded them it was better to accept the ways of the Bushmen, welcoming them when they showed up to help finish that half-dug well, make bricks, tan hides or fashion riems. Oom Jimmy and his young Bushmen friends particularly liked the riem-making. These strong, thick thongs made of rawhide were useful to hold parts of the donkey-carts and ox-wagons together, to tie bundles of firewood, tether animals, lower a person or a bucket into a well.

The rawhide with the hair still on it was cut into strips, several strands wound around a large, flat stone and hung from a sturdy branch of a tree. This was the perfect plaything for young boys. With a long stick pushed in between the stone and the wet riems, they wound up the strips by going round and round, until the stiff cord could be released to spin back the other way, the stone whirring in a mad circle. What fun it was to get onto that stone and hold onto the riems until the contraption came to a standstill, your head spinning and the world tumbling head over heels!

The games which amused him and his friends gradually developed from shooting birds and mice into more serious hunting. Sometimes the youngsters were accompanied by the older men who taught them all the skills necessary to survive in the veld: how to track animals, where to dig wells during the long, dry months, how to use the medicinal plants that grew undetected in the area. Jimmy was amazed at some of the things people knew, such as the time of year to cut wood for building houses so that the insects would not eat it. They knew that the poisonous larvae used on their arrow points could only be found under certain trees at certain times of the year, and that the poison would not be potent all year round. They even knew the difference between a lion's roar in the morning and at night!

Many of the things they told him he took as fables. Like the story of the hartebeest which supposedly carried a large, white worm inside its forehead. But the first time they split open the animal's skull after the hunt, he was stunned into silence, because with his own eyes he saw the worm, a slowly wriggling white mass in the hartebeest's sinuses. His friends jeered at his surprise. After that he never questioned their stories again.

Yes, these days his own children do not even know these things anymore, he thought when he watched the young ones playing around Ntcisa. They buy meat in plastic bags from the fridge at the store, or from the butcher tree when someone has killed a goat or a cow. He had taught the older ones some of the skills he had learnt as a boy, but these days he did not have the energy, and where were the animals, anyway?

It felt to him as if everything had gone to pieces around him, if he compared how life used to be when he was young. He remembered how, the night before a hunt, he would sit and listen to the older hunters discussing the eland's expected movements and the direction it would take. They had found its spoor and they were predicting the next day's hunt from experience. "It will cross the big dune, then it will stand still and sniff at the air. Thereafter it is sure to turn west, in the direction of the pans." The old hunter would gesture, lift his face to sniff at the evening breeze. "We'll find it at the third pan." And that was how, the next day, they would find it. But, nowadays, there was no way of telling what tomorrow would bring. Things did not make sense, because everything was broken and life lay in scattered fragments around them.

It was easier to find water, though. Although Ntcisa had to carry the heavy bucket from the pump, the water was always there, not like when he grew up. One of the most important lessons the young Bushmen then had to learn was to treasure water. If, on a hunting trip, they filled more ostrich eggshell containers at a pan than they could carry, they would build a platform high in the branches of a tree where they would place the eggshells out of the reach of jackals and other animals. They would remember exactly where these precious stores were and would collect them on their return.

Later, as their games and responsibilities changed, the boys started talking about different things. The girls, their former playmates, now stayed behind or went out with their mothers. And when boys and girls did get together to play, it was not the same as before. The old games evoked new feelings in Jimmy he could neither understand nor discuss with anyone. There were white girls of his age in the area, but he saw them very seldom – only once every few months when the farmers would gather for Nagmaal.

Lately, more and more memories of the religious practices of his family were returning to him. Every evening after supper his father would conduct *huisgodsdiens*, reading from the Bible in a difficult, formal language, the home-made wax candles flickering in the cool breeze of the Kalahari night. Many moths, attracted by the flickering light, ended up waxed into the sides of the candle. As a boy, he could not keep his fingers off the shapes the dripping wax were making on the candle-holder during the drone of his father's reading, so his mother would pull his hands away to ensure his attention.

He remembered how after the first few years of living by themselves, a new group of people arrived in Ghanzi from the northern Cape. Among them were a few zealous former church elders. These men were very concerned about the neglect of church matters among the sprinkling of families who had remained in Ghanzi.

"We are the children of Israel, chosen to carry the Light of God's Word into the darkness, to the heathendom. You have neglected your duty as torch-bearers for the Word of God," one old man, with white hair and beard, told the farmers and started to organise Nagmaal services every three months. On these occasions all the families would arrive in their donkey and ox-wagons, camp at a shady spot, and stay for a few days. These events became the cycle around which their lives were planned. There was always lots of news to catch up with, gossip to be exchanged, advice to be shared and important decisions to be made concerning their problems with supplies, hunting, water and the Bushmen. During the several services held during the Nagmaal weekend, baptisms, catechism and even marriages were performed.

It was unthinkable that he would not attend. But he thought the white girls of his own age strange. Although in their long dresses and kappies he found them quite beautiful, he felt a little threatened by them. They went about with an air of assurance; they knew what their roles in society were. They didn't seem to mind being called away from their games by their mothers to assist with cooking and caring for the babies. The boys were more fun as they competed with one another, showing off the skills they had learnt from their Bushman friends. Almost all of them could speak Naro or Kaukau, and this they used when they wanted to protect their secrets from the grown-ups and some of the girls who weren't so fluent.

The church service was usually held under a tree, since the homes were too small to hold everyone at once. Sometimes they would span a few of the wagon covers for shade, and everyone would bring their own fold-up *velstoeltjies* to sit on. The elder always stood in front and read from the huge High-Dutch Bible which Jimmy's parents also used at home. Church was a very solemn affair, and the children had to be very quiet where they sat on the ground next to their parents. Although you usually could not see the elder from where you sat, you had to follow the proceedings carefully so that you knew when to stand up to pray with the men, or to sing when it was required.

Oh, how difficult it was to keep down the laughter that bubbled up inside if one of the youngsters jumped up at the wrong moment, or someone sneezed in a funny way. But laughing in church was absolutely forbidden, and you knew that the worst thing you could do was to embarrass your parents in church.

The readings from the Old Testament were taken particularly seriously. "If we do not turn back from our wicked ways, obey God's commandments and refrain from idolatry, we shall incur the awful wrath of God," the old man in front would say in a solemn voice, his white beard trembling. The high-pitched, interminable singing, and long, passionate prayers, too, were solemn, almost mournful. Although his mother sometimes spoke about the grace of God and His love, as a boy he was mostly filled with fear of the omnipresent, angry God of the Old Testament.

"How are you feeling these days, Àboe?"

He had not seen Esta approaching. "Are you sleeping better now?"

She handed him a bag with some tobacco and some biltong which she had already sliced for him. She had always been a good child to him, he thought. Sat at the hospital with Ntcisa all the time he was in there, even though she had a family of her own to look after, and no husband. And, he thought, she always seemed to be so happy. She loved going to church. Even now, she probably was on her way to or just back from choir practice, because she was carrying her song books in her one hand.

She moved over to where Ntcisa was now bathing the little one in a zinc basin. He could not hear what they were talking about. Since he had left his parents' home all those many years ago, he had never gone to any church again. But he still respected and feared the Day of Judgement, because his life had not gone the way the God of his parents would have wanted. At least, since most of his grown-up children had joined the church in D'Kar, perhaps *their* souls would be saved, he thought. But the love and forgiveness his children talked about and of which the young dominee in D'Kar tried to convince him, was not for him. He could never again take the step towards the religion of his parents. The sinful, disrespectful way in which he had chosen to live would never, ever be forgiven by the God he knew as a child.

Often on their way back from Nagmaal, he realised that being with the other Afrikaner children did not give him the same feeling of camaraderie and closeness that he felt with the Bushmen children on their farm. He preferred to be with them. His parents started to complain. "We do not like it that you spend so much time at the huts," his mother cautioned. "It is not a good place for you." Yet he knew they were proud of the many skills he had learnt from the Bushmen.

He closed his eyes. His memories were becoming more vivid than what he could observe around him. One of the games they had often played during their early years was to tease each other with mock sexual conquests, the boys chasing a girl, holding her down while taking turns at a pretended rape. The girls would scream, but it was mostly with laughter, and they would rescue whoever was being held, to run away and hide in the bush. He knew that these games were based on the real thing; he had watched animals, and his friends often joked about what their parents had done just outside the fire circle, or even in the grass shelter when they thought the children were asleep.

It was strange, when he was with the Bushmen children he did not feel guilty about these games or discussions. In his own home he did. The scantily clothed children were all so free about them. They even told the story of how sex was discovered. When the women became impatient with the men for taking so long to discover what their genitals were for, so the story went, they climbed up a tall tree and called the men to gather beneath it. When the men looked up, they could see what the women carried under their short leather aprons, and only then did they understand what they should do.

In his own house these matters were never discussed. He was old enough to know, however, the first time he became aware of it, that the movements of his parents in the dark, the muffled sounds on the other side of the clay wall, were the same game. In his mind it became The Thing. And whenever this happened, he felt guilty and lonely, removed from his family and strangely sad the next day, that the closeness between him and his parents was disturbed by The Thing that happened between them at night.

When the same thing happened between him and Casa it was like a real game, and it did not make him sad. That particular day the chasing games grew wild, the girls and boys became scattered, and he found himself alone with Casa behind a group of dense acacia bushes. One moment he was still play-acting, waiting for his friends to appear from the thicket so that he could boast that he had caught another girl, the next moment he realised it was Casa, and within a split second his mind dazzled with a sudden understanding. The glances they had exchanged lately suddenly made sense; so did the brown duiker eyes that had disturbed and teased him. He saw the meaning behind the little gifts they had exchanged, and the reason why she always seemed to be there when he had killed something. He suddenly knew why her dances sang of praise, and why, when they were together in the group, he sometimes found himself with juicy berries or roots to chew that seemed to have come from nowhere.

His body knew what to do. Her little skin apron was so easy to brush aside, and her body was as smooth and alive as a little lizard under his hands. He was filled with tremendous confusion, even fear, when it was over, but what he saw in her face gave him unspeakable joy. They became suddenly shy as they separated, and she started walking back to the group, casually picking veldkos as she went. They approached their friends from different directions, ignoring each other. He noticed that her laughter sounded shrill among the girls, while he himself started to rough and tumble among the boys, surprised at the spurt of energy he felt, as if a fountain had erupted inside, flowing under his skin.

He could not think of much else after that, and lay awake deep into the night, listening to the night sounds, hoping to make sense of the torrent of thoughts that rushed through his mind. The house had no ceiling so he could hear the measured breathing of his parents and the younger children. He shivered as he realised that he had forever stepped out of the tightness of the family circle. The rough walls of the house, the feeling of his mother's arms around him, these were the familiar things that had always meant being inside. Suddenly it had changed. He knew with certainty that he could never, ever tell them what had happened. The more he tried to understand it himself, the less anything made sense, but it was as if he had returned from a long journey and was watching his sleeping family from outside a circle of light, without them being able to see him.

He did not deliberately look for it to happen again, but he was always surprised afterwards at how naturally it did; how she just happened to be there when he was alone; how they would reach out for each other without words and be silent afterwards as well. Later, it started happening almost daily and he found himself needing it so badly he would find any excuse to be alone with her, even pretending sometimes that he was sick so that the boys would leave him behind in the shade of a tree. His eyes would meet hers, and he knew from her look where she would be waiting for him. The others started to tease them. He didn't laugh because it annoyed him that they could even imagine that they understood anything of what he shared with her.

It was when the first rains started when he realised that something had changed: for a few days already she had been avoiding him. She no longer beckoned him with her eyes. Instead her expression was pleading, and then again accusing.

Then came the day that he found his father waiting outside the house when he returned from the veld. He could tell from a distance that something dreadful had happened. The way his father fidgeted with his hat and clenched his fists made his stomach contract into a tight knot, even though he had no idea why.

He heard very little of what his father was saying, just noticed his utter dejection because of the terrible thing he had done. There was going to be a baby. There was no denial possible. What upset him most was that his father's anger and grief was tinged with guilt. He could not understand it. Surely *he* was the guilty one? His mother had stayed inside, but through the open door he could see her sitting at the table with her baby on her lap, her face distorted with sorrow and her eyes swollen with crying. When his father had calmed down he pulled him into the house and made him sit with them at the table.

"If she is your choice, we must accept it," his mother said. "You cannot run away from this responsibility. We'll have to take care of the child."

Many hours of talking followed, most of which his parents seemed to spend with Casa's parents, uncles and grandparents in the shade of the trees outside the house, discussing what each side should expect. He often had to translate. As he now rested his back against the wall of his and Ntcisa's house, with closed eyes, he remembered with fresh emotion the painful struggle to make his voice pass the lump in his throat. He had felt imprisoned by these adult matters. Weren't he and Casa just playing?

He remembered the day the church elders came to visit, the serious talk in the house, the oldest man's hand on the big, black Bible. He was not allowed to be present, but from where he crouched outside the window he could make out fragments of speech: "Others also do it ... not so serious ... will pass." There was talk of the people of God, and he caught the phrase "children of Israel and the heathens" a few times, and wondered what it meant. The elders came only that once.

After that his mother prepared a little space for him and Casa in the corner of the kitchen. They were sleeping on a kaross, but had sheets to cover them and a second kaross for cold nights. Casa would not come into the kitchen while his parents were still in the room. While they ate she would squat outside the door, the last rays of the sun reflecting on her glistening thighs and on her delicate cheekbones. His mother tried to make her wear the dresses she had made for her, but Casa would wear them self-consciously for a while and then go back to her buckskin clothes in which he too loved to see her. The dresses reminded him of the bossy girls at Nagmaal, and he was embarrassed on her behalf.

There was no more playing. His father took him along with him every day now. He had just turned fourteen. He had often accompanied his father before, but now there was no question of not doing so. When they came home in the late afternoon, Casa would be lying under the trees, girl friends visiting her. In the mornings his mother made her help in the house, teaching her the duties of a wife.

Casa's friends always came to her; they did not live far away. You could see the glow of the fires at night; sometimes hear the dancing and the laughter. He and she would often slip out at night so that she could join in the circle of clapping and chanting women. From where he stood outside the circle of firelight, he would marvel at her complete absorption and the serenity of her face.

He felt uncertain of his own role there, however. He would eventually lie down on the sand to wait for her until deep in the night, when the dancers had gone into a trance, and the rhythm of the clapping and the stamping of feet had become an irresistible pulse that dominated his heartbeat and made his mind sway. The women's intent faces, the intoxicating singing rhythm and the feverish urgency, excluded and bewildered him.

In this world he could not reach Casa. She was so much a part of it and it of her that she could not explain to him what had happened. He knew that the trance was vital; the main dancers had to keep going until they were foaming at the mouth, their eyes glassy, and they collapsed in the sand. This was the only way they could get the power to regain

39

some of the "medicine" that had been stolen from their people – the fat of the eland that would bring health, harmony and success back to the clan. Afterwards she would be able to talk about the dances by name, "the ostrich", "the eland", but she could not or would not tell more about the dark, unseen power that threatened her people's existence and which they were fighting through the dance.

His parents did not approve of these nights out. They were trying hard to bring Casa into the family. They did not say anything, but he could sense their apprehension about him becoming part of her life. After a while he gave up. She would rise from their bed and go out alone, returning at dawn and warming her freezing body against his sleep-warm chest.

When the birth was near she went back to her mother's house. He was lonely, worried and self-conscious about being in his parents' house on his own. When the longing became too great he would go out to her. Without a word the men would move over to make space for him at their fire; she would sit on one side with her grandmother. Here it was not allowed for him to talk directly to her or to touch her. Instead, the conversation would go round the circle, including everyone. Still it was comforting to be there. He relaxed with the endless repetition of amusing anecdotes, the teasing of a weak hunter, or of a man who tripped and fell while herding cattle or displayed fear during an encounter with a lion or leopard.

The baby was brought to stay at his parents' house when it was a few weeks old. Soon after the birth, Casa's grandmother had called him over to see his son. He felt embarrassment at the sight of the tiny head sticking out from under the soft duiker-skin blanket wrapped around Casa, unsure of what was expected of him. Casa looked so different, even a little bewildered, squatting in the morning sun next to the hut. During those first weeks his mother also went to the hut daily, taking milk and food for the mother, advising on washing and cleaning the clothes she had made for the baby.

By now he had built a small clay and dung hut next to his father's house. He was assisted by the young men who were once his playmates, and this is where he moved with his family. Casa carried the baby on her back while helping his mother in the house, but once finished with what was expected of her, she would be off to the huts of her people, only to return when he came home. Some evenings he would have to fetch her. He could sense his parents' growing impatience. He himself became a bit concerned that she showed so little interest in the things his mother was teaching her. Her presence in their house was seldom spontaneous and she wore a constant expression of sullen endurance. What he had taken in the beginning to be shyness had clearly turned into reluctance, a stubborn discontent. He could no longer be happy either. Some nights they clung desperately to each other, but with the morning light came a passivity, a tiredness in their being together.

Then one day the clan prepared to move on. Casa was told to stay, although she protested loudly and cried as she watched the line of brown-clad figures disappear into the bush, their skin bags loaded with their few belongings, the click sounds of their conversation growing softer as they moved away. For many days she sat around looking bewildered and unhappy. She made angry sounds when addressed, and mostly went outside in the daytime and played with their son.

When he woke one morning and found her gone, he got up, fetched his coffee from the house and sat in the early sun for a long time before he told his mother. His parents convinced him not to follow, even though he was sure he would be able to track them.

"The clan will return, we know that, so let her go," his mother said. "You cannot force a woman's love. Let her decide for herself if she wants to stay with us."

This was the unhappiest time of his entire life. He had to carry on, help his father, be a man, while inside he felt lonely and scared. He could not help but feel angry towards his parents, suspecting them of hoping that she would not come back, that he could pick up again his old life as their son – as if he could just forget his ties to Casa and her family ...

He had stopped going to Nagmaal after the visit of the elders. There were tears and threats from his family when he continued to refuse, but in the end they left without him. He had somehow worked out a pattern for his own life, he would not be part of theirs again. He slept in the hut he had built, shared their meals, but did not go along when they went visiting. Their discussions had turned to the cattle, how to prepare for the winter, the digging of new wells. The unspoken thing, the question of whether she would return and what they would be to each other then, crept into his dreams most nights, but never entered the conversations with his parents.

After many months, Casa's people were back, quite suddenly. One evening as the sun was setting, a line of people filed in from the bush and started to busy themselves with repairing what was left of the little grass shelters they had abandoned two seasons ago. But she did not come to him; he had to go over to their group. His son was so big now that he could walk. Looking down at the child he was overwhelmed with emotion, knowing he would not recognise his father. The little boy was naked, except for his small skin apron, his belly round and shiny. He sucked on his fingers and clung to the legs of his grandmother, half-hiding behind her skin apron. Something restrained Jimmy from approaching Casa. He was waiting for a cue, hesitantly trying to read messages in the faces of the people who joyfully shared with him some of the experiences of their long trek.

It was only when she stood up slowly, turning to pick up the child, that he noticed her large abdomen. He felt bewildered, surprised, but the faces of the people around her confirmed what he feared. Then Cg'ota, one of his best friends, moved closer to her, his eyes challenging Jimmy without a word. Nobody said anything. He could not bear it any longer, he turned back to his hut with his heart pounding and his mouth dry. That night he cried himself to sleep.

This time the clan did not stay for long. Shortly after they left, his father and some neighbours measured out a new piece of land for him, and they trekked some cattle over to the spot on which he had chosen to build his own house.

Soon, a new band of Bushmen moved close to where he was staying, to help him with the work and to share the milk. He knew some of them from before, and on lonely nights sought out his comfortable place in their fire circle. He had crossed some sort of border; his mind was at ease now. He was still on polite terms with the other farmers, they even passed by his house sometimes to enquire about his well-being, but he knew the boundaries. When he had occasion to go to one of their farms, he would not enter the house; some would offer him coffee outside. His parents and sisters would come on horseback to bring him supplies from time to time. He appreciated their visits, but their worlds were growing further and further apart and they had less and less to say to each other.

Within a few years he had fathered two more children with a girl called Bau. Her clan had moved their huts close to his, and gradually their periods of absence became shorter until they hardly moved around at all. They were getting used to the benefits of sedentary life; the constant availability of water was making them reluctant to trek far, and hunting was becoming more difficult in any case as the game in their territories grew scarcer.

When his little sister Martha came of age, it became necessary to divide the farm again. She married a neighbouring farmer called Jan Vermaak, and she had to be given a piece of land that would extend both the farms. Jimmy was given the other third, and his parents continued farming on their own third. He had five children by now and Bau's uncles, aunts, brothers and sisters, as well as the sons-in-law that always joined their brides' families, resulted in a rather large clan of whom he, too, had become a part. When Bau became sick and died, he took another young wife, but she also left him after a couple of years. Although he was sad, he was not as devastated as when Casa had left him.

After his parents died he finally abandoned most of their ways. He was now in his mid thirties and found that the farming methods he had been taught by his father failed to meet the needs of his large family. By this time the people on his farm had increased to a whole clan and the demands on his livestock were high. He barely had contact with Martha and her husband and knew it would be a mistake to claim his parents' land, since his farming successes were dismal in comparison with his brother-in-law's. Eventually he abandoned his own piece of land and joined his children on the farms where they worked as hired hands. They were sought after, for he had taught his sons all the skills he had learnt from his father: tanning leather, making harnesses, saddles, digging wells. They also spoke some of his own language, Afrikaans, and understood the ways of the white man, which made them even more desirable as workers.

It was after a long spell of work on a distant farm, when they were moving back to their own group of huts, that they had found an Englishman measuring large stretches of land with instruments on wooden legs, shining in the sun. Since there was hardly anything left of Jimmy's own farming efforts, he was happy to accept the sum of money offered by a neighbour for his small piece of land, and for the next few years he and his sons took on the task of erecting fences all over the district to signify ownership of the pieces of land indicated by this man's measurements.

In his old age he often reflected on the irony of the fact that he and his sons had eventually depended for their living on the very thing that had strangled their previous way of life. It did not take him long to learn the trade of fencing, and he took great pride in his skill at folding steel wire into neat knots with pliers, erecting a sturdy, shining line through the bush. Yet, sometimes the members of his clan were saddened by the memory of days gone by, when their people could move everywhere without hindrance. But mostly they accepted what life offered from moment to moment, passing the time making good use of the skills he had taught them.

When the malaria took hold of Oom Jimmy in his old age, he did not fight the disease. He felt too weak to direct his wife and children on how to care for him, and he felt the power flow from his body hour by hour, as he was dehydrating. Lying in his hut, his whole life was passing before him and he waited for it to be over. Sometimes he had fearful moments trying to imagine where he would be going after he died and when the fever was at its peak, he would call out, to Casa, and to his mother. Ntcisa held up his sweaty body and tried to feed him spoonfuls of tea and soup, but he vomited up every drop. To break the hold of the fever, the children had called others who still knew how to dance and one night they danced for him right through, just outside the hut. Once, that night, during a brief moment of consciousness, he imagined that he saw the face of the eland in the glow of the fire, just outside the dancing circle.

When they could not wake him the next morning, the children went to call Moruti: "He did not want us to take him to hospital, but now we can see that we should not have listened to him. Can you help us?"

The young pastor lifted the old white man from his kaross on the floor. He was as light as a child. In the vehicle they made him comfortable on the back seat. He lay with his head on Esta's lap. "He is so old now, Moruti," she said. "And so weak. This time only the Grace of God can save him."

FOUR

# Embers in the Milky Way

The geckos met the night with a metallic din; darkness was moving in rapidly. Dina sat outside her hut, pounding leaves and nuts with a pestle in her wooden *kika*, watching the red dust settle on the thorn bushes. The last rays were slowly being drawn into the setting sun – as if the fiery body was gathering up the folds of its red cloak before disappearing over the horizon, exposing the blue-grey veil which now covered the face of God, she thought. Then she saw the young boy approaching. He had been running.

"Please, Auntie, it is Qasa's baby. My mother asks if you could come."

She had been expecting it. Village news travelled fast. She sent the boy back to say that she was on her way, and went into her hut to collect her bag and walking-stick. On her way to the new mother's hut, trying to avoid the thorny arms of the shrubs as she hurried along, she looked up again and thought of how her grandfather had explained to her why they called the sky God's face. "He is ever present," he said. "He watches from a distance and there is nothing He cannot see. But He does not interfere."

It was always said that God was very far away, and although she sensed something of the immensity of the distance, she believed that He could still see her. Even at night, when the coals of the fires of all the dead people lit up the sky, His eyes could pierce the darkness and peep into the huts of those on earth, see the good as well as the evil in their hearts. The old people used to say that God was no longer interested in doing anything, He just watched and allowed the spirit of Dxãwa to play around with the people, to steal their peace and their health. Dxãwa could not be seen, but he was everywhere, and although he was not really evil, he was bothersome and responsible for many of the things which made their lives miserable. Moruti had explained to them that Jesus had come to build a bridge to allow people to get closer to God again, to give them power over Dxãwa, but she often wondered about that. Life certainly did not get any better; if it was true that Jesus had brought God closer, wouldn't He have done something to make things easier for them?

The house was at the other end of the village. It was quite far, but she knew the way well. There was still no moon, but the stars were lighting up. She had better be careful of snakes, she thought, it was not really wise to walk around at night. Since she was wearing only sandals, she poked with her walking-stick at the shrubs ahead of her as she walked.

Her grandfather told them stories every night as they sat in a circle around the fire, stories of the old people, their forefathers. The stories were about the animals, about the reasons things were the way they were. He kept on talking, until one by one they had all nodded off. Fast asleep, they would be carried over to their mothers and put down next to their siblings, all curled up around the fire.

He used to point at the broad stripe of stars that runs halfway across the sky and show them the smoky patches inside and next to it. "Those are the fires of our old people, you see? They have been there a long, long time, which is why they are only smouldering ashes now. The loose, bright little stars are the black and the white people's fires; they are still shining brightly because they are newcomers to this world."

Dina approached the cluster of huts where the young boy had said Qasa was in labour. As so often, it happened at night. She had always wondered about the significance of it; wondered why God wanted us to be born in darkness. Could it be that He wanted to spare us the shock of where we were coming to, just for a few more hours?

Going out at night was difficult sometimes, especially when she had been still a young girl learning the ways of a midwife from her old aunt. Still, she always appreciated the quietness of the night, the privacy it afforded her and the other women who were toiling away together. They would be secretly working while others were unaware of the small miracle that was happening, the arrival of a new little body amongst them. It was as if the night threw a cloak of darkness around them in their small pool of light, protecting them from all eyes while they completed their precious task. Only God could see them very well; she sometimes felt their little circle must be shining like one of His other stars; perhaps all those other star-fires were also people doing precious, secret tasks which only God knew about at that quiet hour.

If her old aunt had not slowly gone blind, Dina thought as she walked on, she would never have known all the things she knew today. Old Meraai had been such a trusted and popular midwife, she could not afford to admit she had problems with her eyesight. Instead she had said she was getting old and asked Dina's mother if Dina could become her helper. This is how it happened that at the age when young girls were really curious about such things, Dina was happily trotting along to each birth, a skinny twelve-year-old next to the respectable old woman in her dark clothes and headscarf, and thick, black-rimmed glasses.

No doors were closed to them, Dina soon learnt. Old Meraai delivered everyone's babies, her own people's as well as the white farmers' wives', and many of the black women's too. When she was on her own, Dina knew that her place was outside the farmhouses, that she was never to enter the front garden or the house, or to use the white people's mugs or chairs, for fear of being shouted at or even beaten with a stick. But it was different when she was with old Meraai. Then they would be welcomed on the stoep, be given tea while they were busy with their task, and afterwards served food in the kitchen, sitting on chairs in front of the big old woodstove. Often a farmer would go so far as to send his donkey-cart and driver to pick them up, and she would get a special place next to old Meraai, since she was under instructions to stay close – so close that no one would notice that the old woman's sight was failing.

Young as she was, Dina knew that keeping this secret was her entry into a world which other children her age could only imagine. Furthermore, she was becoming as well known as old Meraai, which brought unexpected little rewards such as a lolly being thrust into her hand at the grocery store; sometimes an old dress was even passed down from the farm children.

She learnt to watch closely, to observe as much as possible and to ask very few questions. She knew she had to be very careful to avoid giving the old woman the idea that she could be a threat. She sensed that her aunt still needed to feel irreplaceable. But her eyesight was becoming so poor that soon she was doing everything by feel and instinct alone. Before starting to work with someone in labour, she would cover the lower part of the woman's body with a cloth to keep Dina from seeing things too shocking for a girl of her age. However, the old lady could not see well enough to know when the mother was properly covered, so Dina ended up having a full view while pretending to keep the silly cloth in place. Gradually her confidence grew. This was why she could walk up to Piet de Wet that night and say in all honesty and faith: "Don't worry, I can help her."

The farmer, whose wife had been in labour for a few hours already while he was in the veld, was beside himself with shock and anguish. His wife's labour was so far advanced that there was no time to get a midwife. He was torn between the need to stay with his distressed wife and an urge to get on his horse and gallop into the night to find someone who could help.

In between his bouts of rushing to her bed and kneeling beside her to feel the contractions, he ran out onto the stoep, cursing and screaming at the workers gathered outside the house. "Why didn't anybody come to fetch me? Why have you not gone to look for help already yourselves?"

Only a small group of labourers lived on the farm. Their women were afraid to come into the house to offer help; none of them had the courage to face the man's fury if something should go wrong. Lily, who worked in the kitchen, was panicking too much herself: "I don't know, Baas, I don't know, I 've never done it," she whispered.

Now was the time to test her knowledge, Dina quietly decided. She happened to be visiting a cousin on the farm, so neither old Meraai, nor her mother, nor her older sisters were there to keep her back. There was no reason why she, even if she was only thirteen years old, couldn't and shouldn't do it.

Confidently she walked up to the red-faced man on the stoep. "I know how to," she said. "Let me help her."

"You must be crazy!" he shouted, pushing her aside, beckoning the women to come inside. Frightened, they moved away, behind the kitchen wall. He turned to Dina: "You will kill my wife!"

She remained where she was, telling him how she was the assistant of old Meraai, lying about how she had actually done a few births herself under the old woman's supervision. Piet de Wet saw there was no way out. The damn cowards who worked for his wife were as untrustworthy as one would have expected them to be. So here he was, forced to put the life of his wife in the hands of a mere child. "If she dies, I will kill you, you understand!" he shouted before he allowed her into the house.

Of course she was a little afraid. There had been emergencies with old Meraai and she knew what to do, but would she be able to recognise the problem if something did go wrong?

Bertha de Wet's eyes opened wide with fright when she saw Dina. Dina had learnt a lot, however, about how to pacify adults: working with grumpy old Meraai was not always easy.

Yes, she smiled to herself as she quietly made her way in the dark, that was probably the reason she still managed to get along with anyone and everyone. Over the years she had helped so many people – her own kind, whites, blacks – and they had all accepted her. But she knew, too, what each group liked and disliked, and what they expected from her.

Piet de Wet had given her a goat afterwards, and a lot of clothes. For a while after that first time, whenever she was in Ghanzi, or even at the shop in D'Kar, the farmers would point to her and talk among themselves. Sometimes the women would come over to where she was waiting for her parents' employer in the back of his pick-up truck, saying to each other: "This is her. See, just a child. It is quite amazing, isn't it?"

She recognised Qasa's hut from a distance, even though it was now quite dark. It could barely be called a hut. A collection of cardboard boxes, plastic bags and tufts of grass had been worked into a frame of oddly leaning sticks. She stooped and entered. This was going to be hard again. She had grown heavier lately, and she did not bend so easily any more. Her knees were now starting to give her trouble. She had knelt on them too many nights, bringing countless babies into the world.

Still, she loved doing this; she even loved the element of fear and apprehension she experienced every time. There were just so many things that could go wrong; you had to be able to think fast. Mostly, the mother and the aunts of the woman knew what do themselves, so unless there was a problem of some kind they would not call in her help. Peering ahead of her, she thought: Yes, every birth I attend holds some sort of challenge.

On a cardboard box a small flame danced on a piece of rag pushed into the neck of a bottle of paraffin. It smoked, but she could make out the faces of the people inside. Three women were sitting behind and next to the frail young woman lying on her back in their midst, naked, with knees apart and eyes wide, panic on her face. Qasa's head lolled against the chest of the aunt in whose lap she was resting while she rubbed her forehead and held her in position. Her sister was massaging her huge abdomen.

This looked like real trouble. Labour had clearly gone on for hours, and the girl was very young and delicately built. They start so young these days, Dina thought, barely out of the hut after the menstruation dance and then the babies start coming. If only they would listen. The problem is the big men with whom they slept nowadays – tall, dark Herero cattle trekkers; stocky, strong, black council drivers; even the white farmers with their huge hands and feet. And then we have to save them, tear these large babies out of their tiny, young bodies.

"We have also called Mmamoruti," Ncõx'ae, Qasa's aunt, said.

As if Moruti's wife can help! Dina thought. She tried her best to be involved in everything, but she knew so little. It was like teaching a young girl, even though she already had three children of her own. Anyway, let her come, she can at least go to find help if we can't manage with this one, she thought.

Dina started massaging Qasa's groin. She was widely dilated. It was clear the birth was not far off. It was equally clear that the young woman was at the end of her strength. Her body was really very small. If a hand or foot were protruding, Dina would have known what to do. She had had to deal with that many times in the past: pushing a baby back into the womb, putting her own hand inside and pulling the arm or foot back alongside the little body before manoeuvring it into a different position for delivery. This was always dreadfully painful for the mothers, and they tore and bled awfully, but it was the only way to save their lives. Sadly the babies sometimes did not make it. If she did not do something soon, this one might also not live.

Mmamoruti entered. At least she had a torch with her, Dina noticed.

The hut was now positively crowded, but the women moved up, letting her join their circle.

More than anything else Mmamoruti seemed concerned about the cloth band the women had tied around the upper part of Qasa's abdomen. She seemed disturbed by the fact that they were pulling on this band to push the baby down. Usually Dina would not have minded that, because it gave the other women something to do, and when it was someone's third or fourth birth it actually helped to speed up the process. But this baby was clearly stuck, and it could become dangerous, so she had to give Mmamoruti her way. "Stop pulling," she told them.

They were running out of time. Dina sent Mmamoruti home to fetch Moruti with the car. They might have to cut this baby out in Ghanzi, she silently feared. Qasa cried, holding tight onto her mother. Silly girl, look what you've got yourself into, Dina was tempted to say.

Outside, they could hear the murmur of the men round the fire. Dina went out to tell Qasa's father that she had sent for the vehicle. The men immediately started clearing the area of water canisters, wooden stools and logs so that Moruti could stop as close as possible to the little shack. The other women were putting clothes on Qasa; in soft tones they comforted her and packed a little plastic bag with her clothes and clinic card. Finally they wrapped a blanket around her. Ncõx'ae would accompany her and Dina.

When the vehicle lights flooded the little house, they picked her up and lay her down on the mattress Moruti had put in the back of the Landrover. The back seats had been taken out to make room for the mattress, so Dina and Ncõx'ae squeezed in at the back and sat beside Qasa. Her father slid into the front seat with Moruti.

Qasa did not cry, but she looked as if she might faint any moment. Dina peered between her legs every now and then, rubbed her stomach. But there was not much she could see under the blanket in the reflected light from the windows and the dashboard. The Landrover bumped and swerved to avoid stones and potholes. Occasionally Moruti stepped on the brake to prevent them bouncing up and down, but still Qasa winced from the uneven movement of the vehicle. Moruti kept apologising. Dina wished he would not; they should rather not acknowledge the discomfort, it was always easier that way.

Suddenly, Qasa grabbed her hand and pulled her forward. The words were hissed into Dina's ear in a hushed voice: " I think it is coming!"

Dina looked at the backs of the men in the front, wondering if she should stop the vehicle. The lights of Ghanzi were showing ahead of them already. "Give me the torch, quickly," she asked Qasa's father.

On her knees, her head under the blanket, she could see the baby's wet black curls encircled by the stretched flesh. Blood was dripping on the blanket and the mattress; Qasa had started to tear. The girl pulled her towards her again: "Not in front of Moruti! Please help me!"

Dina suddenly knew what to do. She was in control again. She pulled the blanket away and pushed hard against the protruding bulge, both hands across the dark patch of hair. With her mouth very close to the baby's head, she whispered: "Oh, no, little one, not here. Men are not supposed to see you arrive. You are going back until it is the right moment."

To get a better grip, she took off her shoe and pushed against the bulge with her foot, gently but steadily.

With her one hand she massaged the young woman's abdomen, all the while talking to the little body waiting to be born. She knew it would not be long, but the seconds felt like hours. Qasa was whimpering like a small puppy. "Hold her, talk to her!" she ordered Ncõx'ae.

Moruti and Qasa's father still had their eyes fixed straight ahead. They hadn't noticed anything; the old vehicle rattled too much from the corrugations on the dirt road.

They were almost there.

The Landrover turned into the hospital grounds, stopped right at the front door. So close that the porch light fell into the back of the vehicle. Moruti jumped out to get a trolley. Dina took her hand away, but pulled Qasa's knees together. The nurses lifted Qasa onto the trolley, Dina still keeping her knees together. Once outside the vehicle, she let go but followed close behind, her hands under the blanket. As they started rolling Qasa towards the front door, a tiny body, covered with blood and mucus, slid into Dina's outstretched hands. The baby was very still but she could feel it was alive. It had arrived, it was safe, they would know how to revive it inside!

Dina held the little body, the umbilical cord still attached. She placed it on the mother's chest as they wheeled her away and turned back to

Moruti and Qasa's father who were still standing beside the vehicle: "You can go now. Ncõx'ae and I will stay here with Qasa for the night. You will hear from us tomorrow." As they drove off, she hesitated a moment before she entered the hospital. She looked up. All the stars were out now, and the old people's fires were smouldering above her. She turned her eyes from the one horizon to the other, scanning the wide black expanse of night sky. "There you are, God," she said softly. "Another one. Did you see?"

FIVE

# A dog's life

So, then, Nqaba was a *bitch*, Mmamoruti thought and laughed softly to herself as she drove away from the hospital. She had somehow always known that there was something more to Nqaba than just her stubborn differentness. Some kind of mystery had always surrounded her. But now it all made sense.

As long as she had known Nqaba the woman had been wild. And completely honest about her dreadful life – which was in such a shambles that most of her family just sighed and turned their eyes skyward when you enquired about her well-being. Yet, Nqaba's honesty was fresh and reassuring in a society where so many people tried to pretend they were different from what they really were – for the sake of acceptance by the other groups, and especially to win the approval of the church. Mmamoruti found herself always forgiving Nqaba, again and again, no matter how terrible her last misdeed had been. It was as if Nqaba could never really see the full impact of what she had done, so there wasn't much sense in kicking up a fuss. She was so carefree, so full of self-confidence and courage, in spite of the chaos of her circumstances.

In D'Kar there were very few secrets. The houses were for storage and for rainy times, but mostly people lived outside, in the spaces between the huts which were built fairly close to each other. It was common knowledge who had beaten whom, who slept and ate with whom. And what you could not see with your own eyes, the sand would tell you afterwards: "See here, Moruti, this is where they had walked. Here he met her and from here they walked on together. Here they took off their shoes. Do you see this round hollow? This is where her buttocks lay and here his arms pressed down. They may tell you that they do not sleep together, but anyone can see ..."

Nqaba seemed always to be involved in some or other conflict. But instead of trying to disguise the reason for a black eye or scratch marks in her face, she did as she pleased: told everyone what had happened and took the consequences.

The same freedom was displayed in her choice of clothes. She never wore a doek. As long as she had known her, Mmamoruti had never seen her cover her hair, even though a doek was worn by most women who had children and these colourful headscarves were beloved items in every respectable woman's wardrobe. In fact, Nqaba was mostly closer to being naked than clothed, even in church. Sitting in the pew behind her one day, Mmamoruti wondered why she even bothered to get dressed. If her dress had a zipper, it would be open, but mostly the zipper would be broken and the buttons gone. That particular day she was barefoot and her hair hadn't seen a comb for many a day. The frizzy knobs of hair were dusty and littered with pieces of grass. Into each one of her ears she had stuffed a coin, her offering. No wonder nothing being said here seemed to have any effect on her life, Mmamoruti thought, amused.

At least she had spared the church members her beloved shorts, or the way she pronounced it: "tjorts". Unlike the women around her, she loved to wear the women's shorts that sometimes arrived with the old clothes people donated to the church. She wore these boldly; seemingly unaware that the men found it profoundly disturbing when women wore what they regarded as "men's clothes". Tswana men in particular, Mmamoruti knew, found such dress indecent and provocative.

Bare breasts, on the other hand, were totally acceptable; they were there for feeding babies. Men thought nothing of playfully grabbing at another man's wife's breast, or to annoy a suckling baby by pulling the nipple from its mouth, even in a large, mixed group of people. Mmamoruti had had her own initiation in this regard when one of the most respected church elders unexpectedly tugged her by the breast and said, "With such flat tits you can't have enough milk to give the child, no wonder she cries so much."

Her own pairs of shorts and those of her daughters she packed away for holiday use only, shortly after they came to live here. It was clear that in this culture naked thighs were another matter altogether. The women's thighs were usually quite large; the rounder the more beautiful to the men, it seemed, but instead of silently enjoying the prohibited pleasures displayed by a defiant woman like Nqaba, they showed open annoyance. Nqaba had one pair of blue Crimplene shorts in particular which fitted so tightly over her generous behind that it seemed to say "one for you, one for me" when she walked. She ignored all comments that this piece of clothing drew as if she was deaf. Could there be a connection between her provocative dress sense and the fact that Nqaba perpetually seemed to be in a state of either pregnancy or breastfeeding, Mmamoruti sometimes wondered.

Although she had no permanent home and no income, Nqaba had about five living children. Nobody was quite sure of the number she had given birth to. Two or three of her babies had died very young. No one really knew why. The little corpses were buried the very evening of their death in the floor of Nqaba's mother's hut; no one was even called from the church to say a prayer or hold a short service. It was as if people had expected Nqaba's children to die. But Nqaba was heartbroken each time and tried to drink her sorrows away.

Her mother and sisters had long ago stopped taking responsibility for her children. They were tired of her carelessness and were in any case overloaded with their own responsibilities. So Nqaba's remaining children seemed to be raising themselves among the families in D'Kar. As a result, each one of them was an amazingly independent, though shockingly neglected little person. These kids were remarkably resilient and seemed to have survived without any visible signs of trauma or abuse. Nqaba was notorious for her drinking spells. However, while she was walking through the village, shouting and crying and looking for trouble, or otherwise lying under a bush sleeping off her babalaas, her children seemed to get fed somewhere in the village. They were, after all, masters of charm, knowing when to start performing little dances or comic acts to get a few crusts or a sip of milk. They knew to choose exactly the right moment to appear from underneath a bush or from around a corner, fixing those eyes on you with a meaningful gaze, enough to make your food change direction between your hand and your mouth and end up in an outstretched little paw.

Clara was such a miracle child. When Nqaba was expecting her, she went on a drinking spree for months on end. It often landed her in terrible fights. The people of D'Kar grew accustomed to seeing her with bruises and cuts, a black eye, even burns; but Mmamoruti and the clinic staff were extremely concerned about the effects on her unborn child. Their dire warnings could not shock Nqaba out of her sad state. Immediately after such discussions, she would passionately agree never to drink again, only to greet you a day or two later with another shiner. "Nqaba has failed again ..." she would announce, "but this time God talked to me. He has heard me. *He* is the one who will help me, not you lot."

Nqaba's relationship with God was as unconventional as her clothing. She loved singing in the church choir. The lovely hoarse quality to her voice and her completely individualistic style of singing always made her stand out. Moruti tried his best to keep her in the choir, while the choir members did their best to make her feel unwelcome – for understandable reasons: her dress sense, or lack of it, was a blemish to the image of the choir, and a drunken member made practice evenings most uncomfortable. The choir members were often more successful than Moruti.

Mmamoruti had never heard and had forgotten to ask if Nqaba ever managed to join a choir in Ghanzi, where she had been living lately, before she became ill. She wondered if she could have been as free with her singing in an overpopulated place like Ghanzi as she had been in D'Kar. As Mmamoruti drove past the Kuru office on the sandy track through the thorn bushes just before the turn at the gate to her house, she remembered the time she came across Nqaba right there, singing all on her own in the veld.

Mmamoruti was on her way back from the office when she heard this beautiful voice. There were almost no huts on that stretch, so she stopped in surprise. Where could the sudden song, so clear and close by, come from? There was a strong, honest appeal in the singing, a purpose in its loudness. Mmamoruti recognised the words, but Nqaba was interpreting the song in a unique and special way. Mmamoruti felt as if she was eavesdropping on a very private and intimate prayer.

"Speak to me oh God, please do not leave me, speak to me, speak to me ..."

She recognised Nqaba's voice, but could not see her because she was on a different footpath. Mmamoruti stood still and waited where she knew the paths had to cross.

"Speak to me oh God, please do not leave me speak to me, speak to me ..."

Nqaba's face was turned upwards, her eyes focused elsewhere. The ever-present baby clung to her hip, rocking with the special rhythm Nqaba was giving to the well-known song. The child's face was quiet and wide-eyed.

To Mmamoruti this was one of the most beautiful moments she had known in D'Kar. One night, long after this, when her own mongrel bitch stretched herself out to the full moon and sent her howling song towards the heavens, she got shivers down her spine. For a second she saw Nqaba's face, lifted upwards, and remembered that song, just as unearthly and beyond comprehension.

That day in the veld she had stood still until Nqaba noticed her. "Nqaba," she said, "you sing beautifully. I am sure God must hear you."

"It's true," Nqaba replied. "He does hear me." And she walked on. Mmamoruti envied her such a simple faith.

"I had better go over to her sisters first and tell them what has happened at the hospital," she told her husband and children after she had put her parcels down. "And the clinic nurse. They've all seen me arrive, I think."

Mmapula accompanied her mother to the huts. She skipped and frolicked in the path ahead of her. When they passed the churchyard, she came running back. "Ma, remember the night when Nqaba shouted so loudly when they showed that film?"

Indeed she remembered. A visiting church group from South Africa once stopped in D'Kar on their way further north. Their luxury four-wheel-drive vehicles were decorated with banners, shouting out the words JESUS NOW in stark red letters. They asked permission to show a film about the life of Jesus to the community. The D'Kar church elders agreed. The visitors walked around the village informing people, and at the Kuru offices Moruti helped them put up some notices. At sunset the elders started ringing the church bell every half an hour to call the villagers.

Since it would have been too hot inside the church building, and the visitors' equipment needed lots of space, it was decided that the show would take place on the grass outside. As always in summer, the night was pleasant and windless. In the dusk, people slowly appeared in small groups from all directions, bringing blankets to sit on, the mothers carrying babies on their backs and the fathers carrying toddlers on their arms. The grown-ups found a place to sit while the excited children joined the ever-increasing crowd of youngsters kicking up dust and doing cartwheels in the sand, a few yards away. The twittering of laughing children filled the air.

The whites in their fashionable holiday clothes had already set up the projector and screens, and were sitting on camping chairs in front of the locals, who had started to settle themselves on the grass. Kelebetse took it upon himself to call the crowd of children together and gained the attention of the crowd by starting with a prayer. Then the generator was started behind the vehicles, and images started appearing on the screen.

The pale faces of the visitors were lit up by the reflected light of the screen. They looked almost as strange as the scenes projected in front of them. From the behaviour of the villagers sitting in a group around and behind Moruti and Mmamoruti on the sand, they could see that the visitors themselves were as interesting to the audience as the film they were showing. The eyes of the crowd, some squatting and some sitting flat on their buttocks, were fixed on the almost surreal scene in the pool of light in front of them, illuminated by gas lamps on tall stands. On the screen bearded white men clad in shabby, brown robes were walking down narrow, winding Jerusalem streets lined with tall, square buildings. Such clothes no one in D'Kar had ever seen, and old Jerusalem offered to many of those who had never left D'Kar, their first views of a city. Even the landscape with the arid mountains, placid lakes and strangely shaped cypress trees, offered nothing they could vaguely recognise or identify with.

The soundtrack of the film was in Setswana. But it was a language not known well enough in D'Kar for the majority to make sense of the story; and the dialect spoken was not used or known in the area.

"What must the people make of this?" Moruti whispered to her where they sat among the villagers. "How will I ever explain all of this?" Still, the audience sitting on the sand were spellbound. Only when the crucifixion scene was announced by loud hammer blows and the pale, bleeding face of a white Christ appeared on the screen, his hand being nailed to the cross of wood, was there a commotion. A sudden choking cry rose from the watching crowd. The people on the ground stirred to make way for Nqaba, who came crawling on hands and knees towards Moruti. She was crying uncontrollably. "It is my Jesus," she sobbed. "It's my Jesus they are hurting like that!"

Nqaba's faith was truly out of the ordinary. There was another time Mmamoruti had met her in the village, which she now remembered. She had little Clara, her youngest, on her hip, and she showed Mmamoruti the awful burns, covered all over with strangely dark, dry crusts, on the little one's foot and lower leg. I do not even need to ask how this accident has happened, she thought.

"What is this that you have put on?" Mmamoruti asked instead.

"Chicken shit."

Mmamoruti almost fainted. "Nqaba, how can you! The child will be infected already, you have to go to the clinic immediately. How can you let the child suffer so much!"

She was overcome with shock and anger. Nqaba watched her without expression. A few days later, she brought the child for her to see. The wounds had healed miraculously. New, pink skin had formed over the wet, raw patches.

"See, this stuff is very good," she said.

But, Mmamoruti pondered, maybe Clara's healing had to do with her own survival instincts as much as with her mother's faith. She had been a special child since birth. How would she ever forget the night, Mmamoruti thought, when Nqaba, with the frightened little baby sitting on her hip, stumbled into their house, drunk. In such a state, Nqaba cried with as much vigour as when she sang. Only she would be crying about life's unfair treatment, usually because she had lost a fight she had landed in after insulting someone in her drunkenness or after flirting with some forbidden man. The little baby couldn't have been more than six months old. Her mother was almost naked, dressed only in a flimsy, torn mini-skirt. The little girl was eyeing the strangers from her mother's side, sitting across her hip bone, while Nqaba waved her arms around in protest, wiping tears and snot from her face. The little mite sat there with wide, wakeful eyes like a koala bear clinging to a tree trunk. There was not much to hold on to, just bare skin and a sagging breast, but the baby had been around Nqaba long enough to know that she had to fend for herself. Nqaba had lots of love to give, but care was something a person had to organise for him or herself. All her children did that remarkably well.

When little Clara was a year old, her mother had yet another dramatic conversion. She stopped drinking and made several unsuccessful attempts at finding work. She was a hard worker, moved fast and was not fussy about what she was instructed to do. If only she could stick it out, people said. But after about two weeks Nqaba was usually fed up with the routine. For her, life meant roaming around the village or catching lifts up and down to Ghanzi. Except that this was a recipe for trouble for Nqaba, and it was also not conducive to good relations with an employer.

In the end she moved to Ghanzi. Besides finding a job, the main reason was that she had joined one of the "salt-water churches" which she believed would keep her on the straight and narrow path.

"They hang a string with knots in it around your neck and arms to tie you to the promises of God," she explained to Moruti before she left. "And they hang little bottles of salt-water from the roof of your house to protect you from evil. And they watch you. They watch that you do not go to bad places. And they dance with you right through the night if you need healing. The church in D'Kar is far too soft on sin," she sighed. "And you never give us something to believe in, something that you can see and hold in your hands."

Like her half-brothers and -sisters before her, little Clara became everybody's responsibility after her mother left. Mmamoruti's previous daily contact with Nqaba changed to a distant wave when she saw her on the streets of Ghanzi, and a word of greeting conveyed by someone who had seen her. According to all reports Nqaba was drinking less.

Then, yesterday afternoon, the call came. The clinic was one of the few places in D'Kar which had a phone. There was an urgent call from the hospital in Ghanzi. Nqaba had been admitted and an emergency operation was needed. They needed her mother's signature for the operation.

The nurse at the clinic did not know the mother well enough to carry over such a sensitive message and had come to Mmamoruti for assistance. Early this morning Mmamoruti picked up Nqaba's mother and together they rushed to Ghanzi.

Nqaba was much better when they reached Ghanzi, and announced herself ready for the operation. "I crawled all by myself to the hospital," she told them. "The pain was so bad that I could not walk." Now she was under sedation and she felt much better. She looked almost happy lying in the high, white bed, except that her stomach was still so sensitive that no one could touch it.

She was, of course, naked again, except for a sheet, and without any scruples she bared herself further to show Mmamoruti exactly where the pain had started and what path it had taken through her body.

"Look, it cut me here, it cuts, cuts and then it shoots away and ggoooeeep! Then it sits over here again and it cuts me ..."

Mmamoruti tried to explain what to expect before and after such an operation.

Nqaba was cheerful and relaxed. "Yes, I know, they cut you open with a large knife. Then they look inside you and when they have finished, they take a needle and thread and they sew you up again."

Yes, it was the old Nqaba she knew, Mmamoruti thought. Her reaction was so different from the other patients Mmamoruti had dealt with, who had a deep fear of being "slaughtered" alive in hospital and imagined the operation knife to be a huge axe.

Nqaba was pregnant, the hospital staff had told them on arrival. It complicated the operation even further. There was a chance that she could lose the baby.

To her mother's annoyance Nqaba could once again not say who the father of the baby was. This suited her well, she told her mother, because losing the baby would now be no one else's worry but hers. As a final argument, she said: "Mama, God is with me, so there is no need to fear."

While she talked, Nqaba stretched herself and put her left arm behind her head. The right one was attached to a drip. Mmamoruti was alarmed to notice a large swelling in the armpit.

"How long has that swelling been under your arm?" she asked anxiously. "You must show it to the doctors immediately, while you have their attention!" she urged when neither Nqaba nor her mother seemed to be concerned. To be laughing, in fact.

"No, Mmamoruti," Nqaba said, "don't worry. I have always been like this, you know. This is how I look." She pulled the drip-stand closer and lifted her other arm as well.

There it was, a similar swelling in her right armpit.

"These are my other breasts. Ever since I became a big girl, I have had them. When I have babies, they even get a little milk, just like the other two." With twinkling eyes she pointed to a small nipple in the middle of the lump.

How had she managed to hide them so well, especially with her type of clothes! Mmamoruti was speechless. Suddenly, a lot of things made sense. Now she understood. If Nqaba's newest puppy would survive the operation, there would be more than enough milk. Maybe this time there might even be more than one puppy?

SIX
# Killer child

It feels like I am carrying a child, X'aga realised with a shock. Like the two babies I carried and gave birth to but never raised.

All through the day she rested the heavy mass in the crook of her right arm. It was covered with an old hip cloth which she now kept tied behind her neck. She had to support it on her arm otherwise it sagged and pulled the surrounding skin painfully.

How long has it been? Sometimes, when she thought about the many months she had been waiting here in D'Kar, seeing one moon after the other shrink and swell again, she was overwhelmed with fear. She noticed that her limbs were getting thinner and that her skin was getting paler. Every day. She had come here with her husband, because she had believed that there might be hope. After walking for many hours in the hot sun, at times following the narrow vehicle tracks and other times heading through the veld, they had reached the main road. She could not keep up with him, so they often had to rest in the shade of the camel-thorn trees. They walked from cattle post to cattle post, following the silhouette of the wind-pumps on their way, to find water. After drinking, she washed the thing.

It was a massive foreign growth that oozed pus on her arm and over her stomach. It had a life of its own and it was growing like a child. Sometimes, in the middle of the day, she even caught herself humming to it, slowly rocking to and fro as if she was trying to put it to sleep. At night she was careful not to roll over on to it. But as she could seldom sleep for long periods because of the pain in her back and chest, there was no danger. She was always alert and always aware of it. In the heat of the day the smell coming from it attracted flies, so she washed it whenever she had water, removed the cloth and dried it in the sun.

There were times when the smell got so bad that Cao could not sleep next to her. But he was always there, close by, when she called for him.

Somehow, she was waiting for it to go away, to finish its life just as suddenly and without cause as her two babies had done. In the beginning, while she nursed it, cleaned it and held it, she sometimes found herself wondering if it was still alive.

But unlike her babies, this thing became stronger and bigger, and she started fearing it.

After a long time trying to think what to do, reading the fear also in the eyes of her husband and family, she felt the urge to move off somewhere, to find a place where someone would know what to do.

At night as she stared into the dark, she sometimes had visions of her aunt, years ago, who had started bleeding long after her monthly periods had ceased. They had tried all their roots and pounded leaf mixtures, to no avail. Then many nights in a row they had danced, while the old woman sat in the fire circle, being touched, rubbed, even embraced by the healers. Their dancing had helped so many before. The circle of singing and clapping women joined the healer in his trance, with his writhing body and foam around his mouth, in calling out to Dxãwa for the healing power. With their intense clapping, palms stretched open, and the rhythm in the air around them, in the earth beneath them, and in the bodies of those next to them, the women created an energy which grew and enveloped them all and helped them challenge the unknown power that held control over their lives.

They were all healing her; the main dancer only carried their message. For many hours they would continue, until their voices reached a climax again, pleading for – demanding almost – the peace, harmony and abundance their little group needed to survive in the bush. When the first light broke, they would be singing still, and the intensity would continue to grow with the coming day. Then, when the first rays touched their moving bodies, they would fall out of the circle one by one, weak with exhaustion, to find a shady spot where they could sleep until life flowed back into their limbs.

The first time the little group danced for her and the thing that was growing on her, she had felt a surge of panic. Their medicine, their dancing, had not helped her aunt, who had eventually lain in the hut next to theirs, a hideous smell surrounding her. No one in the clan could bear to be near her. There was no change in her condition anyway, so they had let her be.

If only she could avoid going like her aunt. In her mind's eye she could still see the old woman on the sandy floor of the grass hut, chickens feeding and scrabbling in the sand next to her. One had hopped onto her head, left a dropping there which nobody removed. Although she had been too young to question why they had given up on her aunt, she knew that there was no turning back for the poor, frail body of the old woman. She moved only now and then, occasionally letting out a sigh, until the day they folded her cold body into a grave in that same hut. They had put her into the ground in a sitting position, covering the body in the same dusty blanket under which she had lain all that time. Afterwards they filled the grave with sand, pounded it down and swept the area until there was not a trace of the grave left. Then the whole group had moved away.

She had persuaded Cao to come with her on this long journey to D'Kar. Even if their relatives were no longer there, surely they would find someone else who could help. The first night, after the truck which had picked them up had dropped them at the big blue building with the many children running around it, they moved towards the first cluster of huts they could see. There they asked if someone knew the names of their people, whom they had heard had moved here, long ago.

Those distant relatives were no longer there; some had gone to Ghanzi and others were now living in government settlements. Disappointed and exhausted, they just stayed right there, at those first huts. Later they were handed mugs with sweet, black tea and they lay down beside the fire with the others. It was cold; the fire was much smaller than the ones they had been able to make on the farm where they came from.

The clinic, that was a word she now heard often and where people took them the next day. The memory of her first clinic visit still choked her. Long rows of people were sitting outside, some coughing, others laughing, smoking and passing their crying babies around. People were going into the building one by one, the door closing behind them, and they only came out after a while. Eventually she and Cao were summoned. The floor was a bright, polished red, and tall instruments and metal containers stood around. A young, black woman with a white outfit and strange hair that hung around her head like hundreds of thin, black snakes, talked to them in a language which made no sense. She looked at the two of them with distaste in her eyes and spoke in an impatient voice. Eventually another one in a green outfit who could speak their language came to explain that she would have to go with them to the town where there was a man who would know what to do. She added that the thing would have to be cut off and that she would have to go to a far place called Gaborone. But, the woman in the green outfit said, her husband would have to remain behind.

That was when she made up her mind. She could not bear to think of being alone with these strange people with their strong voices and their big, dark bodies, in more buildings like these, where there is no fire and where one can see nothing of the world outside. No, she could not bear that. Then rather go like her aunt who, though she could not talk to them any longer, knew her people were there, close to her, up to the end.

But Cao and she remained in D'Kar. It was as if they were hoping for something else to happen. For the first weeks she and Cao lay under the thorny shrubs in the sand by day, and at night they would crouch around a small fire which Cao made from the few thin sticks and burnable scraps he could find nearby. They had moved gradually towards the last line of huts in the village, so that they could be close to people yet have the open veld behind them. There was no point in going back to the farm; their people might have moved on and she no longer had the courage to face the whole business of travel and asking for lifts again. Gradually other newcomers from the farms and the settlements moved in next to them, and they helped Cao collect cardboard boxes, and bits of plastic which were stuck in the wire fences and thorn bushes all around, to build a shelter over the *swarthaak* bush where she lay.

Then winter came and they had to huddle as close to each other as possible, all night and even sometimes during the day. Many nights the howling wind blew sand in their faces and they would lie in the early morning sun for a long time before they could move their aching, freezing bodies. As she was always holding the thing, Cao had to fetch water for them at the tap, collect firewood and put a shelter together. He had also started to make small bows and arrows which, with some luck, he could sell for money to buy food at the place they called Kuru. She shuffled around on her haunches, following the shade around her thorn bush in the day, but mostly her body wanted nothing more than just to sleep.

It was when it started getting warm again and the first thundershowers lit the sky and soaked them and their neighbours to the bone that the white woman discovered them. They had often noticed the car passing not far from them on the narrow track winding through the bushes, and the others had talked about the people of the church. This morning the woman had stopped, walked between the huts and offloaded some cardboard boxes for shelter. Since it had rained the whole night, they were wet through and through, their blankets spread over the bushes to dry. New rain clouds were building up.

Someone had directed the woman to their shelter and she asked to see the wound. There was now no longer any breast, the flesh had exploded into a stinking, steaming white thing that reminded her of the brain of an eland. Maggots were eating away at its insides. The woman's hand trembled when she talked to them both, and in her broken Naro she slowly got the story out of her of the clinic and their fear of the strange people with their big knife in that far-away place.

After this the woman and her husband came many times, taking turns. They brought food and medicine to clean the wound, and they talked about God. Their visits became the one thing that she looked forward to every day, hoping for some small gifts of tea or money for tobacco, which had become her only pleasure. The woman showed Cao how to wash the breast. The smell and the flies had diminished and it no longer oozed so much. One day, the woman talked again about the place where they wanted to take her, and listening to her, she suddenly thought to herself it might not be such a bad idea to cut away the ugly thing. It was already so painful, would the knife be any worse?

She often thought about pain where she lay in her shady patch in the heat of the day. Somehow pain always seemed to be present in the life they led in the bush, something everybody lived with. She told herself that the throbbing was normal, that what was happening to her now would also just pass. She remembered how, one day, her little nephew had stepped on a thorn that went right through his foot. When he could not dig it out of the sole, his father had pulled the thorn upwards through the foot, grabbing it by the little stump that stuck out on top. The child didn't even wince. No, she was no longer afraid of pain. Sometimes the only way to end it was to take more pain. If this woman said it would be good to have the lump cut away, she would trust her.

Many days after she had made this decision, as she sat on a high bed in a tall building, she tried to make sense of the journey, recall in her mind how she had come there, but it was just a confusing blur of memories. There had been an endless time in the back of a closed, mad vehicle, which had bumped and sped mercilessly on, throwing her against the other patients cramped alongside her under the roof. Cao had to stay behind. There had been a nurse who gave them water every so often when they stopped, and who listened to people's hearts with a thing that hung around her neck. They had set off from D'Kar early, still in the dark, and it was long after dark again when they had arrived in a place with many bright lights.

She spent a week in that strange hospital in Gaborone with nurses walking up and down and talking to one another in the language of the black people. At least by this time she could understand a few words. And some of the patients who had come down with her to Gaborone could speak Naro and tell her what the nurses wanted. They told her she was being given extra food to build up her strength for another journey, and for the operation.

The second journey went through many towns, on a smooth, black road and there were so many things to see that she closed her eyes against it all after a while. The vehicle brought her to this tall building in a very noisy city, where there was only one woman she could speak to and only because she tried the bits of Afrikaans she had picked up on the farm in her youth.

She learnt that the endless drone of cars outside, the tapping feet in the corridor with its red and black tiles, the clanging of the trolleys which brought their food – this was Johannesburg. There were many people with kind eyes, but their mouths made sounds she could not respond to, so she sank back against the pillows and watched the clouds or the blank concrete wall outside her window. She had brought her little tin pipe with her and longed for a smoke, but when she showed them the pipe, they all just laughed, admired it, took it to inspect among themselves, and brought it back to her empty. She tried to picture Cao in their cardboard shelter, boiling water for tea for himself in an old jam tin and sometimes wondered if he would not get tired of waiting for her. She wondered if anyone had ever told him where she had been taken.

Although she could not understand them, she did what was expected of her when they came for her. She had learned to hold out her arm for their needle, and once, after such a jab, everything grew hazy and she had woken much later with a bad feeling in her head and strips of cloth wound round her body. Blood had soaked through the fabric where the thing had been and she was afraid to touch it, more because of fear of the bleeding than because of the pain. It was quite a while before they removed the dirty strips of cloth and put on clean ones. She was shocked, yet reassured, by the bright red, clean flesh underneath. The broken patch on her skin was large and scary, but such a weight had been lifted from her that she felt strangely young and lighthearted. It made her happy when she realised that she could reach out with her right arm again, now that she no longer carried the thing on it all the time. She was sure that she would soon be able to go home.

Again they brought her extra food and special things to eat, things her fellow patients did not get. Although she could not talk to the others, they had developed a kind of sisterhood in sharing their ugly disfigurements and hearing each other turn and toss at night. She shared her fruit and extra meat with them as she would have done at home with her own family. They were all so very sick; looking at them helped her forget her own pain. One had a growth on her face which made her head lopsided and heavy. She had to rest her chin in her hand mostly, and you could see her head becoming heavier in her hands every day.

Time went by and her own body grew stronger. Yet her heart and mind became sadder and lonelier. She watched the moon outside the hospital window shrink; waited for it to appear outside her window each night until it was just a silver sliver in the sky, like a sad little smile. Three times she saw it disappear and waited for it to grow big again, while she tried to imagine the sounds back home, wondered what Cao was doing, and whether they ever danced for her. She often thought about him and her, and how they had watched this same moon together in D'Kar, covering themselves with their only blanket. She smiled when she thought of the story her father had told them so many times, about the moon and his wife who also shared only one blanket. Slowly, night by night, the wife would pull the blanket off her husband until he lay naked, shining brightly and in full view. Then, feeling cold, he would start to pull the blanket back over himself, gently so as not to wake his wife, until he was completely covered again.

By now she had even started to understand something of the strange languages spoken around her, and people were kind. Every now and then they would come and fetch her, which she feared, but deep down she knew she had to go with them if she was ever to get out of this place. They took her down a long corridor where they put needles and pipes into her body in different places and let her lie in a special room with many faces around her. Afterwards she was always too weak to walk, she vomited and could not eat for days. The other patients supported her while she spat everything that was inside her into the toilet, until her body was empty and she had no power left.

She did not understand what they were doing to her and she feared the sickness which came over her afterwards, but a few days after they had put the needles and pipes into her, she could feel herself getting stronger. She was growing fatter. In the mirror in the bathroom her face looked strange and swollen and she could see that her hair was thinning.

Then one day there was a sudden bustle in the hospital, people were packing, some had already dressed and walked out. Christmas time, they said. The hospital closes for a month, they must all go home. She had nothing to pack and didn't know where to go. Frightened, she sat on the high bed in her white hospital jacket, terrified to be left alone, waiting for something to happen. Eventually they fetched her, and together with some other women she was driven back on the long, black roads until the vehicle stopped.

It was the same hospital she had been brought to after she left home, and she recognised some faces. She was put into a ward with some other people from Ghanzi. They explained to her in Setswana that they were all waiting for transport to go home. One day, a young white man in brown clothes with signs on the shoulders of his shirt, came to fetch her. The others mentioned something about going up, but she did not understand what they meant until she saw the small, metal body of what looked like a big insect. She had seen this thing pass over their home in D'Kar before, people called it the fly. Here they called it the Flying Mission. She knew then that this man was taking her home.

She was used to nausea by now, so when the fly took off and she felt the familiar turn of her stomach, she closed her eyes for the rest of the journey to ward off the fear and the sickness. But then flying low towards the airstrip in D'Kar and over the huts, she could see Cao, the white woman and her husband standing next to their car. Suddenly panic gripped her. What if they did not recognise her? By now she was completely bald and her face, hands and feet were puffy. She also no longer carried the thing on her arm, the way Cao had last seen her. As the fly moved slowly towards the little group of people, after the man had set it down on the ground, a few people she knew came running towards them and children were jumping up and down. She clung to the arms of her chair until the engines were silent, and the man in brown clothes with the signs on the shoulders of his shirt came to open the belt with which he had strapped her to her seat before they had gone up.

This wasn't home, but for her it was the only place she had ever wanted to be. The clicks of her language washed over her; people reached out and took her hands where she sat in the white people's car; children were cheering and jumping on the back of the bakkie.

Their hut was a surprise. Cao had found enough grass to cover almost half of it; the other half was still plastered with cardboard and plastic, but it looked new and tight.

Every day people came to see her, touched her bald scalp. She had to tell her story over and over again. They particularly liked hearing about the high building she had lived in and how she was taken up high by stepping into a tiny, bare room which would move up so fast when someone pressed the buttons inside that she had to hold on to keep her balance. Once this little room was up, it waited for her there, near the room where she had stayed all that time, to take her down again to the place where they gave her the medicine which made her vomit. She also had to tell them about the many vehicles that snaked along the roads way below her window, and how scared she was at first to look down. Those cars on the roads below looked just as tiny and were just as many as the ants filing along their paths after the rains, she told them.

It was hard to get used to the lack of food again, as well as to the cold at night. But Cao was there and they held each other in the darkness. He had gone home to the farm while she was away, he told her. He had told the others what had happened and they had promised to come and visit her in D'Kar. But she and Cao had also become full members of their new community by now and she didn't miss her own people so much any more. Others would join them at their fire at night to share the scraps the whites and other people brought her, and she was contented. She even sometimes went out with Cao to collect firewood, though she tired easily.

But as the moon waxed and waned again she felt her body grow weaker. She had lost a lot of weight now that the three meals a day she had become used to were not there, and although she enjoyed her metal pipe more than anything else, she was coughing badly and her chest burned every time she smoked.

One night the group danced for her again. The sound of their singing and clapping drowned out the music of the gumba-gumba at the drinking place and the sounds of talking and occasional shouts from other houses in the village. She was alone with her people again; the healer rubbed her shoulders and she could feel the power flowing back into her body.

The next day the white woman and her husband came to see them. They brought a dress and some things they said were for washing your teeth. It was time to go again, they said, the fly would soon come to take her back to Johannesburg.

The news took the ground from under her feet. "Táá!" She shook her head. She would not go anywhere again.

Suddenly she was so angry, she moved into her hut and turned her back on them. They sat talking to Cao; others gathered around, but she smoked her pipe, blocking out the voices outside by scratching in the sand with a stick. After a while she got up, walked past them into the bush, talking loudly to them over her shoulder about the things they had made her do, the pain, and the strange world they had thrown her into, the way they had deserted her.

She only came back when everyone had left, muttering to herself as she picked up firewood, until the wild beating of her heart had stopped.

That night, she and Cao made a plan. Far from there, in another village, was a man from the north, a great doctor of his people – the ones who lived next to the water where they made fields and moved on the river in hollow tree trunks, so they had heard. They had often been told of the healing gifts of this man. But they had heard, too, that people must pay a lot to be healed. Those who did not have money must take him goats, sometimes even cattle.

The next day Cao went around talking to people, and that evening, when the sun was pulling in its round, red face behind the last rows of the thorn bushes, he was there with a donkey-cart pulled by two donkeys. They would have to pay for the cart, he said, but the man was willing to wait. In the darkness, afraid that the white man and his wife would find out, they loaded their possessions, put a blanket down behind the bench for her to lie on. Cao sat on the bench with the owner of the cart. It was a terrible journey. She tried to sleep, but the bumpy ride jolted her body and caused terrible pain in her chest. Around midnight they stopped for a while and lay down under the cart in the grass.

The donkeys, whose front legs were hobbled to stop them from escaping while they grazed, tore at the grass tufts on the side of the road while they slept. When it was still dark, they set off again, travelling until the sun, high above them, drove them into the shade of some trees for a rest.

Back on the road, Cao would spread a blanket over her every time they heard a vehicle approaching. He disguised himself by pulling his hat low over his eyes. Nobody was going to find them, take them back, and separate them again.

It was late the following night that they arrived at Kuke, where the black doctor lived in a hut at the edge of the village. They camped close by. She was so tired she did not care where they were. The pain in her chest, which had become unbearable lately, was so bad that she choked on it. And her right arm, which had started to swell during the past few days, was stiff and sore. In her armpits aching lumps had appeared. Cao massaged her chest and arm, but the skin where they had cut away her breast had not healed well, and at the edges of the wound painful ridges had formed which she could not bear to be touched.

The next morning, the black man listened to her story inside his hut. Cao would have to bring him two goats, he said. Then he started mixing all sorts of things he took from a bag made from animal fur with wild cats' tails attached to it. On a fire in the corner a small can was boiling, to which he added the unknown stuff. He returned and made little cuts with a sharp knife in the skin of her stomach, and into these he rubbed a black powder, mixing it with her blood. Then he closed his eyes, pounded on the floor with his open palms and uttered strange words in a dark voice. Later he led them both out of the hut to an open space where low wooden stools stood in a circle. She had to get down on her knees while he rubbed oil into her bare scalp. Then he offered her a tin cup with a greenish broth, instructing her to drink it as fast as possible. This, he explained through his translator, would make the poison leave her body.

The medicine had a dreadful taste. As she paused for breath, he urged her on: more, more! Her body went into a spasm, she doubled over and she retched violently and uncontrollably. He didn't touch her again but danced around her.

When at last she could sit upright, he pointed triumphantly with his stick: "Look, look! There it is, the evil has come out!"

In front of her, in her green vomit on the sand, lay a few hairy clusters. The dark, awful stuff must have come from inside her. Then everything turned black before her eyes as she fell to the ground.

The whole day she slept in the shade of the tree. Cao waited by her side. That evening she had terrible stomach cramps. She had to go to the bush; it was as if her bowels were exploding. Repeatedly through the night she had to get up and go to the bush, until later she was too weak to walk.

All of the next day the cramps continued. Cao had moved her to another tree, further from the man's house. He sat next to her, wiping her legs and throwing sand on the green liquid that ran from her body. The doctor came over to them once and looked at her. They should not worry, she would soon be well, he said. This was just more poison coming out.

She was terribly thirsty. She wanted to go home but knew that another journey on the donkey-cart would be too much. Cao brought her water, washed her legs and dress. That done, he sat next to her and in silence watched her sunken eyes close and her breathing become shallow.

That night he lay close to her and held her tight until her body stopped trembling. Later he felt that she was no longer breathing and had become cold and stiff. He kept on holding her, waiting for the glow of dawn to bring some understanding and courage. He could not sleep. As in a dream he saw the two of them going back to the farm. They followed the road they would have to go, the whole distance to the junction on the main road and beyond, travelling along the sandy tracks to their cattle post. He was carrying her on his back, all the way back to where they had come from. She talked to him over his shoulder of how she would milk the goats, of the veldkos she would bring home. Then he saw her sitting at the fire once more, roasting *cgùi* nuts in the warm ash. She had a baby suckling at her breast. A sob burst from his chest when she looked up and smiled at him.

Later, when the rising sun fired a glow in the east, he covered her body with their blanket and rolled towards the fire to get some warmth for himself. He was so tired that he fell asleep almost at once. He dreamt she was leaving him in a fly, just like the one in which she had returned home that day. He could see her face through the window, but she looked past him. Her face was unspeakably sad. He chased after the fly until his lungs were about to burst, but the little metal insect didn't notice, slowly lifted its wheels off the ground and left him standing there, and disappeared in a cloud of dust.

SEVEN
# What's in a name?

If it had not been for her and Qgam, Mies Betty would have had no one, Turu thought, where she was bending over the zinc basin outside the farmhouse. They were busy packing everything in the house, but Mies Betty wanted all the blankets to be washed before she moved back to Ghanzi. As if anyone had slept in them, Turu thought. For more than four years, these blankets have been lying in the cupboard, waiting for bodies to warm, for people to roll themselves snugly into them; but no one came. Maybe Mies Betty wanted them to be washed so she could rinse out the memories of this place, make them disappear with the soapsuds in the heat of the sun. Turu turned the basin over under the pepper tree and watched the large splash of water shine on the ground for a moment before it sank swiftly into the smooth, yellow sand. She watched the little soap bubbles that hesitated on top of the sand for a few moments, reflecting their colours in the sunlight before they popped and also disappeared.

Mies Betty was returning to Ghanzi, therefore Turu and Qgam could also go back to their people. They had come to live with her in Namibia, when, as a widow and late in her life, she had married a farmer from Gobabis. Turu can still remember how, after this man's first visit to the farm in Ghanzi, Mies Betty's eyes sparkled again and they could hear her singing in the kitchen in the mornings. The old people on the farm were worried. It had been years since her husband had died and they were used to helping her on the farm. There was no need for a new man. "His car is too shiny, and we do not know him. And is he not too young for her?" old Xau said the words everybody was thinking.

After he had come for a few more visits, Jan Liebenberg started staying over for a few days each time. There was talk of the farm being sold to Gert Vermaak. Turu remembered all the workers and their families discussing at night what would happen to them if the farm were to be sold. Some were talking about going to the settlements where the government had promised to make people fat. Others thought that they were too far from everything, they thought D'Kar would be a better option. They were very sure that neither Gert Vermaak nor Jan Liebenberg would let them stay on. Farmers usually had their own Bushmen who worked for them.

Life at Hanahai, where Turu moved with her family after Mies Betty had moved to Namibia, was very different from the farm. Some people were given food rations each month by the Council, especially those who were old or had young children but no husband, but they missed the milk, the tobacco, soap, sugar and tea they had received every week at Mies Betty's farm. It was not even two years after Mies Betty had married Jan Liebenberg, when Paul, her oldest son, came driving into Hanahai to find Turu. He no longer lived at Ghanzi, but he had always come to visit his mother once a year from a far place. Since he had grown up in front of them all, they recognised him immediately when he stopped at the kgotla to inquire, and they sent one of the children to hop onto the back of the bakkie to show him the way to their huts. Turu could still see Paul standing there, one arm on his bakkie's open door and the other hand on his waist, squinting in the sun. He did not want a chair, he said. He was wearing the khaki short pants all white men in this area wore, so Turu watched amused how the children sat next to him in the shade of the vehicle, looking at the hair on his legs while he talked, trying to touch the hair without being noticed.

Jan Liebenberg had left Mies Betty, he told them, and she was all alone on the farm in Namibia, with workers she did not know or understand. Would Turu not come to Namibia to help her?

The family talked while Paul waited in his bakkie for their decision. At last the family decided to send Qgam, her sister's son, along with her so that he could help in the garden. This way Mies Betty would have more people from her own place. Turu's children would stay with her parents and Qgam would keep her company in Namibia. She had often been grateful for that decision, Turu thought. It would have been much more difficult if she had come here all by herself. She smiled when she thought how happy Qgam had been when she told him last week that they were going back to Botswana. He had been talking about his little son so often lately, wondering what he would be able to do by now.

"It's not as if she's not looking after us well, but this is the time a man should be near his family," he said last night, sipping coffee from his tin mug, the glare of the fire on his cheeks.

It was true. Loneliness is a very bad thing, Turu thought, while hanging the blankets over the washing-line, wringing the corners to squeeze out the excess water. She had always thought one would feel less lonely when you became a little older, like she and Mies Betty were, but she had never seen such loneliness in a person as what they found in Mies Betty when they came to Namibia. Not even in the earlier times, after her first husband had died and her children were still small, did Mies Betty cry so much. Gradually Turu and Qgam heard pieces of the story. Jan Liebenberg had started visiting another woman in his shiny car and had then moved to live at the sea with her. He had allowed Mies Betty to stay on in the big farmhouse, but he had rented the farmland surrounding it to a neighbour, so she had no responsibility for what happened to his cattle and no income from the farm. And he had left her with too little money to go back to Ghanzi.

The other labourers on the farm, who lived at the cattle posts, were also red people, but they were from the Kaukau people, so they and Mies Betty could not understand each other. Even Turu and Qgam never got to understand them fully, and so they kept to themselves at the farmhouse most of the time. In any case, Mies Betty needed someone around her constantly, so they could not go away for a long time.

She put the basin away in the laundry room next to the back stoep. This house was huge, much bigger than the one Mies Betty had had in Ghanzi before. So many different kinds of rooms. Turu had to look after the inside while Qgam worked outside, raking the yard, chasing out goats, watering the cannas and vygies. He had to tend the little patch of green grass in front of the house and the huge palm trees which lined the fence. He had to start the generator to pump water for the house and garden, feed the chickens and the peacocks, and every day he had to sweep the little cement footpaths that were laid out to prevent one from carrying too much sand into the house. In front of the stoep someone had pushed green and red bottles upside down into the sand to create a hardened glass base on which to step before one entered the polished stoep. The green and red bottles formed a pattern, almost like a carpet made of glass. Every morning Qgam raked the remaining sand patches in the yard with little patterns which reminded Turu of the carvings her parents did on ostrich eggshells when she was young.

Mies Betty did not see much of Qgam's work, though, because she did not go outside much. Her own bakkie was always in the shed, but she never went anywhere, and trusted Qgam and Turu to look after everything. Turu lived in a small room outside, near the electricity generator, so she could be close by when Mies Betty needed her at night. Qgam slept in an old hut which someone had built inside the yard near the back fence many years ago. He made a fire outside this hut in the evenings where the two of them then sat, looking at the stars and talking about Ghanzi. Once a year, at Christmas, Mies Betty went to her children in South Africa and gave them two weeks off to go and visit their relatives in Ghanzi. That was the only time they saw their people. Now and then, however, they got some news from home if they happen to meet some of the lorry boys of the white people who brought their children to school in Namibia. This was when she and Qgam took the bakkie and went shopping for Mies Betty at the farm shop and petrol station a few farms away, on the road to the Botswana border. Qgam did not have a licence, but Mies Betty told him which back roads to follow so that he had to cross the main road only once.

Turu closed the gauze door of the kitchen behind her and continued to pack the pots and saucepans into the cardboard boxes on the floor of the kitchen. She put water on the gas stove for her and Qgam's porridge. It had worked out well in the end, bringing Qgam along to Mies Betty. Turu had been afraid that because Qgam was still young when they had lived on her farm, Mies Betty would not remember him that well, and that she might not want to have him here. After all, Paul had only come to Hanahai to ask for Turu.

But Mies Betty was glad that Turu brought him along, she said when they arrived. She did not know how to talk to the people in this country. Although her Naro was not perfect, Turu and Qgam could understand her well. They had lived with the whites long enough to know what they meant even if they could not pronounce the sounds of their language so well. Therefore Turu was shocked, the first morning after they arrived, when she heard what Mies Betty was shouting outside the kitchen door, in Naro. Turu dropped everything and ran to the kitchen, thinking that the woman had gone mad. How could she shout "Penis! Penis!" for everyone to hear? It was only when she saw Qgam arrive on the back stoep, looking embarrassed, that she got it. Mies Betty was calling his name, but she said Qam instead of Qgam. She got his name all wrong and she did not know what she was saying! Turu ran into the pantry and laughed and laughed, pushing her doek into her mouth, so that she would not embarrass Mies Betty with her laughter.

At first Qgam was angry and slowly repeated his name for her every time Mies Betty called him, putting stress on the correct sound. But she did not even seem to notice that he was doing it and she probably would not have heard the difference. Later he gave up and they both became used to it. They had never told Mies Betty what she was saying.

Turu and Qgam sat on the ground under the pepper tree in the backyard with their bowls of porridge and mugs of tea. They rested their backs against the wall of Turu's room. The generator was quiet now. Every evening after sunset they had to start it so that Mies Betty could have electric light. The thud-thud-thud only stopped at around midnight, because Mies Betty liked to read in bed.

"Remember how I complained in the beginning about the terrible sound and the trembling walls of my room?" Turu asked Qgam. "In the beginning I thought I would die, but now I might even miss the noise," she laughed.

"One would have thought that some of her children would have come to help us move," Qgam said. "White people are strange."

Mies Betty's children were all grown-up and they lived in South Africa. "Probably better they do not come," Turu said. "This way we at least have peace." Mies Betty's children seldom came to visit her, and when they had once done so, they all quarrelled and there were a lot of loud voices and even some crying. They only stayed for one day. Qgam had said that time that he thought it was because they discovered she had sold the farm in Ghanzi and wasted the money on her new husband. After the children left, Mies Betty cried for days. Oh, she could cry and pity herself! The only thing that could cheer her up, Turu found out after a while, was when she imitated people they both knew from Ghanzi.

Turu had always known how well she could do this – the way people walked, the way they held their faces and hands – you could not help but recognise them. Everybody always loved it when she did that. After that visit of her children, to try and make Mies Betty laugh again, Turu called Qgam into the house and the two of them acted out, first scenes they saw at the shop, then they imitated Mies Betty's children, her neighbours on the farms around her and eventually even her husband coming to the farm in his fancy clothes and new car. That first time. In the end Mies Betty was laughing out loud.

But the most difficult thing was to break through Mies Betty's silent times. When she cried, one could eventually make her laugh. But the times when she just sat in front of the mirror in her bedroom, looking at herself without talking, those were the dangerous times. Turu had learnt how to handle them too, however. Mostly it helped if she just squatted down, took Mies Betty's feet in her hands and started washing them in a basin of warm, soapy water. She would then cut her toenails, cut out the corns on the soles of her feet with her pocket knife. Turu knew she was good at that, she never hurt Mies Betty. At such times, none of them would talk. She always waited for Mies Betty to start talking first. And my, didn't she talk then, and the things she could tell you!

"Whites might just look as if they have no troubles, but they just hide them better. They can also do some very nasty things to each other," she once said to Qgam as they sat around the fire one evening after such a day with Mies Betty. "You know, sometimes when she tells me the things this second husband has done to her, she cries and cries and the only thing that makes her stop is me stroking her hair or rubbing her neck."

Such times, she felt as if she had to comfort Qgam as well. The more Mies Betty cried, the more concerned he became that they would never leave Namibia. She, too, missed her children, and the warmth of other bodies next to her at night, the happy chatter at the fire until everyone had fallen asleep. She missed the walks to the veld with the other women to find veldkos, and the continuous exchange of news and stories. But Qgam was becoming restless, more than she was. Maybe because he had only his rake and the birds as company in the daytime, and he did not see the sadness of this woman as closely as she did. Now he was eagerly helping her pack, and every day he asked her if there was news of when the truck would arrive. He could not wait to go back, even though they had not been told where they would go, if there would be work for them there or not.

Turu drew deeply on the tin pipe Qgam had passed her. It was midday, and Mies Betty would be sleeping, so they could sit a little longer in the shade of the wall. She must admit that it had not always been easy for her here either. Yet she had learnt a lot of things, in the daytime, with Mies Betty alone in the big house. She had to do the washing, sweep and dust, and rub oil into the tables and cupboards until they shone. Mies Betty could not stand anything that was dirty. Even though, with only the two of them in the house, things did not really become dirty. Mies Betty would walk around checking every corner, drawing a damp cloth over the surfaces of the many tea tables and window-sills and call Turu back when there was brown dust on the cloth. Not a speck of sand, not a spider's web, not an ant, nothing, was to be left alone in that house. In the mornings the curtains had to be kept closed and the windows shut. In the evenings Turu had to open the windows while making sure that all the gauze frames were drawn down to keep out the bugs.

"This is how you keep the coolness of the night inside the house, Turu, so that the house does not become as hot as the wind outside," she would complain if Turu dared to open a window. This was difficult, because Turu loved the breeze of the Kalahari on her face, so she would sit on the low cement wall outside the kitchen door, smoking, when she was not needed inside the big, suffocating and half-dark house.

But one thing she took a long time to learn – how to curl Mies Betty's hair with those plastic rollers. She would sit in front of the mirror and show Turu how to take a piece of wet hair, roll it around the plastic tube and stick a small white peg through it. The first time she tried it, she told Qgam that night, "I almost pushed it through her scalp, and she screamed and slapped my hand!"

"Whites have such funny hair," Qgam laughed. "I hate it when it falls out and blows all over the place. If I eat the food she's cooked I always think of how she never wears a doek over that hair."

"Yes," Turu agreed, "and their hair gets stuck in those rollers if you do it wrong, and you think you will never get them out! White people's hair is jumpy, the little strands keep going loose, jumping out of the rollers and standing up straight. Mies Betty looked frightful the first time I did it, like a scared porcupine!"

From where they sit, they can see the main gate to the yard and the sandy track that winds through the veld to the main road. Any day now the truck from Ghanzi will come through that gate to take them home. The gate makes Turu think back to the day it all started, when they knew their lives were going to change and that Mies Betty's loneliness might be over. For a long, long time they had had no visitors, then one day, suddenly, there was the sound of a car approaching. There were several gates to open before the car would get to the house, so Turu and Qgam ran out to watch in the distance who it could be. When the bakkie stopped at the second last gate to the farmhouse, at the kraal, they could already see that a white man was driving, with a red person standing at the back. They both thought at first that Jan Liebenberg was coming back, but even though the bakkie at the gate was a good car, it was not as shiny as the ones they knew he liked.

Turu and Qgam stood outside the house, watching the bakkie approach. The yellow grass and the solitary, large camel-thorn tree on the other side of the fence contrasted sharply with the bare and well-raked sandy yard. The veld here had no small thorny shrubs like in Ghanzi, so one could see quite far. This bakkie was from Botswana, they could see from the familiar-looking number-plate when it came to a standstill in front of the last gate to the house. The person standing at the back of the bakkie looked familiar too. When he jumped off to open the gate, Qgam gasped: "It's Cukuri! From D'Kar!" He suddenly turned and ran back towards the house.

Then Turu recognised the farmer inside the cab of the bakkie as well. It was Frans Botha, who had a farm in Ghanzi, near where Mies Betty used to live, and who used to come and visit her a few times in the months and years after her first husband had died. This could mean something, this visit. She had better go and see that Mies Betty looked her best, she thought, and also scurried back. At the back door, she came upon Qgam and Mies Betty. He must have called her out. She was standing inside the door frame, with a questioning face. Qgam was holding his hat in his hand, and was out of breath from running. "Mies Betty," he said, his voice pleading, "please, from now on, do not use my Naro name. Please, just call me Saulus."

EIGHT

# Girls

The girls were restless. The whole weekend lay ahead of them; school was out but they could not go home on their own. Sometimes it was possible to slip away on a Friday afternoon and get a lift somewhere, since the road passed right in front of the school. Getting to Ghanzi or D'Kar one could sometimes manage, but going to the farms, where two of them came from, was more difficult. The farm roads branched off the main road and then they would still have to walk for a couple of hours to reach home. They did not feel like it today. It was their last year in primary school and the December holidays were just around the corner.

The other deterrent was the punishment that surely awaited those who dared to leave the hostel without permission. The matron did not want to let them go out for weekends, because she believed they would not come back once they had been with their parents, or, as she had called it, "gone wild" again. There were times when they had slipped back home and a council vehicle was sent to find them and bring them back to school. But mostly, once they went back home, the days would just fade into one another until they forgot about school altogether. When they went back, they sometimes would not find their parents living where they had last been, because their families may be out hunting or visiting or perhaps had even moved on. In which case it would take so long to track them down that it would be too late to return to school.

Once, when Tix'ae's parents were still living on a farm, she went home like that. She was very young still, but even now she could remember how she had stayed home from the beginning of the cold time until after the rains returned. She did not want to go back to the hostel afterwards because she could not stand the loneliness, the getting up in the cold of the morning and going to school when it was still dark. At school she longed for the fire at her home where she always sat close to her grandmother's outstretched legs in the morning sun, covered by the same blanket, until their cold limbs had thawed. That time, her parents had been upset when she was dropped on the farm by a family passing by on a donkey-cart. They wanted her to return to school straight away, but she just blindly refused to go until she knew the teachers would no longer take her back because she had missed too much. The most frightening thought about going back to school that time was the sure beating she would get from the big teacher with the very dark skin and the brightly coloured dresses. The one who always told them how much she hated being in a place where people were so uncivilised. So whenever her parents tried to force her to go back, she told them about this teacher. Then they would just sit there, looking at the fire, but they would let her be.

But she was taken back to school the next year. Not so much because her parents insisted, but just before the rains came they had moved to a ranch where the farmer simply rounded up all the kids at the beginning of the school year and took them to the hostel. The teachers allowed her back in without a fuss that time, but she had to sit in a class with younger children.

The three girls were resting under a tree, Khamx'ae picking lice from Koaba's hair, Tix'ae just lying on her back watching the wisps of white cloud pass across the blue sky and the few vultures circling leisurely. They were the three biggest girls in the boarding-school in this village on the main road north of D'Kar now. They kept their distance from the younger girls these days; they had too many things to talk about.

Koaba had come back to school after the holidays with something really big to share. She had been put into the hut, after she had seen the first blood and told her grandmother. For many days she had had to stay in that hut all by herself, listening to the women singing and dancing around the hut, night and day, day and night. She was not allowed out, but she could peep through the cracks in the walls where the pats of cow-dung plaster did not cover the frame of branches solidly. The women circled endlessly, twirling their bodies, baring their buttocks and chanting the songs about the eland and its fat. The men stayed away from the hut for as long as they danced outside and she was inside.

When she was allowed out, a deep track in the sand showed where their feet had stamped out the rhythm for many hours. In the hut she was served by her grandmother. The old woman brought her food and took out the bucket placed there for her bodily needs. Each day she came, sometimes with some of Koaba's old aunts, to rub her with strange-smelling lotions and herbs – her head, her body, her genitals. Her grandmother talked to her the whole time, telling her about the things women have to do, about babies and men and God and food. Every day the old women came to wash her body with the pulp of the *cgùi* plant and afterwards to rub her with the lotion. There were coarse pieces of leaf and pounded root in the lotion and they rubbed her body so hard that her skin was on fire for a long time afterwards. In the half light, her body had shone with a deep glow.

On the day she was allowed to come out, they painted her face – black circles around her eyes and on her forehead. The black circles, the old woman told her, were the rainbow, the many blessings that awaited her and the good rains that she would bring that year. When she stepped out into the bright daylight the desert sun made her eyes squint and she felt dizzy from the long hours of sitting. Some men had joined the dancing women and she was lead into the dance by her grandmother, holding on to a small stick. Everyone was joyful, laughing and dancing and singing with fresh energy. They all took turns to take her small stick and dance with her. She had felt so grown-up, so loved and successful. She could not wait to go back to school to tell the others. Especially that she had now moved into a hut with her grandmother, away from her parents, where her older sister was already staying.

Back at boarding-school, she had them listening over and over again to the story. Khamx'ae had not yet had the experience, and Tix'ae had been in the hut for a weekend only, so that she would not miss school. Since Tixae's parents had moved to D'Kar and were working in the projects, they had a bit of money and were able to arrange transport home when the message reached them that her time had come. These days some teachers allowed the parents to keep their daughters out of school for one day after such weekends.

"For me it wasn't so nice, anyway," Tix'ae told the other two. "The women were shy, because there was a strange white man from another country writing down things and taking photos. And the boys from the soccer team kept on playing videos in my uncle's house right next door, so the noise confused everyone."

She didn't tell them how it had hurt when she overheard the boys next door talking about her and making fun of the old women who were trying so hard to keep on dancing. She had been glad when the weekend was over.

At times like these, when the school was closed and the teachers had gone to Ghanzi for the weekend, they were left with the younger ones and only the matron. These were perfect times to talk about what was happening to their bodies and about what the future held for them. Tix'ae had lots to tell. She had had men before. The noisy soccer boys and the others as well prowled around on weekends and if they had been drinking, it was difficult to keep them away from you.

"It is fun anyway," she tells the other two. She stretches her legs out, points her toes and studies the movement of the muscles in her thighs. "It is different from the games we played in the veld when we were little, you know. One's body knew nothing then." With these boys she could feel her body respond, her heart beating with the thrill of being chosen from amongst the other girls. They would all be wearing bright plastic earrings and would have put black dye on their hair and copper-wire on their arms and rubbed their bodies with the lotion from the shop mixed with the juice of the leaves of the *tshāá* bush which had such a lovely smell when you crushed them. When she was chosen, she would laugh and dash off with one of the boys in the dark, behind the shrubs near the ruins of the old farmhouse. Sometimes the boy she had been with would go off again with another girl afterwards, but she didn't care. The times she had done it were few because she didn't go home that often, and in the boarding-school it was too difficult, and besides, these boys were all much younger than she. The games in D'Kar were quick and rough, and afterwards they would sweep the sand with a branch to cover up the hollows their bodies had made. Just in case some passing grown-ups would guess what had happened there the next day. But she enjoyed replaying these scenes in her mind, feeling her body go moist and warm at the thought.

She loved the other girls' wide-eyed attention and the privilege of her experience. She could not bring herself to tell them of her first time, though. But the memory sometimes did come back, often in the dark of night just before she fell asleep. She had been alone at home, or so she had thought. The grown-ups were all out – her father working at one of the Kuru projects and her mother collecting veldkos with the younger ones – but her brother came back from somewhere. When he entered the hut where she was relaxing, he closed the door behind him. There was something strange about him. He looked so broody and anxious that when he had pushed her over, roughly pulled off her panties and held her down with his right arm across her chest while he undid his pants, she dared not oppose him. It was so sore! His eyes were wild and he pushed hard against her hips.

She could have fought him, he was not that much bigger and stronger than her, but she just felt so sad and deserted. And confused and angry. At the same time she felt sorry for him. She did cry, sobbed hard and screamed a little, but it was more of a protest against him than a real effort to get help. She knew there was nobody around and even if there was, she would not have wanted them to find them like that. Afterwards he was sullen with her, impatient, until he saw that she was not telling. Then he became soft and protective. He never tried it again.

Boarding-school was boring. They felt cooped up and tired of the routine. The hostel room they shared with the younger girls was a long, bare dormitory with iron beds and smelly mattresses, dark stains bearing witness to the many times a child had been be too scared or too sad to get up at night to walk the long, dark passage to the toilet. They were locked into the dormitory every night just after dark by the night watch, who also woke them before dawn. Then they had to go outside to bath in the big zinc tubs waiting at the tap. In summer time it was not so bad, but in winter the icy water stung your dry skin and the wind on your wet body left you shivering violently. The matron did try to warm some water on the fire, but the cast iron cooking pots were needed to prepare breakfast as well, and there were too many children for the little water anyway. At home they would never wash until the sun was high in the sky, but here there was a fixed routine: early-morning prayers and singing even before school began!

The only thing they really enjoyed was the singing.

They gathered outside, watching the matron's wide hips roll with the rhythm of the songs she was leading in her high, tinny voice. She danced with the tune, showing them how to step to the rhythm in the same spot. The songs were all about Jesus and God, and although they were very different from the rhythmic clapping and yodelling songs they were used to at home, the singing warmed them, bound them together. At home their fathers and brothers never sang, only danced in a circle around the fire at night while the women clapped and sang. But here the boys' voices filled in from the back with deep, dark tones while the girls were encouraged to thrust their voices upward to reach the highest notes.

Tix'ae was a song leader; she always stood in the front row. First the matron would get them all to be dead quiet, building up the tension and anticipation. Then she would start to shuffle her feet to the rhythm, the kids following. When the shuffling had gone on for quite a while and just at the right moment, the matron and Tix'ae would look at each other and chant the first line of the tune, all alone in high, shrill voices. The others always drew in their breath, getting ready to join in full force and in different voices at the second line.

This was wonderful team work, it put the energy back into your bones and cleared your heart of the nightmares, the long hours of longing in the dark dormitory and the fear of what the new day in school might bring.

"Nobody knows, no-o-o-body knows, when Jesus is coming," Tix'ae started humming in the shade of the tree. She kept the rhythm with her head and upper body. Very soon the three of them were totally absorbed in their song, bodies rocking. Their eyes remained on the road, though, following each passing vehicle until its dust had settled where the road disappeared around a bend on the horizon. It was going to be a long and boring few days till Monday.

NINE

# Boys

Eric, Peter and Johan had been watching videos all morning in Johan's uncle's farmhouse, sprawled on the carpet with their beers. They had gone through the whole range available: comedy, rugby, a steamy one about a Taiwanese prostitute. Their empty cans had grown to a heap where they had tossed them in the corner.

It was a rather large house. Since his uncle and his family had moved down to his other farms in the south of the country, Johan had been the foreman on this farm, the only one to live in the house. But he found the empty rooms down the long corridor so depressing that he preferred to sleep in the living-room with the large autumn-leaf carpet and stuffed animals on the wall next to the built-in bar. The horns of the hartebeest were the perfect place to hang his hat! On the same wall there were two large paintings – one of a bright sunset on the Okavango river and the other of a broody buffalo staring at you from between two thorn trees. The other walls carried framed certificates for prizes taken by his uncle's bulls at the Ghanzi agricultural show. Between the imitation-leather sofas the ashtrays on their metal stands overflowed with stubs. He had moved his single bed into a corner, where the maid woke him each morning with his coffee and beskuit.

"I'm glad you two came to see me," he said. "There's nothing you can do here by yourself on a Saturday." And thought: The water-pumps had all been started at the different cattle posts. The young tollies had all been branded the past week and the dehorning was finished.

The large ranch was divided into camps with a cattle post in each, so it wasn't even necessary these days to herd the cattle or put them in a kraal at night, like they used to do before the farms were fenced in. He had so often heard the old farmers talk of then, how lions were a constant menace and a young man still had the challenge of the wild. Hunting had a real purpose, was more than just a sport. These days there was little game left on the farms and you needed a permit to hunt, even on your own farm. And hunting was only allowed during the cold season anyway.

It had been quite hard work in the sun, this past week, making sure the young animals were all branded with his uncle's initials and registered number. But it offered him no challenge. The Bushmen, who had been living on this farm as long as and even before he could remember, knew the work so well that he had to do little more than supervise. Sometimes he got the uneasy feeling that they regarded him as just a kid, although he was already on the wrong side of thirty.

Through a haze of smoke he watched Peter reach for yet another can of beer. Eric's eyes were glued to the video of the prostitute which he had put on a second time. How similar their situation was! Every other day he drove around the farm to check the fences, usually at sunset when the golden grass waved softly in the evening breeze and an occasional kudu hopped over the fence or a jackal dashed ahead of the vehicle. That was his favourite task. He loved the cool evening breeze on his face and the colours of the clouds in the wide sky, a bustard tumbling down from its upward flight with a loud cackle, because he had passed too close to its nest.

Occasionally he was asked by the labourers to assist with an emergency, such as a cow that wasn't able to give birth. They knew what to do but wanted him to take the responsibility of deciding which to save, the cow or the calf. Sometimes they would sweat for hours, trying to pull the dead calf out with ropes; at other times they had to resort to cutting the dead calf into pieces to relieve the poor, bellowing cow.

A second task the Bushmen were under strict orders to leave to him, was the fixing of the water-pumps and the wind-pumps at the house and cattle posts. When a mechanical problem interrupted the pumping of water from deep underneath the Kalahari sand, they would come running for him, because it was the availability of this precious silver liquid that made it possible for both whites and blacks to live in this vast, dry grassland. But even for this task, he thought, they did not really need him. The farmers often talked about how skilled some of the Bushmen were with mechanics, even though they had had no formal schooling.

In the olden days they managed to live off the veld during the dry months, the older Bushmen told him, without surface water, because they knew which tubers to dig out for moisture, and where the sipwells were. He doubted that they would be able to do that still. Like the farmers, they had become completely dependent on the thud-thud of the engine and the creaking of the wind-pump.

He and Peter and Eric had often complained to each other about how unexciting life in the Ghanzi district had become. The farms were so vast and widely spaced that it took at least half an hour of driving along some fence on a sandy track to reach any homestead. And with no telephones at your disposal, one would make such a journey without any guarantee that you would find your neighbours at home. Many of the farms did have long-distance radios, but all broadcasting was done on the same frequency and it took a lot of courage for a young man to announce himself over the ether and state his business in clumsy sentences, knowing that the whole of Botswana could be listening.

To get to the bar in town he had to drive about a hundred kilometres – a long distance, which was quite a bother if you got too drunk to drive yourself home. The other farmers around him were all settled with families, so for unattached young men there weren't many meeting places or distractions. The only regular activity was the rugby match once a month, followed, if you were lucky, by a meal and a barn dance on some farm. But the single guys didn't always feel at ease with those families, and the few young, white women in Ghanzi were either already snugly and arrogantly involved with some or other educated fellow from outside, or got married within a few months of returning from boarding-school in Namibia or South Africa. What was more, the recently married young farmers didn't really welcome their visits and eyed them with suspicion if they arrived unannounced. As a young single man, you dared not risk letting them catch you on their farm alone with their wives after they had been out during the day!

Johan lay back in his chair. He was feeling drowsy from all the beer. What could he suggest next? They could go for a swim in the large cement reservoir in the orchard, but would that satisfy the deeper need, the longing he had been carrying for quite some time now? For a man his age he had accomplished all there was to be done in this wide, harsh land. This place, which he used to see as offering the maximum freedom when he was younger, had now become a prison, a fenced-in path from which he could not escape.

Sometimes he yearned for his days at boarding-school in Gobabis, just across the border in Namibia. The white Ghanzi children, who every three months had travelled back and forth to school on the backs of the supply trucks, had formed their own little community at the school. The memories of the companionship, the playful competition at sports events and in class, gave him a warm feeling that now only heightened his sense of loss. He used to be so good at rugby, athletics; he was something at that school and he had had many admirers. The Namibian boys couldn't boast about as many adventures as the Ghanzi boys, because life here was still much wilder and there were many brave tales of hunting with which to impress your young listeners.

He would have even more to boast about now. He had his own bakkie, enough cattle, everything he ever desired back in those days. But somehow, it meant nothing. Why, he wasn't really sure. He did venture outside the district sometimes to collect supplies, but he never felt that he fitted in anywhere else. Women scared him; so did groups of other young people. He always needed some booze to dampen his fear of social situations. Yet, in his bed at night, he longed for a change; in his dreams he had wild adventures in strange places.

"Let's get out of here, guys, I can't stand this house any longer. I hear there are a few nice overseas chicks at the Kalahari Arms, should we drive there and see what we can get?" he suggested with a wink.

"No," Eric said, "we'll run into too much competition at the hotel. Let's go the other direction and see if Jan de Klerk's niece is still visiting."

In the Landrover Eric passed the two-litre bottle of Coke around. Peter had mixed the contents with a good-sized bottle of brandy. The sweet tinge on the tongue made life look a bit more exciting. Very soon, they had to stop for a pee. Standing in a line next to the road, aiming over the smaller shrubs, Eric asked, "So, when did you guys last get laid?"

They looked at each other. Admitting one's deprivation or lack of success was never easy, because you never knew if the other guys were lying and if you were truly the only one leading such a dry life.

"Come on," Eric said, "we all know it's fucking hard to get anything around here, but surely you guys are creative enough?"

Johan's head was spinning from the alcohol. He did not quite trust the situation. These were things one did not talk about. Dare he think the other two might be solving their problems the same way he did? He had often calculated his risks, deep in the night, when he had gone out to the fires, carefully approaching the group squatting in their peculiar way in a circle around the fire. He remembered the very first time, how intimate it had looked from a distance, how utterly lonely he had felt from where he watched the smiling, softly lit faces. They were passing a pipe around while his foreman, Cukuri, described a hunting scene with such vivid gestures that he could recognise it without understanding a word. A dog started to bark and growl, betraying his presence, so that it would have looked foolish not to join them.

That first night he did not ask for anything, just sat there in their warm company. But he could not keep his eyes off Nqose, Cukuri's youngest daughter. Every time his gaze would return to her – the glow on her skin, the reflected firelight in her eyes. Damn it, these Bushmen girls were fucking pretty!

He went to bed much later than usual, but he couldn't fall asleep. The next morning he asked her brother outright to bring her to him. That night he lay waiting, the front door ajar. His heart bounced when he heard the soft steps on the stoep. The brother had disappeared quickly, left her standing shyly just inside the door. He didn't dare take her in the living-room or in any of the bedrooms. Somehow it didn't seem proper. In the end, he did it on the bathroom floor, so that he could wash himself afterwards. Would these guys understand? Could they also smell the mixture of musk, dust and wood smoke at the very thought?

He had been quick with her, but he had been far more excited than ever before with any white girl. Afterwards, she regularly came to the house at night. He would sometimes buy her a dress, but mostly she was happy with a twenty pula note and some tobacco or tea.

Eric laughed while zipping up his pants. He gave the other two a challenging glance. "Well, if you haven't been brave before, shall I show you how? Come on!"

Johan looked at Peter. Did he imagine it, or was he hanging back?

Peter smiled crookedly and gave a strange, choked little laugh. But then his eyes met Johan's and he said, "Let's go," as if he was in a hurry.

His eyes kept returning to the splash of colour on the flyscreen on the outside of the window. The purple bougainvillaea blossoms against the iron gauze were a speck of sanity, a reminder that life was carrying on outside, of better days and unblemished nature. It was stiflingly hot in the courtroom. The wasps, annoyed at the sudden restricted access to their clay nests on the ceiling, droned above the heads of the fifty odd people who had been filling the benches for the past three days.

"So if you say that these girls consented, how did you actually ask them?" The magistrate looked straight at Johan. He started stuttering again; he'd been feeling such a fool ever since the beginning of this dreadful ordeal because he had never learnt to use the English language comfortably. For the Bushman witnesses they had arranged translators. But he had to battle to express himself in English, in sentences that would make sense to the court as well as to him, while in the back of his mind frantically trying to remember what the young lawyer from South Africa had advised them *not* to say.

"I cannot speak their language, but Eric can and he said that they had said it was OK, Your Honour," he finally uttered. If only he could fend off the images that kept floating through his mind, one superimposing itself on the other. There they were in the abandoned farmhouse on one of Eric's cattle posts, sitting on bare mattresses in what once had been the living-room. By this time the three girls were really drunk. They only had on their panties, and they were dancing, giggling and clinging to each other. It had not been too difficult to persuade them to come along when they passed them on the road. Eric knew the one well; they were chatting away in Naro. She had a cheeky, free air about her and he remembered how she had looked them straight in the eye, as if to say: "What's in it for us?"

The other two watched shyly from behind her, and when they darted around the Landrover to scramble into the back, they giggled and pulled at each other to be the first one in. They were awfully young, he could see that, but their breasts were full and firm, pushing at the cotton dresses.

Eric was waiting for his turn to testify. But first he had to listen to the accounts of others. The man from Gaborone – they said he was a human-rights lawyer – had the floor and he was describing in an angry voice

96

how the Bushmen were abused, in general as well as in this particular case. "I can clearly see, Your Honour, how these three Afrikaner men had gone to the school with the sole intention of making these young girls believe they would take them to their homes; give them a lift. In the meantime, they had already prepared the scene of the crime, in a spot as isolated as possible, where these girls could not get help no matter how much they might have screamed. It is by such acts that the San people are being persecuted, day in, day out, by black and white alike. They have no choice in life, neither of where they might live nor of who might govern them. Their land not only has been taken by settlers and their resources used up by others, but their very lives have been taken over in a deliberate, merciless process of discrimination. I beg the court to make this case a turning point in their history, to show once and for all that justice can be done for all the people of our country. The San included. Our constitution promises us all equal rights and opportunities, yet we allow cultural genocide to be carried out daily, right before our eyes."

Old Komtsha was called as a witness. Over the years he had become a crumpled little figure with a walking-stick and grey peppercorn hair, Eric noticed, but his eyes were still fiery as he grabbed the stand determinedly. He had always been a strong and stubborn man, even in the days when he lived on their farm, before he moved to D'Kar with his family. His impertinence was probably the reason why his father had sent him off the farm, Eric thought. He had grown up in front of this old man, and now he stood in front of him as the accused.

Komtsha talked animatedly. The translator had to hold up his hand every few minutes to slow him down. "Our children have to learn, they say. We are told by others to send them to school, we are told when they should go and when they may come home. When we do that, we cannot understand our children any more, they do not want to live the old way, and they do not listen to us. For long periods we do not even know where they are; our women can no longer teach the girls the things about life they need to know. When they come back from school they are ashamed of us. Other people are stealing our children from us, like they have stolen our land and our lives."

The old man shook his finger. "They take our daughters, but they never marry them. They leave their black and their white babies for us to raise; they never come forth and give them names; they never pay us anything for looking after their children. To them we are lower than the donkeys and the dogs. They treat us as if we are nothing."

The South African lawyer gave Komtsha a fierce look. "Your Honour, I want to put it to you that this man as well as his daughter, rather than having a legitimate case, are being used by people with their own political agenda. I put it to the court that this was not a case of rape, but just one event in a continuing relationship. Both parties knew what was at stake and it could well be that it was not the first time that this act had taken place between the same people. We have no proof yet, but it is a possibility, especially between Miss Tix'ae Qgam and Mr Eric de Beer, who, according to the evidence, were the two leaders in the group."

He paused and turned to old Komtsha. "Sir, can you explain to the court why your daughter Tix'ae and her friends did not go straight to the police? If this was rape, why did they tell the matron about it only after they were caught for having been out without permission? Was this rape story not simply a red herring to deflect disciplinary steps by the school authorities?"

The translator battled visibly to put this argument across. The old man listened intently, then answered: "Your Honour, we do not know the paths to follow if we want to change something which is wrong. We have many things we would like to report, but where should we take them? The people in the offices laugh at us, they do not know our languages and we do not understand their laws. We only agreed to take these children to the police because there were people who said that they would help us and who would represent us."

A tall, darkish man with sallow skin now took the old man's place on the witness stand. Eric recognised him; he had been in court every day. He didn't know his surname, but his name was John. His father was an Englishman and his mother a Bushman. His English father actually married John's mother, something which always astonished the Afrikaner farmers. Because of his background, Eric did not have much social contact with the man, but he knew that after his father's death, he had been sent to school in England. Ever since he came back a few years ago to take his father's place on the farms the other side of Ghanzi, rumours had been circulating that he was leading a Bushman revolt, that all the farms were going to be given back to the Bushman people. Apparently he often went overseas with some of them, and even Komtsha had once accompanied him to such a meeting where they complained about the way the Bushmen were treated in this country.

When they heard about it, the farmers were upset; they talked among themselves in little groups, over the shop counters when they came to town, and when they met elsewhere. Leaning over the fence at the auction kraal, one foot on the bottom slat and hats pulled low over their squinting eyes, they asked in indignant voices: Did the first settlers not find the land deserted? There were no Bushmen settled here; they were always on the move, so how could this place be called theirs?

The man was clearly used to addressing an audience. "There is a movement, world wide, to recognise the injustices done to the first peoples of this earth. This case may be just one incident, but it is symbolic of something much bigger, an evil undercurrent of prejudice and discrimination. An indication that in this corner of what is supposedly one of the most democratic countries in Africa, feudalism is still being practised. A system which enslaves people to the extent that they are unable to distinguish their own will from that of their masters."

All these arguments were going beyond Eric's understanding. His mouth felt dry. It had been going on for days now. Inside the court they were being humiliated in front of everybody; outside the court they had to hide from the reporters and their cameras. People stood around in small groups every time the court dispersed. Everybody's eyes turned to them when they came out, but they were always quickly whisked away by the lawyer Johan's uncle had found, a clever man whose full plan he hadn't been able to follow completely.

Eric was overcome with shame and confusion. Now and then he stole a glance at the small frame of his mother, her shoulders hunched. Where she sat in the back row she looked completely out of place. The floral dress she normally wore to church contrasted oddly with the formal clothes of the law people and the safari fashions of the reporters. Damn, it was the drink! So often on a Sunday night, after he had been visiting elsewhere for the weekend, he had seen the deep sorrow in his mother's eyes before he slammed the door of his bedroom behind him. He had stifled the remorse when he recognised her grief. Because she had suffered before. The look in her eyes when she was holding him as a child, the two of them watching his father breaking furniture and hurling his brandy glass against the wall in drunken rage, always came back to him. He had often wondered how much she knew about his visits to the huts at night.

"I was too drunk to remember, Your Honour," he now answered as he had been instructed. How he wished that it was true. Would he ever forget? The girl was a virgin; he realised it the moment he entered her. He was very drunk but she was just about unconscious at that stage. He had to roll her over and open her legs; she was lying on the mattress in tiger-print nylon panties. In the one corner Johan was busy with Tix'ae, but Peter had either finished or he never made it; he was snoring with his mouth open.

The girl's eyes had been open but she made incoherent sounds as he pushed feverishly, feeling sweaty and nauseous – just as he was now, clutching the wooden railing of the ridiculously small box he had to stand in.

Peter had finished testifying. Now he sat in deep thought, trying to make sense of what was happening to them. For him it was the first time with a Bushman girl. He always knew that some of the other farmers did it, and he had once or twice heard gossip about the light-skinned children you sometimes found at cattle posts. He had even heard jokes in the hotel about how many children were being passed off as old Jimmy's. He was such a randy old bastard, they said, it wouldn't dent his reputation to have a few more children attributed to him.

He would never have dared to approach a Bushman girl. No. Even though they could speak each other's language and had always played together as children. Because everybody knew it wasn't right to mix with Bushmen or black people in that way. It was written in the Bible. He had to admit, he wasn't even sure how one would go about it. What if the girl's parents found out, or someone told on you? Everyone knew that in their drinking sprees these people could get completely out of control, and the things a drunken Bushman would say!

That afternoon he hadn't dared admit his fears to the other two, once it had become clear what their plans were. And to be quite honest, he was wickedly excited at the thought, given courage by the booze and by Eric's obvious experience. In a way it was a pity that he was so drunk. He couldn't remember much at all, only that when he was through with her, he fell asleep. Now he wasn't even sure which one of the three it had been.

Johan had been very quiet all through the hearing. In the evenings they all went their separate ways. Except when they had to meet their lawyer in the hotel. The other two had their families with them; he had only the fat purse of his uncle who had bailed them out but afterwards refused to discuss the matter further. He had so far spent every night during the week of the court case entirely alone under his mosquito net in the chalet he was renting at the safari lodge.

It was the third day already. He glanced around at the other whites in the courtroom who came to support them. If only other people would talk more openly about it! After they were granted bail four months ago, the three of them had not done much together. Every time they tried to discuss the thing, it brought bitter arguments and accusations as to who was to blame. So they mostly avoided each other, except for the one time they had to travel down to South Africa to meet their lawyer.

When he had to come to town people avoided his eyes. Not a single person, not even those with whom he had grown up or his friends in the rugby team, ever referred to the case. At night he struggled with bitterness and fury about their silence.

He tried to imagine what would happen if tomorrow he walked into one of the shops in D'Kar or Ghanzi where the men usually drank tea on their weekly trip to get supplies, and asked out loud: "What do you think about what I've done? Who will stand by me and admit I'm not the only one?" He'd like to see the faces of the men slouching and sitting on the counters with a tea-cup or pipe in the hand. But of course he could never do it.

Instead, people would continue to slap him on the back, laugh a little too loudly at his silly jokes and talk about the weather or the coming rugby match against Mafikeng or Gobabis. But the silence of the men did not disturb him as much as that of the women, whom he thought were now even kinder to him, even more silent; serving and bowing to their husbands. Driving home these last couple of months, his eyes would sometimes fill with tears of frustration. At night, rolling around under his mosquito net, he would recall Nqose's visits to his house, remembering her smell and the comfort he had drawn from her.

Now these other whites were sitting here, pretending they had nothing to do with this case. Yet he knew that they, too, often felt freer amongst a group of Bushmen than a group of people from outside Ghanzi. He just wished this whole thing were over. He no longer worried what the outcome might be, they were destined to be the scapegoats and they would have to carry this burden anyway.

The lawyer now had Eric's mother on the stand. Eric felt as if his heart would break. Never in his whole life had anything been more painful. He knew how much courage it must have taken her. There were many other women like his mother on the farms, and the saddest thing about what had happened was the shame it brought on them. In his grief he knew that this act of theirs had violated the trust and kindness of all these women, who were as able on the farms as their husbands. From their simple homes they offered their gentle hospitality to every stranger who came by, and they were constantly working, preparing food – baking bread, making sausage, cutting biltong from the kudu carcasses their husbands would dump on the kitchen table. They always had to be ready for the unexpected visitor or emergency trip that required provision.

Now his mother had come all this way, left her home and farm to be here with him, in spite of what he had done and was still doing to her. How bravely she carried on after his father's death! How he had always admired her way with the Bushmen on their farm and the trust she had won. She had girls helping in and around the house sometimes until late at night, yet they never complained. Although their huts were close by, they often rested under the tree in the yard when they had finished sweeping or doing dishes, in case she might need them again. She, too, was always ready to help them. Many a night she was called out to assist with the birth of a child or to treat a feverish child in one of the huts. Even as he sat here in the stifling courtroom he could see her delving by flashlight in her medicine cupboard with its wealth of tiny bottles, the secret contents of which only she understood.

In the daytime there were always people around their house. When he was small, they seemed to be an extension of his own family. Except that they were always in the background, always got onto the back of the bakkie when his father drove somewhere, squatted outside, behind the kitchen door when they ate instead of sitting at the table. Sometimes he imagined he could remember how, as a baby, he was carried on the back of old Xau while she was doing his mother's washing or sweeping the yard. Maybe he only remembered it because she always teased him when she saw him at the shop in D'Kar where she and old Komtsha now lived, about how she used to give him the breast to comfort him when he was little. Maybe it was not even true, or maybe he was too young to remember, but old Xau's story did evoke feelings of warmth and contentment, and vague associations with the very distinct smell he got to know on his visits to the huts on their farm at night. It made him wonder about this need for comfort which he could not resist.

He had often watched his sister's children with the Bushmen outside the farmhouse, the women sitting together under the trees playing with the children's blond hair and chubby pink toes and fingers. To put the little ones to sleep they would wrap them in blankets and tie them onto their backs, the little bodies warmly tucked in. Only when a child cried inconsolably would the women take it back to the farmhouse and to its mother, who was just too glad to have been relieved of the baby for a few hours while she was trying to cope with the household demands of a big ranch. No wonder so many of the white children from Ghanzi spoke a Bushman language before they could speak their own!

"Mrs de Beer, you have known the parents of the girl in question for many years, have you not?"

The lawyer had moved to right in front of the witness box and was looking his mother straight in the eye. Now it is coming, Eric thought. They are going to find out. "This is your only chance," the lawyer had said to them earlier. "If they cannot prove that the girls are minors, they do not really have a case against you. Then it just becomes a sexual act between consenting adults, and nobody can prove rape. The girls do not have identity papers, therefore it is your mother's word against theirs."

"How long have you actually known Miss Tix'ae Qgam and her parents, and how can you prove it to the court?"

His mother's voice trembled as she answered, "Your Honour, when the girl was born I was called to help the mother. They were living on our farm at the time."

"Mrs de Beer, according to your statement about the year in which you assisted with Tix'ae Qgam's birth, the girl would now be eighteen years old. As we have no record of the birth dates of the other girls, your testimony will have to stand as an indication of their ages as well since they seem to be age mates. You appear to me to be a good, trustworthy person. Can you assure us that your statement is the truth, and nothing but the truth?"

The creaking noise of the ceiling fans was the only sound in the deadly silence in the courtroom.

"It is the truth, Your Honour," his mother said in the direction of the magistrate. Her face was a sickly pale colour; she could not lift her eyes from the floor.

Warm tears ran over Eric's face. Something fluttered in his chest and then died slowly. A feeling of barren solitude took hold of him. The magistrate's voice was still droning in the background, but he no longer heard anything. It seemed as if all the other people in the courtroom had disappeared, except for the three girls and their families. And his mother. Through a haze of tears his mother's face faded away, and the wrinkled features of old Xau settled in his mind.

TEN

# Milk and money

I have really had enough now, Turu thought, and impatiently shook out her dishcloth. She was sitting with the others in the cooking shelter, watching her sister Ncaoka stir the black three-legged pot with her long stick, eyes screwed up against the smoke. But Turu's mind was elsewhere. She was thinking about her job. How long would she still have to wait for her money? Michael had told them the other day that the exhibition in Gaborone had gone well; many people from overseas came and bought the pictures she had painted with Xuse and the others in the sun outside the workshop. He always took their work away to go and sell at such places, sometimes even over the sea. But why did it always take so long to get their money? Michael came from overseas, like so many of the white people who had come to live with them in D'Kar to help them in the projects, so he should know. He kept on telling them that the money was on its way, but how much longer could it really take, and what was the chance of their money getting lost on the way to D'Kar?

She had seen their pictures in the gallery in Gaborone; she had also noticed the red dots on some of her works. That meant that some of the many people who were walking around with wine glasses in their hands, looking at the pictures on the walls, had bought her paintings. But Michael said that these people would only pay after the exhibition was over, and then their money still had to go through the bank and the mail to get here.

She had even seen her face in the newspaper the day after the opening. Michael had made a copy for her to put on the wall of her hut, but the children took it down and played with it and in the end it got soaked with rain. What she disliked most about waiting for the money like this was that the others started to blame her because there wasn't food in the house. At the same time the white shop-owners, who were always making fun of her, were saying to each other: "Look, here comes the big artist again, let's show her our new radios, blankets." Things like that.

She knew she owed all these shops a lot of money. She even owed money to the *semausos*, the black vendors' little shops at their homes, where one could always buy food, even at night. And she owed money to Mmamoruti as well, because she paid for her granddaughter's school shoes the other day. They would all just have to wait as long as *she* had to wait. In the meantime everyone around her expected her always to have money for food!

The porridge was now almost done. She watched the little bubbles coming to the surface in the boiling, white mass, like little mouths puffing out steam. Ncaoka has cooked a large pot, because she knows the children from the other huts in Oom Jimmy's compound will soon join them. That's the one thing about marrying into such a large family as Oom Jimmy's, like Ncaoka did, she thought. You always need to make a lot of food. And they definitely all have high hopes about what she would contribute, she thought wryly.

The other day she went to the Kuru office, and there was this Dutch woman who had started working there recently, who refused to give her a further advance, saying she's already taken more than the other artists in the project! Going to that office was always like that. Mostly she already knew what they were going to say when she asked if there was any money in her name. Mostly she did not even listen to the translator, but pushed the impatience rising inside her down and put on a smile and nodded as if she agreed.

"No, Turu, you cannot have any more money in advance. You should not have used up all the money you got last time so quickly. You knew the next exhibition was only in a few months' time ..."

What do they know after all? This woman who came from far away, what does she understand of Oom Jimmy's grumpiness when he does not have tobacco; or about the children of her dead daughter's need for shoes. They were growing so fast. What was this work business anyway? You had to walk a long way in the hot sun every day; you had to sit and please everyone, and on top of everything you had to answer silly questions the whole time about what it was you were painting. You worked as hard as anyone else in the project, but the others got paid salaries. You just got money when someone bought your paintings. But they didn't pay *you*, they paid *them* first. And what happened to that money when it eventually came? They took off so much for this, so much for that and in the end you were left with so little you couldn't even pay the shops!

She can get so furious! Those others in the office, some even her nephews and nieces, they get money for just being there. Then they make a big fuss about how thick the envelope is when she gets her money. As if it was going to last, and as if they ever showed *their* money to anyone!

She moved a log out of the way. The small spiral of smoke rising from a crack in the wood was burning her eyes. She could not stand the smoke these days, her chest burnt and the cough that kept her awake at night was much worse when she had been sitting at the fire.

Suddenly the soft chatter of the children is interrupted by a load roar, and they see the belly of the Flying Mission fly go over their heads. The fly always flew so low over the village when it came in to land, it was quite scary. The little plane turns around, makes a wide circle over the village, dipping its wings to the one side as it turns. Soon it roars over their house again, now even lower as it prepares to land. The children shriek with pleasure and run towards the airstrip.

"Come back, the porridge is almost done!" Ncaoka shouts after them. "What is this now again? Either someone is sick, or someone is going some place far again," she says.

The fly reminds Turu of the time they went to England to sell their work. There was an exhibition and she and three others had gone with Michael. First they had left in this little fly from D'Kar. It was hot and bumpy, they could not talk to each other and she felt quite sick. Then they had to climb into the body of this huge fly in Gaborone with many lights and soft chairs inside. In those days she didn't know it was called an aeroplane. They were up in the sky for a long time, but before it got dark they had to leave the soft chairs and get out in a big, noisy place with even more lights and chairs. They walked around looking, and looking at everything while Michael tried to get them a lift with another fly. When he did, they had to run down a narrow passage like a big pipe and up the steps to the second fly. Off they flew again. It was just like the first time: you felt dizzy and you felt your ears go full. But this time they flew for a long time, right through the night, and when they stopped, they were in this cold city with the grey buildings and the fast-talking people.

London. What a strange name, she thought, rolling the sound around with her tongue. There were so many houses, yet they found some people sleeping outside on the streets, covering themselves with cardboard boxes, just like here! She and the other artists could not understand why these people did not stay with their families, or why they did not at least make a fire to sit around! Michael laughed a lot when Coco asked why those lonely men didn't just get themselves some girlfriends so that they could have a place to sleep.

They had met such strange people in London! She smiled when she remembered the one woman. Michael said she came from a place called Spain. One morning they found her in the gallery trying to dance to the music of the *dengho* and the *dqòmà*. The gallery people played their music, which Michael had put on a tape when they were still in D'Kar, every day, while people were looking at their paintings on the walls. This woman from Spain was dancing so oddly; she and Xuse decided to show her some steps. But in the end they were learning the white lady's clapping steps and hip swirls as well. It was such fun! A whole crowd of white people who came to see their paintings gathered around them. White people love watching other people dance. Perhaps it is because they never seem to get it right themselves!

She didn't mind. She likes to perform for people. Whites get so embarrassed and stiff if you try to pull them into the dance, but afterwards they are always much friendlier with you and they give you something more easily if you ask. Dancing and asking are always easier if one is a little drunk. Then you can forget yourself a bit and just have fun. The day that music man – Michael said he was from Norway – came to D'Kar to make a programme for the radio in his country, she first went to the drinking-place before she went to them. She knew they were waiting for her that day, but she wasn't sure what this man wanted from her and the other musicians. They were all just told to come and perform in the cultural centre and be filmed.

But one has to be careful with the whites if you've been drinking. If you are drunk and you are funny, they forgive you, but if you are drunk and noisy, they push you out. No arguments.

It is easier if you're a little tipsy on Fridays when you have to go to the account office to beg for your money. Usually they tell you that you've already taken more than what you should've; and that you have to wait for your money to come from strange places like Australia, America or Holland. But she and the other artists have discovered that some of the people in the office have soft spots, they just need to be pushed a bit. And the beer took away the fear to do that. And it helped you to give them a bit of your mind if they did not listen to you! Afterwards she sometimes remembered how she'd cursed them, and then she always enjoys remembering how brave she was to say all those things. One day they actually pushed her out of the office into the road and closed the door behind her. It didn't matter, she laughed so loudly outside that they had to close the windows as well. She really told them some things that day!

Michael can't stand to work with her and the other artists when they're drunk. It was funny to see how he tried to sneak away when he saw them coming from somewhere. He was such a soft man; she sometimes felt sorry for him. But he also kept telling them that they were making a lot of money while they never seemed to get any. So it is good that he sometimes hears how unhappy they are and that they think they're not making any progress with this job.

He always talks to them about the animals they paint, wants to know why and what. Just like the many strange visitors who come to see them work. One really gets very tired of trying to find something to say that will light up their eyes and make them scribble madly in their little notebooks. They've noticed quite a few things, she and the other artists, and they now know what those people want to hear. Especially those with the cameras. She knows how to handle them now, but it just makes you so tired. Sometimes she has to think really hard to find words to talk about her pictures. Why do these white people have such trouble understanding the animals and plants and people she and the others painted? None of her own people ever ask her questions about her work!

She remembers how proud she felt that one time about Coco's words. Someone asked him at an exhibition what it was they were painting.

"Why do we paint?" he said, standing up and facing all the people. "Sometimes the pain in our hearts makes us pick up the brush and the paint becomes our tears that cry onto the canvas ..."

If she didn't truly love to sit down in front of her canvas, trying out and playing with the lovely colours, she would have moved away from D'Kar long ago to somewhere where there was more fun and not so many things she didn't understand. She could even go back to Hanahai or to the farms. But she loved to paint. Sometimes when she was busy painting she could hardly breathe – feeling the brush going over the canvas, and the little ridges of paint that formed when you put two strong, bright colours next to each other with a clear line.

It was true that the creatures and many of the plants she painted were no longer around or did not really exist like that. But they were still living in her head. The moment she let them out she was surprised herself at what came out of her hand. She could get completely lost when she painted! Sometimes it felt as if she was a child again, trotting behind her mother and her aunts in the veld, running from bush to bush, watching them collecting food, digging out tubers with their long sticks and sharing handfuls of sweet berries. When she felt like that she painted those things she longed for, trying to put them down on her canvas.

She couldn't teach even her own children half of what she knew as a child. There were no fences then. Their family roamed freely across a huge area where their game and the cattle of the farmers sometimes grazed together. There was always meat hanging from the trees where they had built their grass shelters. Every day it was an adventure to see what they would find in the veld, and in the late afternoon, when they all threw what they had collected on the karosses, there was genuine excitement and joy about the insects and roots and berries and leaves people had found.

They didn't see many whites in those days, only occasionally when they needed to get water from the wells or when they were needed to help with something on a farm. She couldn't remember seeing many black people either. Just the occasional black horseman or hunter, yes, and sometimes they came to barter with the white people. Now there were so many of them, so many different kinds of people!

Before she started working for the project, at the time Moruti found her in Ghanzi, she was employed by a Herero woman. She had to fetch water and the woman paid her with beer. It was bad; she was really sick and thin then. It was just after those two long years in jail. The drinking was getting her down, and the only way she could survive was to beg from her neighbours. And to satisfy a man here and there who would pay for it. No, it wasn't easy, but sometimes she thought that she was more free then than now.

*Áiè*! Life has really tossed her around. She still felt bitter about the jail story. It wasn't fair, especially when that magistrate said that she must go to jail because she was a bad example. If he put her in jail, he said, it would serve as a warning to other people. But nobody talked about what Tshabu had done to her! No matter how hard she tried to explain to the court how this man had sneaked out of her hut at night when he thought she was asleep, how he afterwards always said she was just thinking up things. She wasn't thinking up things. In the end it was all true, but the magistrate made as if that was just nothing. It didn't surprise her. After all, he was a man too.

Now that she thinks about it, there were only men in that court. Weaklings, men are. She's had such silly men in her life. She has a way with them, though, and even now that she was old and quite thin, they still wanted to sleep with her. Yes, usually she was the one who controlled a man; she was not going to be pushed around. That was probably why she was so very, very angry at Tshabu when she found out that he had been visiting Ncaku for a long time. It happened at night mostly, but she knew he also sneaked away during the day sometimes. That was one thing, but when she saw Ncaku wearing the bright new doek that she had seen him buy, that was when she knew this man was really making a fool of her. She had almost burst with rage. He and Ncaku had made a bioscope of her! For all to see!

What really hurt was that Ncaku was her friend, her age mate. Ncaku had always been pretty, though, she must admit, quite beautiful with that long, graceful neck and delicate hands and ankles of hers. Her bottom was the best, however. And she knew it, of course. She always showed it off during the dance. She would keep her body quite still, only tapping her feet, until the lovely round buttocks started to move, to vibrate in time to the music, lifting the back seam of her skirt just a little.

So there! she remembered thinking that night as she pushed the first tuft of burning grass deep into the thatched roof of their hut. So, I have a sagging, floppy behind, and I don't have other beautiful things, but I have power! Did I not build this house myself?

111

She was talking breathlessly to herself, that night, running feverishly to the other side of the hut to light more grass. Tshabu was sleeping inside. So let him burn, let him see what he had done! The higher the flames shot into the sky the more pleased she was. That will show them!

"Did I not build this house myself?" she shouted to the people who came running, who dragged her away from the fire, and to Tshabu who crawled sheepishly out of the burning hut, pulled out by several hands. She could still see the little specks of burnt grass in his hair.

She laughed softly, feeling herself glow at the memory. She lost a lot, that time, that's for sure. All their clothes, her clinic card and her O Mang card, things she had a lot of trouble replacing afterwards. Especially when she suddenly needed a passport. But the biggest thing she lost was her man. The rest weren't really so important. Those long months in jail weren't so bad, there was always food, the prison people taught them to do all kinds of things, and sometimes the women had great laughs among themselves. Only the nights, alone on a blanket in her corner, the cement floor hard and cold, almost killed her. Maybe that is where the TB really got her. Maybe because her chest was already weak with the pain of longing. How she missed the children's voices that time, and their soft bodies cuddling next to her on the kaross; how she wanted to sit around a fire again and to be able just to wander off into the bush.

"Those shoes you bought me, Áiè, they are really the best," her grandchild says. "Nobody else in school has such nice ones."

She gently patted her grandchild's fat little cheeks. "That's good, my child. Now you just look after them well, you hear?" What would life be if you were always alone, no children's voices, no company of your own kind?

"Ncaoka, give me the stick," she said and took a turn at the pot with the stick. The soft porridge was now cooked, but now came the stage to make it thicker. So she tipped more dry flour from the paper bag onto the simmering mass. It was hard, hot work stirring this lot in without making lumps, and you had to churn vigorously, hanging over the fire, until it reached the thick consistency they all loved. All the children have moved closer by now, they cannot wait much longer. To amuse the children and Ncaoka she chanted a few of her strange English phrases, while she stirred.

From listening to all the visitors to the art project, she had mastered the sound of the English language so well, that it sounded as if she was speaking English although she did not know a single word with any meaning. She knew she could always use this gift to make people laugh when things were not going well. Now Ncaoka, Ntcisa and the children joined in delightedly, mouthing the incomprehensible words, pulling their lips forward as they mimicked the people who work in the projects until they were all laughing hysterically.

The other children had come back from the fly. Visitors to the church, they said. White people with cameras and long-sleeved shirts and long trousers. Turu took the little dishcloth hanging from a twig on the shelter to dry the cups and bowls her grandchild had been washing in an enamel bowl at her feet. She had in the meantime hung all the wet cups and bowls on the branches used to make the shelter.

Only porridge today. They do not even have sugar or milk to mix in. They had even finished Ntcisa's baby's food, which the clinic hands out every week. It's nice and sweet and helps to give the porridge some taste. On their trips with Michael they at least always had lots to eat. She's never really liked the white man's food, but the worst is when they take you into one of those big rooms with the many tables where you have to sit and wait until someone brings you a big piece of paper and asks you to choose what you want to eat. Of course you cannot read, so someone else must choose for you and you never know what you are going to get! Sometimes when they bring you your plate it is full of something you have never seen before! In London she got so tired of the bread; they seemed to eat it all the time. They hardly ever got meat, and she knew they must have meat somewhere in those houses because she could smell it.

What she liked almost as much as meat were those bowls of nuts on the tables when all the people came to the opening of one of their exhibitions. And the glasses of wine, of course, which she and the others would quickly drink when Michael wasn't looking. He didn't want them to drink that wine, because one night Coco drank too much and tripped in the gallery and broke the glass, and they all had to go home early.

But actually she didn't mind the strange food. To be hungry is much more terrible than to have to eat bread and funny food like fish in those cold and busy countries. There is just so little to eat these days if you can't buy food in the shop. Every afternoon the girls go out to collect firewood and usually they come back with some berries and roots, but it is as if no one ever gets enough, as if you are still hungry when the pot is empty. Sometimes, if you really got desperate, you could always talk the girls in the Kuru shop into giving you some tea or sugar for free, but the manager watches them so closely that they complain a lot if you ask. They always say they're not supposed just to give things out, the shop has to make money. But why should the shop have money if the people don't? As far as she is concerned, some people just do not understand life.

Not that she got hungry so much these days. The TB probably had something to do with it, and the swollen bumps in her neck and armpits. The whites keep urging her to go to the clinic, to start taking those dreadful tablets again, like she had to do a few years ago when Mmamoruti took her to the doctor because she was so thin. She did get better that time, but she won't take those horrible tablets again, they make you feel sicker than the TB does and if you skip a day or two the clinic people make such a fuss, they even refuse to treat you again, or they make you start all over again, just when you thought you had finished the course. It was just too difficult to do the things they tell you to every day. Where was she supposed to get food every morning before she took the tablets? How could they expect a person to remember all the time? Sometimes you just felt like going somewhere, and it was only when you got off the truck that had given you a lift, far away from D'Kar, that you remembered you were supposed to fetch your stupid card at the clinic. And without that card they won't give you medicine at the new place.

She snorted. What was so bad about dying anyway? She looked at Ncaoka, smoking next to the fire. "Pass me a smoke. You know, I refuse to drink that medicine any more. Maybe then, if I get really sick they will feel sorry for me and pay me my money. Anyway, I can't trust them. They say it is all my money, but if it really is as much as they say, why is it always finished when I need it?"

"*Tseegu ka*," Ncaoka said. "You are right. Did they ever give you your money back after that time when they tried to give you red notes instead of the green ones you had given them?"

Just the thought of this made Turu angry all over again. There was this man in the office – she did not know which country he came from because new people came and went so fast she could not always keep up – and he was actually laughing at her, telling her that the red notes he was handing her were exactly the same as the green ones she had given him to save a week ago! The worst was that the children who worked in the office made fun of her too, and even though they gave her her green notes in the end, she felt mixed-up and cheated. If she could not trust that man with the colour, how did she know the amount was the same?

At the accounts office they always told her how much she had in her savings, and at the shops they told her how much she owed them, and then she could not make out if she owed more or had saved more and if the one amount was bigger or smaller than the other. Or if all the amounts she owed put together would eat up all her money coming from the exhibition. What if her exhibition money was less than all the shop accounts? What if everyone who'd been waiting for her money to come wanted something and there was nothing left for *her*?

"The problem is there aren't so many safe places where you can put your money," Ncaoka said. "Q'ane has an account at the bank where she sometimes puts money, but she says they're stealing it from her there as well. Would you believe it, they took money from her when they thought this money had been in the bank for too long! They told her they *must* take it because she has to pay the bank for keeping it for her! They also told her that she has to pay more if she keeps a small amount in the bank because it's easier to look after a lot of money. Such robbers!"

Turu didn't bother to answer. She and the other artists had also tried to save their money at the bank once. It wasn't worth it. It was even more terrible to go to town and stand in those long rows of black and white people than to face the Kuru office people. In the bank they all looked at them as if they'd lost their way and the Tswana bank officials made fun of them. "Ah, a rich Mosarwa! Can I send my daughter to work for you?" one said to her, and to Coco he said, "Soon you people will probably not want to milk our cows any longer." Going in there and coming out there with your money was just too difficult. Because inside were the bank people and outside her town relatives waited. They wanted their share, and everyone knows what happens if you don't stuff a few notes in every outstretched hand as you pass.

"Are you getting something again this week, Áiè?" her grandchild asked, her little face shining with expectation.

Clever little thing, she thought, she's listened to us talking. How she wished she had money, right now, for she remembered the last time she had some pulas left. She had paid everyone the money she owed, and she had bought some clothes for the relatives who were standing around the shop, and in her purse there were but a few notes left. She knew they could not buy a lot, but she still needed to buy food.

On her way home, she stopped at the Kuru shop. She looked at the shelves for a long time. There were the usual things – packets of sugar, tea, soup powder, mealie meal, washing powder, soap, cooking oil, matches. All things they needed. But taking them would swallow all the money in her purse and they would still not have anything really nice.

On a side shelf a big, yellow tin caught her eye. It was the largest tin of Nespray milk powder she had ever seen. That was it! She emptied her purse in her hand and held out her palm to Anna, the shop assistant. "Will this money buy that tin?" she asked.

"This thing is very expensive, Turu. We keep it for the pre-school, they buy it for the children. You'll have no money left if you buy it."

The little ones danced around her when she came back from the shop with the shining tin balanced on her head. She called them all and with shining eyes they crowded around the tin. She made them sit down, and one by one they dipped a spoon into the rich, creamy white powder. It made her heart sing to see them like that: the little faces covered with the milky, dusty goodness, the littlest one also smacking her lips and sucking on her spoon.

"Do you remember the day I bought that big tin of powdered milk, Cgõa?" she asked.

Her granddaughter's face lit up. "Yes! You know what was so nice about that milk, Áiè?" she said. "The powder stuck to the inside of your mouth and when it got wet you could go on licking for a long time after the tin was finished!"

Turu laughed. Even that same day, she was sorry that she didn't save some of the milk powder to put in their tea later. And that she didn't buy mealie meal and sugar and all the other things they needed, because for many weeks afterwards the hunger stayed with them until they went to sleep at night, no matter how she struggled to get advances at the office.

But so what. It was a *real* treat. They are hungry again, they are always hungry, but it pleased her to know that Cgõa still remembered that day.

ELEVEN

# Red skin

If they wanted to see the speakers, they had to stretch their necks and peer between the bodies, big hats and hairdos. They were almost at the back of the gathering, sitting on the low chairs that were borrowed from the primary school nearby. The flaps of the huge yellow and white tent were beaten about by the wind which shook the whole structure every now and then, making it tremble and sift fine sand down on everyone's head. The tent came from somewhere else and was specially erected for the meeting in Ghanzi.

Kelebetse and the Jimmies sat at the back with the other church council members and senior people from D'Kar. They would come to listen, they had said to each other beforehand, but also to talk. Komtsha, Tshabu and Debe were in the row just in front of them.

Kelebetse was waiting for the right moment. He was listening very hard to the loudspeakers, but the din of children playing outside and people selling fat cakes, meat and other things in the stalls next to the tent, made it difficult to hear. Their Kuru stall was there too, with the products they made in D'Kar: saddles and harnesses, bows and arrows and little wood carvings, the shirts painted by Dina's children and the paintings done by Turu and the others. Moruti had said that if the people saw what they could do with their hands, then they would listen better to what they have to say. Many of the people who would talk against them today, he said, had never produced anything that could compare with what they had to show. That was why they had taken a stall and why Q'ane specially wore one of those patchwork dresses the sewing group made. She was outside, selling all their things today, including those dresses which the women from Gaborone loved to buy.

He was happy to be here with the people from D'Kar, Kelebetse thought. He liked sitting with them, even if he looked different. They still teased him about his black skin and big hands and feet. Then he would tell them, "Man, look at my heart, not my feet."

Strange how the one thing he used to consider a thing of pride as a child, now in his later years here in D'Kar had come to stand in his way. His blackness. On the cattle post in the communal grazing lands in the west where he grew up he didn't look different from the other people, but he had always felt different. At D'Kar it had more to do with how he felt, not how he looked. He felt that he belonged.

He couldn't remember how old he was when he first realised it, but he knew that it had cost him many hours of trying to work it out, once he discovered that the people he stayed with were not his real family. The old woman who looked after him was not his own mother, even though he called her Mme and she fed him. She was his father's mother. His father worked in town and now and then brought diesel for the water-pump so that the cattle would have water. He also brought mealie meal, soap and tea for the old woman and him, but he never stayed.

Early in the morning Mme would sit at the fire and stir the black pot. When the porridge was ready, she stirred in the sour milk and gave him his cupful of *motogo*. As he grew up, he was told to sit outside the cooking shelter when he ate. Only he was looked after by his Mme, the other children had an older sister who looked after and cooked for them. They always told him he should know his place and not sleep or eat with them. At night they sat at their own fire. The problem was his mother, Mme later explained. His mother's people and the Bakgalagadi, his father's people, did not belong together.

At such times he would sit and stare at his black skin for a long time, trying to see if there was something he could see that was different. He also looked at his hair in the smooth tin sheet that they had wiped until it shone so much that they could see their own faces in it when they combed their hair. What was the thing that Mme had said, that his mother was not right? In what way was she not right? Sometimes he put his hand next to the hand of one of the other children and tried to measure the difference in the depth of their blackness. Their skin looked the same to him. But they always teased him about his hair, said that he should try to comb it out so that it could be softer. Their hair was thicker and woollier; his grew in tight little nodes right against his skull. Then he would pluck at it with Mme's wide-toothed comb, but the next day his hair was again clinging close to his skull.

When his father came from town he was kind to him, always called him towards him and asked if he still looked well after the goats. But he would always be standing and looking down at him while he talked. He had watched the children of his uncle swarm all over their father when he came from town, everyone grabbing at the things he brought while he laughed and let them sit on his lap. Now and then his own father would bring him shoes or a shirt, but mostly it was only food and sometimes something for Mme.

He liked to go out into the veld with the herd of goats during the day. Then the others could not tease him. "Mosarwa! Mosarwa!" they shouted, and laughed. At that time he was not sure what it meant.

One morning his Mme did not sit at the fire, cooking his porridge. The embers were still cold. Nobody told him anything, but the oldest daughter of his uncle went in and out of Mme's hut, crying. Each time she closed the door behind her and chased the little ones out. Later a bakkie came to fetch his Mme, and a few days later they brought her back in a big brown wooden box. After the funeral his father and his uncle sat talking on an old oil drum under the big *moshu* tree and he knew they were discussing him. They didn't tell him anything, but his uncle came to stay at the cattle post. After this things changed in his life, like night and day. He could no longer sleep inside the cooking shelter in front of Mme's hut, and he had to cook his own food. They gave him Mme's little black pot and some mealie meal. And even though he was still small, he knew what he could pick and eat in the veld and what not. He drank the goats' milk straight from the udder. But in the evenings, when the animals were in their kraal and the other people were sitting at their fire, the smell of meat lured him and he moved closer to them, even though his uncle would sometimes say, "Make your own fire, Mosarwa!" Sometimes they shoved a bowl of meat his way, though.

When the cold time came that year, they did not give him a new blanket like Mme had done every year. The fire he made helped, but to keep the winter wind from his back he squeezed his body into the open side of a hardened piece of folded hide he had found outside. He moved it around so that the open side was facing the fire and his back was shielded against the wind. He could not understand why he had to sleep outside like this. What was wrong with him? His Mme was never playful with him, like his uncle was with his children, but she did not mistreat him. Now that she was dead, his father stopped coming back from town.

The people who one after the other stepped onto the stage of the big yellow tent, all talked about the Basarwa. He had wondered so many times, why they were always called names by others which they did not choose themselves? The blacks called them Basarwa, the whites called them Bushmen. But they, the red people, wanted to be called by the names of their family groups, and of their own languages. It was because of that hateful name, Basarwa, which he had to hear all through his childhood, that he was here. He had told the others in D'Kar already that he was ready to speak about what it meant to be called a Mosarwa. He had a lot to say. The Botswana government had called this meeting, but it was not the first meeting of its kind. Some of them had already been taken to one in Windhoek, a few months ago.

The woman who now talked looked familiar to him. She was a young and fashionably dressed Motswana woman. Debe turned round and explained to him: "It is the same one who was sent by the Council of Churches in Gaborone a few months ago to go around the district and ask people how it felt to be a Mosarwa. She was also the one who came to pick up Tshabu's son to give evidence before the police how he had been beaten and tortured by the officials who caught him hunting," he whispered in his ear. "Remember, she took photos of the scars on his back?"

Kelebetse remembered well. Tshabu's son had to tell the police how they put a plastic bag over his head until he fainted and how they had twisted his balls around until he screamed with pain. Just because he was looking for meat.

"This is 1993, the United Nations-declared Year of the Indigenous Peoples. Why should our own first people be denied the world's attention?" the woman in the front was saying in English. They were translating everything in Setswana. She was so brave, he thought, to talk against her own people like this. They said she had even opened her own office to be a representative for the Basarwa. But he had heard that she also helped other people who were badly treated by the law, to know their rights. The red people at first did not trust her at all, they thought she had come as a spy. But when they saw the thick book that she had written about their problems, everyone who could read talked about how brave she was. She had written down the things just as they had told them to her. Now they believed what she said.

The Motswana woman was still talking, but one of the important people sitting in one of the rows of seats on the stage, facing them, had jumped up. He was talking and shouting at the same time as her!

She stopped talking, stood aside and looked at the angry man. Kelebetse could not believe his eyes. He sat forward to take a second look. It *was* him. Truly, it was the uncle from whom he had run away so many years ago. And now he was sitting there, among the big people of the district, the ones who made all the laws and decisions! Once, long ago, he was told that his uncle had become a councillor, but he couldn't believe it.

Kelebetse shook his head. The man had changed a lot from those days at the cattle post. It looked like he had done well for himself, if you looked at his big stomach. The suit he was wearing fitted too tightly over his back and it pulled the front of the jacket away from his hips in a funny way. You could clearly see his large belly hanging over his pants.

"Lies, they tell lies! I refuse to listen to this any longer!" he shouted. "Who can tell me anything about the Masarwa that I do not know? Did we not live with them all these years? They work for us! They belong to us! They are the biggest liars you can get. And who says they were here first! Those are also lies!" He looked exhausted and sat down in his chair with a sigh.

Everywhere in the tent people were now shouting and talking to each other. Kelebetse's heart was beating fast. Some had turned around to look at their two rows of people, sitting in the back.

He did not hear what the others were shouting, he only saw his uncle. It was so many years since he had run away from this man and his ways. He thought he had almost forgotten about everything. It all came back to him so clearly now. One night he let the goats walk back to the kraal on their own. He stayed behind in the veld and started out in the opposite direction early the next day. He walked until he came across a wind-pump. He drank some water and lay down to rest in the shade of the small tank. He woke up when the shadow of a horse and rider fell over his face. It was his uncle. He was furious about all the trouble he had put him through, having to track him down like this. He made Kelebetse sit behind him on the back of the horse and galloped home with him.

Kelebetse clung to the back of the saddle, frightened that he might fall off. He was too scared to hold onto the waist of the man in front of him. That night he was fed from the food at the other fire and he did not need to cook for himself. The next day one of his uncle's sons took the goats to graze and he was told to wait for his father. When he arrived that afternoon, his father pretended not to see him. This time there were also no shoes and no food.

The two men sat under the *moshu* tree again and talked about him. "Back to his own people," he heard his uncle say. "I do not know why you took him away from there in the first place."

That same afternoon his father and his uncle mounted two horses and set off. He sat behind his father on the back of the horse and held him around his waist. It was the longest he had ever been that close to his father. Late that afternoon they reached a small group of huts. His father and uncle got down from their horses, but they remained standing next to the small, light-skinned people who were squatting on the sand.

Kelebetse scrambled down from the horse and looked around. The huts were made of grass only, and he remembered thinking: One would have to bend really low if you wanted to crawl inside. The walls were not very solid, he could see through them, even from the outside. Mme's house was made of clay and dung, and the door opened into the cooking shelter. These people lived very differently! In Mme's cooking shelter there were clay benches all along the walls for people to sit on and onto which she stacked the pots. Every so often the floor was smeared with soft dung and Mme swept it every day with a grass broom. Here there was no cooking shelter, no floor, only sand and the bare huts. It looked as if these people owned nothing, or as if they were only camping there temporarily.

His father called him. "We brought back the child," he told the people. Then he pointed to a very old woman, wrinkled from top to toe, and said, "This is your grandmother. You have to stay here with your people now."

The people offered him food after the two men had left, but he could not eat. If only it were not so dark already, he would have set off again at once. But they gave him a blanket and after a while he sat down next to the fire. He tried to understand what had happened to him. His mother had died long ago, his father told him on their way here. That was why he had fetched him when he was little, to take him to live with his father's people. But now his Mme was also dead.

He felt nothing when he thought about his own dead mother. What did he have to do with her anyway? With these Masarwa he could not even talk. They used Sekgalagadi, the language of his father's people, when they addressed him, but among themselves they spoke a language which bewildered him, with many tongue clicks and noises coming deep from their throats. They discussed him every time they talked, he thought. It looked like they had nothing more than the two miserable little huts. Everyone, young and old, slept around the fire.

The blanket they had given him was made of soft leather and in the end he lay down a few yards away from them on the sand. "Mosarwa. Mosarwa, child of the Masarwa," he said to himself, over and over, before he fell asleep.

Very early the next morning, with the stars still shining brightly and the call of a jackal in the distance, he quietly got up and took off into the night. He could remember that they had crossed a gravel road the previous day with the horses, and he tried to head that way. In the darkness the thorny shrubs scratched his legs, but he ran, dodging the thorny branches and holding his hands in front of his face to protect his eyes.

The day was breaking fast and the stars were fading. Soon there was a pale glow in front of him on the horizon which became brighter and brighter until the sky turned red. Later the sun showed a small red edge among the trees, and then suddenly it shone brightly, straight into his eyes.

He followed the sun, remembering the direction from which they came the previous day. He ran for most of the day, it felt, occasionally resting under a tree when he became too tired. He was afraid that they would follow his spoor, so he kept on running. Then, unexpectedly, late in the afternoon, there was the gravel road in front of him. He must have been running parallel to it for a long time, he realised. To go back to his father he would have to cross over this road and continue east, but that he could not do. His father's people did not want him, and he did not want these new people, his mother's people. He would have to follow this road. He had no choice, it did not matter if he got run over by a truck.

When the sun started to set again, he spotted a dark object some distance down the road. At first he wanted to hide, but as he got closer, he saw that it was a vehicle. Later still, he saw that it was a big truck. Two men were sitting next to it on the ground, repairing a flat tyre. They were white people, like the ones he had seen on the scarce occasions when the clinic car visited their cattle post.

He sat down at a small distance from them, waiting for them to finish with the tyre. They looked friendly and tried to talk to him, but they spoke a language he could not understand. It was getting dark again. He could not stay by himself next to this road, he knew. The lions would eat him, there was no place to hide. He would have to go with these people, no matter where they went. When they started packing up their tools, he anxiously indicated that he wanted to get on the back and started to hoist himself up the side of the truck. But the men pulled him down. They shook their heads and pointed down the road where he came from. He burst out in tears. He could not stop, all the pain and confusion of the past days went into that crying. With tears running down his face, he tried to scramble up the back of the truck again. It did not matter where they went, he could not stay here.

This time the men let him be and even helped him up. He got in and looked for a place to sit between big bags of sugar, boxes of tea and canned food, tobacco, rolls of cloth. The truck was already rocking from side to side on the dirt road when he found the two soft bales of clothing and wedged himself cosily in between them. Seeing all the food around him reminded him of his hunger, but everything was wrapped in plastic, and they would in any case immediately see if he took anything. He soon fell asleep.

The red glow in the east had returned when the truck stopped in front of a big, blue building with pillars and a veranda. He sat up. He was very cold and stiff. A white man and a black man with a lantern came to the truck and the two men who had given him the lift, opened the back and started off-loading the goods. He tried to hand them whatever he could pick up, but soon it was too difficult and he jumped down and waited on the veranda with his back against one of the pillars. The white and the black man with the light looked at him and exchanged words about him with the other two. Then the black man took his hand and took him to a room where he gave him coffee and bread, lots of bread, until he was satisfied and felt so tired that he fell asleep on a blanket in the corner of the room. When he woke up later that day, the truck had left. The two men wanted to hear his story. They could both speak Sekgalagadi, and they looked at each other and sighed while he was talking. The white man, whom he later heard he should call Mr Eustace, took him to a zinc bath with hot water, helped him to undress and wash himself. When he had finished, Mr Eustace came and scrubbed his neck and washed his hair and ears. It was the first time in his life that he was scrubbed like that.

When he was dried and dressed, the black man, Abel, had already left for his home in the village. It was called D'Kar, he later heard. Mr Eustace was the manager of the Ngamiland Trading Company store. He had no children nor a wife. That same night he gave Kelebetse a small room next to his back door, and it became his home for many years. When Mr Eustace died many years later, Kelebetse was working in the shop; a grown-up man who had already fathered some children in the village.

Why did he have all those relationships with the Basarwa women, but never married any one of them? he now asked himself. He had children with three different women, but like him, they also didn't live with their father.

"Liars, they are all liars! ..." The words of his uncle on the stage in front of the tent raced through his soul and pulled him back to the present. When did he start seeing who he really was? It was only after he started going to the church in D'Kar that he understood what love and forgiveness are. He had received love from people who owed him nothing, and he had to forgive those who denied him the love they owed him, he realised. He now knew that he was forgiven for hurting those people who wanted to take care of him, his mother's people, and he had to forgive those who hurt him.

"We know them, we own them," his uncle had said on the stage and many people in the tent shouted "yes, yes!" after he had finished talking. That awoke old, buried thoughts in his heart. After he became an elder in the church, he had started here and there to pay a little bit of money to the mothers of the children he had in those grass huts in D'Kar and on the farms, but in the end he married a Motswana woman. Hannah. She was pretty and clever and taught him some reading and writing. Her parents and brothers and sisters did not like him, however. Before they got married, her family made him walk with his head bowed down; for weeks he was not allowed to look them in the eye. When he passed them, they shouted insults: "A poor beggar like that, how would he look after our daughter! We do not even know his family!" He knew this was the Tswana custom for a family to test a prospective son-in-law to see whether he was patient and wise enough to marry their daughter, but the words opened up an old hurt. The pain in his heart from the things his uncle and father had said about him and his mother when he was young, started throbbing again.

Now and then, as he walked through the village, he would come across some of the children of the women he had had before. The look in their eyes, the expectation in the tone of their voices irritated him and the guilt made him rash and impatient with them. At night those same eyes brought fear and sadness in him. He was lying next to a Motswana woman, and the two children he had with her would sometimes lean over the fence and shout at the other village children: "Mosarwa! Mosarwa!" Even though they knew that some of them were their half-brothers and -sisters.

His wife also knew of those other children of his. She had been in this village as long as he. She even sometimes sent food or clothing over to their houses. She was a good person, and also a woman of the Church. At night she was sometimes different though, and when he turned to her she would push him away, saying, "You smell like a Mosarwa." The next day she would give him extra meat on his plate and made his reading lesson a little longer. But her eyes would still be saying the things her mouth had said in the night.

And then she had died. Within five days. A disease that went into her head and made her shake with fever took her and before the tablets from the hospital could work, she was gone. For many months he had looked after their two children with the help of his sisters-in-law and two girls his wife had hired to do the washing and to rake the yard. During this time two of the mothers of his other children made it very difficult for him. When they saw him, they would say things like: "So, you're free now. Do you now look down on us? You remember my blankets, don't you?" All he could do was to carry on walking and pretend he did not hear, but in his heart their words shamed him deeply and increased his sadness.

But then came the time that his and his wife's common possessions had to be divided, according to Tswana custom. The elders from her family came to see what they had. He had to declare everything: the cattle, the old bakkie he had bought after he started to work in the leather project, the stock in the small *semauso* they started together, even the supplies he got from the government that time for his dairy, which had failed. She too had had other children before they got married and then there were the two they had together. Everyone had to get something – her parents, her sisters, all her children, everyone. He did not mention his other children in the village to the elders, though.

After their common possessions were divided, he had to start from scratch.

Maybe it was because he was now so poor that the gap between him and the red people in the village was no longer that big. A year after Hannah died, he took Esta as his wife. One day, when Nqaba was drunk, she came walking past his house and yelled at him: "Yes, you pretend you're someone special. You lie with our women, but you would not marry one of us, not so? Now you take one of the half-blood Jimmies, so that you can pretend you are a real Mosarwa!" Even though he laughed, he felt ashamed and angry. Nqaba was not even one of the mothers of his children, so what was her business humiliating him in front of everyone? But her words stayed with him, would not leave him alone.

But Esta was a good wife. She talked Naro to him, his mother's language which he by now understood but never spoke, and slowly he started to use the language himself. He came to this meeting with his brothers-in-law. "Man, this is our chance to speak up," they had said. "Can you imagine, the government invites us to talk! You're one of us now, man, come along."

"Are there any of the Basarwa who'd still like to say something?" the chairman called from the front. "Please, feel free. Come on, the government is giving you a chance, so that you can no longer say you are not heard."

They looked at each other. They lacked the courage. It was quite a distance to walk to get to the front, and there were so many people you had to pass, what if they laughed at you?

"The laughter is not the worst," old Komtsha had said earlier. "It's their anger. There are some people here who have great power."

The chairman urged once more: "Anyone else?"

Debe had already talked, earlier. He was used to this kind of thing and he was wearing a tie and jacket, like all the other people in front. But he alone could not talk for all of them; no one would believe that they all felt the same.

Kelebetse's heart stood in the aisle long before his legs followed. He held on to the back of Tshabu's chair before he ventured further. It was a long way and people were already starting to turn around to look at him.

As he walked towards the stage he suddenly became aware of his tattered shirt and the patches on the knees of his pants. He didn't have socks on and his shoes could not close properly. But it was too late. He could no longer turn back.

On the stage they gave him something to hold in front of his mouth. He got a fright when he heard his own voice coming out so loud and stopped and looked around for help. People laughed. But the chairman pushed the black thing back in front of his mouth and told him: "Continue!" If only his legs would stop shaking.

"I do not look like the red people," he said. "This blackness of my skin was like a blanket that covered my heart for a very long time. But now I am free of that blanket and I can tell all of you who I am. This man, who says he knows the Basarwa so well and that they are all liars, he does know me well. Yes. I do not know if he knows the other Basarwa, but he knows me and if he says he doesn't know me, then he is the one who is a liar. But he also knows the thing I tried to hide for a long time. This thing: that my black skin which you see, is actually a red skin. This redness made him throw me away when I was still small, just like people are still throwing us away, even today. This is not a lie, everyone knows it. Ask him, he knows that I am speaking the truth today, here in front of all the people and before God."

He turned to his uncle. The thing in his hand made crackling sounds as he moved.

He felt his body becoming light and his heart beating in his neck as he said in a clear, measured voice, facing his uncle: "I want to tell this man that I am standing here today not in the name of my father, who is his brother. I am standing here today in the name of my mother."

TWELVE

# Two letters

It must have something to do with the letter he had written to the Queen. It had taken a very, very long time and still no one had answered that letter. But he had been waiting. Now he has been called, he is not sure why and by whom, but he hopes it is in connection with the letter. He has to go there all by himself. But he isn't afraid, he knows he can do this thing on his own. He will just go; he will see at the other end what is waiting.

He was sitting inside the fly, listening to the humming of the engines. Someone whom he could not see was talking somewhere, the voice trying to rise above those of the other people around him. To him it was just more sounds mixed in with all the others. He couldn't understand any of it, but he was not overly worried. The note, which he carried in his top breast pocket, had brought him this far, and it would carry on working for him. The first one he gave it to, just after he got onto the plane in Johannesburg, was a smiling white woman, who took hold of his hand after she had read it and led him to this seat, strapped him in and snapped the lock, now lying on his lap. For a brief moment he had panicked, thought he had been led into a trap, but then he noticed that the two people on either side of him as well as those across the way had locked themselves in like that too. It must be the law of this place.

As soon as they were all tied up, he showed the note in his pocket to the people sitting on either side of him. They smiled and nodded, and then turned back to the big papers they were holding in front of them. The one on his left was a black woman, but her hair was different from the black people's hair back in D'Kar. It was longer, all fluffed out and soft but standing straight, unlike the straight hair of white people which mostly hung down. She wore a tight, very short skirt, which moved up

131

over her thighs as she sat. He could not help comparing her heavy black thighs with old Xau's thin ones, which always showed when she squatted down, her patchwork skirts neatly gathered and pushed down between her legs. Pretty, colourful skirts which she made herself from little pieces of cloth she gathered from everywhere. Xau would sit like this to smoke, eyes fixed on a world only she could see. Her old thighs were the colour of a calabash and the wrinkled, sagging skin looked just like a spider's web when she sat like that. Then one could also see the little black lines on her upper thigh clearly, markings of ceremonies and healing sessions during their years together. He couldn't read a book, he thought, but few people could read the story of her life, of their lives together, better in those lines than he and old Xau could.

Komtsha looked down at his own frail body which looked almost childlike next to the other two people's. The man was also bigger than he, but the woman was huge, her arm took all the space on the arm of his chair so he had to hold his hands in his lap. The man on his right was a white man, but much whiter than the ones he was used to. Komtsha could not help peeping at his face and hands. You could almost see through them, like the petals of the lilies you found on the pans in the rainy season. The white people he knew were tanned by the sun, their skins as brown as his own, but much rougher, more hairy, and usually they were covered with dark spots and marks. He had to remember to tell those whites to take better care of themselves, now that he had seen how their kind was supposed to look.

They were now moving, he could see through the small window on the other side of the woman. But if it weren't for the buildings, the vehicles and the people running around on the ground he could see passing by, he would not have known. He grabbed the arm rests. The fly had left the ground! He could see only see the redness in the sky where the sun had set and the small line of lights on the ground that were shooting past. Mmamoruti had warned him about what would happen, but what was it she had said? He put his hands over his ears, and the fat woman smiled and gestured reassuringly. Soon the funny feeling in his ears disappeared, the noise of the engines died down a little. The fly was turning and out of the corner of his eye he caught a glimpse of many, many small lights that were coming on everywhere. The springbok on the plains of his youth had not been so numerous. Not even the wildebeest when they started moving north were so many. There were more lights here than the stars, he thought to himself. Would anyone ever believe his story when he got home?

Every time one of the women who were walking up and down inside the fly brought him something he handed her his note. She would smile, give it back to him, and hand him plates of things he had never seen before, so he watched his neighbours closely to see how they got to the food and how they ate. He tasted everything carefully to try and work out what it could be. Because he didn't know how long the journey would take, he decided he'd better save some food. He wrapped a piece of bread in the soft white papers they gave him and put it in his pocket. Some of the other food tasted so odd that he wrapped it too, to take along to give away later; someone somewhere might want it.

Deep in the night, when everyone around him was asleep and the little window was pitch black, he again thought about the letter. Over the past years he had been on several journeys, everywhere taking the opportunity to tell his own people about the problem of the land. He was quite sure the situation they found themselves in nowadays was the result of a simple misunderstanding. If only he and others used the chances they were given to speak out about how his people no longer had land for their families, and how the game had gone away because so many other people were now living on their land, then someone would realise the mistake and take the other people from amongst them.

The letter had been sent long ago. It had gone ahead of him like an arrow following an animal. Hopefully it had reached its target by now, he mused. Maybe he will now be able to find the place where the arrow had hit. Then he will be able to pull it out and wipe it clean and go home and tell everyone what he had shot and killed, just like he did in the olden days when he used to bring back so much meat from a hunt that he first had to cover most of it with thorny branches so that he could go and find help, because he could not carry all of it at once.

The trouble started with the fences. He can still remember when they put up the first ones. He was a young hunter, and he loved life and was respected for his skills. His father was proud of him, he knew, although they no longer hunted together and the old man challenged him and his brothers each time they brought meat home by scoffing at the bounty. But they knew it was his way of encouraging them to try even harder, because a hunter was only a leader while he was the best, and that could change in a moment. Tomorrow someone else might find the eland and you lose your position.

At first the fences were just a slight bother, causing unnecessary delay on their journeys. They soon learnt to crawl through them, even how to lift the poles from the sand and stand on the wires to make the whole fence lie down when they were herding animals or carrying a carcass, or when many of them wanted to pass all at once.

His people had not understood at first, he pondered to himself. They even welcomed the fences because so many of the men were given work to help put them up. Although old Jimmy and his sons got most of the contracts from the farmers, they, in turn, hired other helpers, so they all earned a little money in the end. How they enjoyed buying those things they could see in the shop in Ghanzi, or D'Kar, the canvas shoes, the belts with shiny buckles, the shirts, pants, bright cloth! Those things brought a man more honour than the finest antelope brought back from the hunt.

And the drinking! Nowadays he seldom drank, he had seen what it was doing to his people, even his children. But those days! He chuckled a little as he remembered the fights after they had been to the shop. Drink was usually the first thing they bought; it was the most desired, the most exciting thing in the shop. There were tiny little bottles with stuff that looked like water, but that water would take your breath away completely! Whatever money was left had to cover the other things they wanted. Holding their change in their hands and letting the shopkeeper count it out, they bought one item at a time until they were told that there was no money left. With their little bottles of liquor they would then walk a small distance from the shop, just out of sight of the white people who usually shooed them away from their homes and shops when they were drinking. Here they would share what they had and laugh a lot until the fighting started. Quite often they would find themselves under those same bushes the next day, the sun scorching down on their sometimes bloodstained bodies, their heads throbbing as they tried to remember how they came to be there and what they had bought to take home.

It had taken him many years to figure out what was happening to his people. He had laboured on many farms; he knew how to work with cattle and he had come to love the farm life. There were the regular milk and tobacco rations and the few animals he had accumulated during the years as part of his wages. However, he still grew restless when he remembered his hunting days, the time before the fences. Because very soon these fences became a big thing in their lives. The fences cut them off from the areas they knew so well and from their old hunting routes. No longer did it help to burn parts of the veld to make the wild animals move to the new, green grass that sprouted after a fire, because the fences restricted that movement as well. Later the farmers stopped allowing them to pass on their age-old routes through their farms. They had to stick to the sandy tracks made by the donkey-carts, which usually ran along the fences and went in quite the wrong direction. They knew where they wanted to go, the old route that would take them straight there, but the farmers – and later the police officers – forced them to stay on these tracks, which took great roundabouts and made their journeys very long.

When he started to talk about these things with his fellow workers a few years ago, the baas on the last farm where he was working fired him. At first he only discussed the problem with them of having to travel a few days on a journey that should only take half a day, and of farmers putting padlocks on gates across the roads they did not want them to use. There were times early on when, in a drunken fury, he had broken these locks to get through. But he had received one too many a lashing as a result, and had to change his tactics. That was when he turned "politician", as Jannie de Beer called him when he gave him his last month's wages. "Take your family and your donkeys and everything, and go and join that crowd of law breakers at D'Kar. You are a troublemaker and a politician, a good-for-nothing!" he shouted.

He took his wife and children, but also his father- and mother-in-law along, because he was responsible for them. He had left his own parents many years ago, when he went to live with his wife's family, like a young man had to do. His parents were now living in one of the government settlements far away, but he did not want to move that far from the farms where one sometimes could get a job. When they reached D'Kar, they lived in the veld for a long time, sleeping under their donkey-cart, tying plastic sheets from old stock-feed bags around it to keep the winter winds out. He wanted to make sure that they would be able to settle there, that they would not be chased away again, before he made a more permanent home. There were many of his relatives in D'Kar, and his wife and children enjoyed visiting everyone, but none of them had ever known such hunger as in those first months in D'Kar!

When they were still living on Jannie de Beer's farm, his parents-in-law often attended the services that the church people from D'Kar came to hold under the cluster of camel-thorn trees near the kraal. They were therefore considered members of the church in D'Kar. As "old people" they could receive the rations of sugar, mealie meal and tea handed out by the church every week. They all survived on this food, although it usually lasted only from Friday to Monday. By the middle of the week they had nothing left and had to survive on the little veldkos old Xau could find or beg from their neighbours. Later, Komtsha discovered he could also register his in-laws as "destitute" at the clinic, and that gave monthly rations from the government, which at least lasted for a week.

At first the fight for survival took so much time and energy that he almost forgot about this thing of the land and the fences. He tried to get some money by joining the tanners. The tannery, where a group of Bushmen worked together in a big shed not far from the church, was behind the old farmhouse where the Moruti now stayed. Komtsha learnt that you first soaked the goat and cow hides in some lime, then you scraped off the hair and soaked the skins in pounded *mosetsane* root until it became the nice brown leather the other men in the tannery used to make shoes and harnesses for donkey-carts and bridles for horses. The money they got for their products was never enough, but the leather was useful for their own needs as well.

This was the time when he began going to church on Sundays with his family. There were the benefits of the food rations for his parents, and the work, but he also went because he had started to ask himself too many questions about life and death. He had started talking to his father-in-law at night about how it was that the traditions and the spirits of the past did not seem to have any power any longer.

The young Moruti, who had come to live in D'Kar with his wife and children not so long before Komtsha moved there, made a lot of God who had come back to His people. This was just the opposite of what they had always believed, which was that God had made the people and animals and then went away to watch their struggles from a distance. For a while he tried with his whole heart to get to know this God, to see if He could really change something in their lives, and in the end he became a church-council member. Not long after he was chosen, the Mission Church from Namibia gave up the patch of land they had owned among the cattle ranches in the district. Moruti brought them the paper with a red blotch in one corner, which he said was a seal showing that this land, this farm, was now theirs and could never be taken away from them again. The Bushmen Church Council was now the legal owner of D'Kar! They bought a small iron box for the church and they locked their paper in there, taking it out only when they needed it to demonstrate their power at kgotla meetings or to visiting government officials.

Having title to the land, as it was called, meant a lot, but it also caused quarrels and pain. There were things he could not understand, but he had stopped discussing them because he had seen that his arguments were not heard. He wanted to know, for instance, why his people had to pay for pumping the water and for keeping the fences in order now that the land was theirs. Imagine stealing all of someone's land, then giving him back a small piece and telling him that from now on he must pay for the things others had put there, like the boreholes and the hateful fences! He soon saw that the fences could also have a good purpose, though, also keeping his own animals from mixing with the neighbours'. And it was good to have water from a tap all year round – but to expect money for such things from his people who had lost everything, that was going too far.

Being a landowner gave him and the others new courage. They were becoming quite reckless, standing up at the long, boring kgotla meetings where before they had just sat quietly at the back, playing games in the sand and mocking the speakers among themselves until their laughter made those in front look at them angrily. Now they started moving to the front, daring to say things that could get them in trouble. But how tired they were of listening to the government officials and politicians who brought new promises, new rules, always telling the Bushmen how little they knew, how lowly their ways were and how disrespectful their behaviour! In the past their only way to get through these meetings was to watch carefully and to plan little imitation scenes which they could act out to each other later at home. Often at these meetings they were asked to choose a "chairman" for some or other "committee" which they knew would never meet again. But they had such fun in proposing people like old Petros or Maria, whom they knew would turn up drunk or say all the wrong things. Komtsha sniggered to himself. At least his people had always known how to have fun.

He had worked out how things happened in the kgotla long before he talked there for the first time. The circle, built with tall logs planted next to each other, had an open mouth. The Bushmen usually squatted near the mouth in the thin line of shade cast by the logs. Inside the closed end there were a table and some chairs where the important people – the Kgosi and the councillor, usually – sat in their dark suits. They had a water jug on the table, some plastic flowers, and papers which had to be held down with stones because the wind always blew on kgotla days. Then there were a few chairs in front of the table for other important people – the teachers, the clinic staff and the few Batswana who lived in D'Kar because they were selling beer or providing lodging for their own and their relatives' school-going children.

Next came the school children, who were made to sit on the sand, and then there were the Herero women who also did not mind sitting on the sand in their long dresses.

Komtsha smiled to himself. The Baherero were easier to get along with than the other black people, although they never gave you any money if you worked for them. But at least they spoke the red people's language and did not mind sharing the same cup as you.

The first time he spoke in the kgotla he was mocked and laughed at by the Batswana and the Baherero. Even by some of his own people. That was when he told them that the black and white people had stolen the land from the Bushmen, that they were all newcomers and that the black people's government did not honour his people. He told them, as he was told by his father, that Mmamosadinyane, the great English queen, had given the rule of the country to their first president, Seretse Kgama, expecting him to govern the land in a fair way when her people went back home across the water. He also told them that they were ignoring half of the people in this country now – his people – and that his children did not want to learn other people's languages and their ways in school; that he did not want to speak those languages either, and that to be fair, they should also learn to speak his. Then he wouldn't mind speaking theirs. That first time the jeering and shouting and laughing were so loud that he had to give up. But later so many of his own people told him how they liked his courage, and promised to join him when the opportunity came again, that he knew this was what he was meant to do.

It was not long after he had started talking like this that he was chosen to become the chairman of the red people's own organisation, which they called the First People of the Kalahari. Now, he and others believed, they would be taken seriously. There was the meeting he was called to attend in Namibia, where for the first time he saw other red people like himself, whose language he could not follow, but whose words he recognised, not through the translation alone, but through the fire in their eyes and the trembling of their bodies when they told of how their land had been taken, how the animals were getting fewer, and how the Baherero people were moving into their areas with their many heads of cattle. A few white people were present; one was introduced as a man from the government in England, where Mmamosadinyane lived. Komtsha suddenly had an idea and he was sure this was the right thing to do. He stood up, asked for translation, and pointed to the man from England.

"This man, this representative from the Queen of England, must take a very important message back to her. I am speaking on behalf of the people of Botswana only, because I understand the people of Namibia did not lose their land under English rule. But maybe the King of the country which gave Namibia away to others will also be told by Mmamosadinyane about my message."

He must have slept even though he had thought he would never be able to. Suddenly there was bright light inside the fly, and he felt an urgent need to stretch his legs. He also needed to go to the bush! Then he remembered how Mmamoruti had explained that this would not be possible. Just then, as he was starting to panic, the friendly woman who had shown him to his seat came to call him. She stretched over, loosened the straps round his body and led him through the rows of people to a tiny room at the back of the fly. She showed him how to make the water run for washing, and pointed to a bowl that was standing lower. Although he felt embarrassed, he knew what to do because he had seen and used toilets on his travels. He was a little scared that he would not know how to work the door, so he did not close it completely but turned his back to the waiting woman while he relieved himself and washed his face and hands. Another problem was solved.

Later, when he could feel they were going down, he started to see the ground outside again. He had the same funny feeling in his ears. Then the fly stopped moving forward. When all the people around him got up, he waited until he was led out of the plane by the same woman. Was he happy to see John standing at the end of a long, winding passage! John was from Ghanzi; he was the one who had sent for him, asked if he would come to this meeting to support him. John's mother was related to Komtsha, but his father was a white man. He said he needed Komtsha's support to show the world that the things he was saying everywhere he went on behalf of the red people, were true. Komtsha was so pleased to be able to speak to someone who understood his language that he did not even look at the many new things they passed in the vehicle. All he saw was that the roads were black and hard, the land was flat and very green, and everywhere he could see thin, tall white towers with two arms at the top, sometimes so many that they looked as if they were growing there. John explained that the people caught the power of the wind with those towers, to make the many lights burn. It seemed also as if there was water everywhere, even more than after a heavy thunderstorm in D'Kar. After a while he became tired of seeing so many new things. He just wanted to sleep; after that he would try to work out where this big fly had landed.

On the day of the meeting, John prepared him for what would happen. There would be many people from many countries, he said, even some who would look like white people though they were actually red people. Like the Naro, John said, those people would be there because they wanted to tell others how their land had been lost, just as had happened to them in Botswana. His heart stopped beating so fast. This sounded just like the kgotla in D'Kar, so he would know what to say.

He sat next to John in a large room. The chairs were soft and the rows of people in front were lower than them, so everyone could see the person talking in front. It felt a bit like church, but the people were more showily dressed. Some in very colourful clothes had stuck feathers in their hair. There were badges with small signs fixed on their clothing. Someone had also hung something around Komtsha's neck, a leather strip with the tooth of an animal they said they hunted in the sea. It made him happy to wear it, even though he did not know the animal. The "white" red people, as John had said, looked very white – even more so than the man on the plane. They wore bright red and blue coats, boots and woollen caps. John explained that they were also hunters who lived in a kind of desert, but instead of sand, there was ice, ice as far as you could see.

Some other people, he noticed, had brown skins but long, straight black hair which hung softly down their backs in long plaits. Their eyes were narrow, a little like those of the Japanese people who often visited D'Kar to write books about the red people.

Most of the people who spoke began their talk with something to catch people's attention. They burnt something to their gods, or they drew circles in the air – to invite the good spirits, John said. Others spoke about having the same troubles as the red people, but Komtsha found it hard to believe since they looked fat, just like white people, and did not even need translation. The one said he came from America, and yes, he looked and dressed just like the other Americans Komtsha knew, who worked as volunteers in the Ghanzi district. Those ones had little caps on their heads which they sometimes turned back-to-front; they wore mostly white shoes and socks and those soft shirts with writing on their chests. This man was a little darker in the face than the other Americans, but he had quite a stomach, which told Komtsha that, even though this man might also have lost his land, he had managed to find a good living somehow.

There were some people who lived in a sandy desert, just like them, John said, also from Africa. Once, when all the people went out to drink tea, they showed him and John photographs of their homes, which looked like tents. But these ones scared Komtsha. They wore headscarves and earrings like women, but they talked about fighting and guns, and said that the time for talking was over. They said the newcomers on the land should be killed. Komtsha hoped this would not be necessary for the red people, for they had never made war to protect their land before. They were lucky he had written the letter to Mmamosadinyane, because he was sure that letter would help them to avoid war.

Komtsha and John were called to the front. It was far to walk, and they had to go down many steps. He also thought about the many eyes that were watching him and was glad that he could just follow John. When they reached the front Komtsha sat on a chair while John stood up and spoke in front of a tall stick, holding his mouth close to the round ball at the top. He had told Komtsha earlier that this stick would carry their voices to the far end of the big room. Although John spoke in English, Komtsha could hear that his heart was in the words. Sometimes he raised his voice, other times he spoke softly and bowed his head. He kept his eyes on John's back. He didn't want to look at the rows and rows of people in front of them, because they were not the kind of people he knew. The whole time John was speaking he tried to think what he would say to these strangers.

The people clapped their hands for a long time after John had finished. Then he beckoned to Komtsha, who moved over and stood beside John. He did not know what to do. He reached up and felt the leather band with the tooth around his neck. He folded his hand around the tooth and held on, while John set the long stick lower so that it stood right in front of Komtsha's mouth. John looked at him and smiled. "Just tell them what is in your heart," he said to him softly.

Komtsha looked up and saw the rows and rows of strange faces. This meeting was not like the kgotla or the church. John was standing next to him to translate, and the people were so quiet it took him a while to get used to having only his own voice in such a large, quiet open space. He spoke the words he had spoken many, many times before, but now, suddenly, he could feel that the people in front of him really listened. He could feel their respect. This encouraged him to mention the letter again. Even if this was not why he had been called to this place, there might just be someone from the Queen's country in this meeting who could remind her of the letter she had received. He clearly remembered what he had told them to write down that day and he repeated the words one by one to the ball on the stick:

> Dear Great Queen
> My name is Komtsha. I am an old man. I am a Bushman. If we are too unimportant or if you have forgotten about us you must ask other people what a Bushman is and where we live. People call our lands now Namibia or Botswana. When I saw a man from England, I asked him to give this message to you. It is a message about

our pain and suffering. The people are stealing the land from us. I must answer my people. I say I do not know why they can come and do this. The Great Woman from England will know. She will know the truth.

I will ask you now. Not very long ago you gave the Tswana people their land; when you came to our land at that time, what did you see? Were there only trees and black people there? Maybe you did not notice the red people, because we are small. Is that why you did not talk to us? The Tswana people think you have given us to them. They do not understand that you did not see us and that it was a mistake.

If you did not give us to them, then you must tell them now that they must let us go. The white and the black people are killing our land. They do not understand the animals or the land. They are wasting everything and soon nobody will be able to live here. We have always lived with the animals. They are our friends. Other people are chasing us away from the animals. Some land is now kept only for animals. The other land is for other people, but not for us.

We Bushmen are many. We do not all speak the same language, but we are friends and we are all Bushmen; you must help us all. This is my word to you.

Afterwards, many people wanted to talk to him. Some even cried. John was busy talking to other people, so he was not always there to translate. At such times, Komtsha took the note from his pocket and handed it to the person. It always made them smile and nod, or pat him on the back. He really had to remember to tell Mmamoruti what a good note it was she gave him. He did not know what she had written in that note, but it had really opened people's hearts and made them help him. He must make sure that he kept this letter forever. Even if the other letter may never have reached Mmamosadinyane, this one at least had opened many gates for him.

THIRTEEN

# The Teacher

Mpho loved walking with her dogs in the village in the late afternoon, especially after a difficult day at the Kuru office. Her dogs, knowing the footpaths well, ran ahead sniffing at the scents that mark the territories of other dogs and defiantly cocked their legs against the thorn bushes. Occasionally they performed a little growling dance with the pathetic, slinking and wire-thin dogs who tried to challenge them; but the challengers soon crouched down before the superior force, tails between their legs.

Here and there she stopped for a few moments at the hut of someone she knew; paid fleeting visits to parents of the children who had passed through her hands over the years. She enjoyed most talking to the older people. Their Setswana was limited, but their faces were open and their laughter came easily. With them she felt none of the animosity she had increasingly become aware of these days, especially from the younger ones who had been to school.

Some of the mothers were stamping away at their *kikas*, preparing a mush of leaves, insects, or whatever they had managed to find during the day, to go with the evening porridge. She noticed a group of children returning from the water-pump carrying buckets on their heads. With them was a chubby little boy, proudly carrying two small buckets with wire handles made from soft-drink and beer cans. The soft light of the setting sun caught the splashes of water spilling from the buckets onto the girls' faces.

At other homes people were gathering their washing from the fences, chopping wood or burning garbage. This time of the evening, but particularly on weekends, a peculiar smell hung over the village, wood-smoke, sometimes mixed with the acrid scent of burning hair and excrement. Outside each yard there was a big pile of ash mixed with burnt cans, on to which was tipped more rubbish every time the yard was swept. In the moments before dark there was a distinct hum to the village, punctuated every so often by the sharp shrieks of children playing. It was the sound of activity, of people shaking out blankets to make beds on the ground outside their huts; of women and older girls chatting on their way home from the veld with meagre bundles of sticks for the night's cooking and for keeping their families warm. Their silhouettes against the darkening sky always brought a sad peace, a sense of longing into her heart.

They did not know, they did not believe and they did not understand. When she walked among them here in the evenings they showed respect and greeted her, but she could feel them keeping her at a distance. Still, after all this time. If only they realised how similar they all were. To them, her strong heavy-set body spoke of an abundance they did not have. Her healthy, assertive dogs symbolised her confidence, the success of her life. When she stood in front of a class of young people who complimented her on her clothing – and she knew they copied her style in so many ways – they saw only the accomplished teacher, the one who had it all. Yet she had tried to tell them of the cattle post of her youth, the struggle for survival when she was a young girl out in the veld with the boys for weeks at a time. But her stories were met with expressions of doubt or frank disbelief.

She stopped at one compound and addressed the young woman taking down washing from her fence: "Q'ane, why hasn't Qabo been to school lately?" She also worked at the Kuru office, got a fair salary; she should know better than to let the child drop out.

"I don't know. I cannot control these kids. I have talked to them, but ..."

"But you *must* take control, you know! They must not be allowed to overrule their mother's wishes! You are killing the child's future if you do not force her to go to school."

The mother bundled the clothes over her shoulder, looking away. "You do not understand our lives. You have everything; you are strong. People listen to you." She turned and went into her house.

Exasperated, Mpho walked on. These people were oppressing themselves. How often had she told them they could change their fate if they stopped thinking and acting so negatively? At times it was so painful working here, suffering the constant accusation that it was her people who were oppressing the Basarwa, keeping them poor just so they could have cheap labour at their cattle posts.

She did not always agree with the policies of her government, but neither did she believe the laws and regulations that most affected the Basarwa were motivated by malice or indifference. Were not the Batswana themselves oppressed for centuries, first by the Matabele and Msilikazi and then by the whites? Hadn't the Boers, too, experienced oppression by the English, and just look how they have managed to improve their own lives? These were things the volunteers from Europe and America, all the many she had worked with over the years, did not understand. They were so quick to judge, and to talk about injustices. When she told them her side of the story she could feel the prejudice, see the scepticism in their eyes. Yet when she was with her own people she also felt accused.

"Why do you waste your time working with people who will never be able to help themselves? Aren't you interested in the children of your own tribe? What about our old people who are as poor and suffer as much as the Basarwa?" they asked.

What could she say?

As she walked on, watching fires being lit everywhere, she thought back. How well she remembered these rituals, the hasty preparations before dark! When you slept outside, a dependable fire was crucial, especially on winter nights when the stars seemed to be stacked in layers, when the cold crept into your feet and lower back until your body was stiff and aching. Your face and hands felt scorched from the heat of the fire, while the cold ate at your back so badly you wanted to roll into the flames to warm yourself up.

When she was about four years old they had simply sent her along with the boys to the cattle post one day. She was never sure if it had had something to do with her mother going away to town and leaving her grandmother, her Mmemogolo, with too many little ones to care for, or if it was just that her brothers wanted her along. But she was happy, though she knew that most girls her age stayed home and helped with chores and baby care. The boys had to herd the cattle, milk them, and take them out grazing, which was sometimes so far away from their hut near the water-pump that they had to sleep out. In summertime some pans would fill up with the rains, which meant the cattle could stay out in the veld. Then the children had to stay with them, for weeks on end sometimes, to keep them from wandering into other people's areas.

One difficulty she remembered, though, was the hunger. They seemed to be perpetually searching for food. Throughout the day they collected berries and roots, but as soon as they spotted a hare, the hunt was on. The bigger boys could throw their sticks so fast, with such deadly accuracy, that they killed many hares, birds and even now and then a duiker.

Her biggest shock was the day they roasted a live tortoise on the fire. She had watched the creature's frantic clawing at the air, the neck stretched out in a bow as if trying to break free from its shell. Once it managed to roll over in the red-hot coals and tried to crawl out, but it was pushed back over by one of the boys. Upset though she was, she was too hungry to resist when they offered her a morsel of tasty, stewed meat, scooped from the burnt shell. The days when they had meat were special; there was happy chatter throughout the rituals of skinning and braai-ing on the coals. On such nights they would lie down to sleep with their tummies full and warm, like when she was with her old Mmemogolo who fed all the children sour milk and soft porridge in the evening before they settled round their Rremogolo's feet for their evening story.

When she was in the veld she missed those story nights in the village; she missed the care of adults and the company of other small children. When her grandfather or one of her uncles told stories, the little group around the fire became cocooned in their pool of light, cut off from the night outside, full of sounds, figures, eyes watching. In their little nest they felt transported into the story world. They knew they were visible to the darkness outside, yet they felt strangely protected. The stories were mostly about animals who could speak, who became human or who controlled the human world. They were so scared of the jackal! He knew everything they did during the day, he watched over all their activities and even controlled their thoughts. If you misbehaved, he would come and get you!

The little ones would listen wide-eyed until the voice of Rremogolo sounded further and further away, their bodies became limp and they toppled over. Later they would be carried to their Mmemogolo's hut, one by one. In the veld she missed her grandparents' care very much. At night she had to make her own little hollow beside the fire, wriggle herself into her blanket and move the burning logs if the smoke drifted her way. Those creatures her Rremogolo had talked about felt even closer at night in the veld. The bigger boys enjoyed telling scary stories to make her cringe with fear. And when she heard the cry of a jackal or hyena, she would scurry up to her older brother and close her eyes tight.

But she got so tough! My, she learnt how to fight with sticks, how to set snares and follow tracks. She also learnt how to milk a cow straight into her own mouth when she got hungry and thirsty. She was just a little tot, but she was quick and clever and the boys took great pleasure in teaching her skills, showing her off when they got home. She got so used to being with the cattle that their smell and their quiet lowing at night comforted her when the darkness became too threatening. Those big, warm bodies would protect her from the jackal as they protect their own calves, she believed.

"You know, you are becoming a real farmer," she remembered her older brother saying to her one day, watching her with the cows. And look how far from the cows she had gone these days, she did not even own one herself.

Her people's warm, strong bond with their cattle had existed as long as anyone could remember, so Rremogolo used to tell them. Therefore, their work in the veld looking after the cattle was the most important work there was. A man was not a man if he had no cattle, she thought to herself; his happiness lay with the well-being of these animals. In those days, before the government introduced a programme to dehorn cattle, big-horned cattle were the proudest mark of quality, of strength and wealth. Now their horns were trimmed so that they could be transported more easily and did not damage each other's hides. But when she was little, my! they were immensely scary, those snorting beasts with their sharp, white horns set on wide, heavy foreheads which they would lower threateningly to warn off the children. Later she developed a pride in their beauty. She marvelled at these animals which provided them with meat and milk, whose hides could be tanned to make ceremonial dress, mats and chair covers. Even their dung was precious!

Funny how her people's love of their cattle was the very thing which set them apart from the Basarwa, the single thing for which they were most criticised by the world outside. But rather than blaming the

Batswana for having cattle and therefore getting more land, she thought, why don't the Basarwa get cattle for themselves? Change their lives so they can all be equal? Instead, the cattle they were given by the government to start farming, when their people were moved to the settlements, were mostly sold or eaten before any calves were even produced.

So deep ran this difference between her people and them that even the name they had been given by the Batswana – Basarwa – was an old word meaning "down under". People said it referred to the fact that they did not keep cattle. Well, it was at least better than the other name her people cursed them with – "Motshuba naga" – which referred to their old practice of burning the veld. She had noticed that some people were not even offended by it, probably because they did not realise the implications. Imagine burning the precious grazing of the Batswana cattle! She smiled, shaking her head. They did not understand that farming with cattle was different from the way they managed the game; they maintained they used to control the game migrations by burning the veld. But these days, she pondered, so many of them had an income that if they used it to buy a cow each time they had spare money, instead of wasting it as they did, they would soon become rich, and the politicians would have to listen to them.

How could she make them understand? When she went to secondary school she was sent far away to Mochudi in the eastern part of the country. There were so many strange things in that place that the young girl from Ncojane village in the west felt as if she was four years old again and alone in the veld, adapting, surviving, utterly lonely. They laughed at her for so many things. Every time she opened her mouth, she was ridiculed for being from a lowly tribe, for speaking ancient Setswana and for using strange proverbs. Her dress, too, was considered strange. And the food they made her eat! If only other people knew how the Batswana oppressed each other!

However, the more they pushed her down, the stronger she felt herself become, until in the end she feared nobody. She was determined to show them who she was, so she studied hard and spoke her mind. To this day she is considered a tough woman. Men mainly try to ridicule her, and they tell her she should behave more like a woman. Having worked to free herself from prejudice and discrimination, she has become stronger than the men of her tribe. She knew now that she would never marry; she was not prepared to be the slave of a fat, lazy man who had authority over her only because he was a man. Nor was she prepared to bow to the tradition of becoming the personal assistant of a mother-in-law. She knew it was mainly because of her pride and independence that the fathers of her children had eventually left her, but she did not care any more. She feared nobody, except sometimes herself.

It was this quality she'd been trying to cultivate in her pupils all the years she had been working with Basarwa people. If only they would fight back, they could change so much. Sometimes she wondered what had become of that boy in the first school where she had taught, way out on the fringes of the district. Had he learnt anything? Sometimes the memory of what she did shamed her, but it turned out to be the right thing, because they had ended up as friends.

How furious she was that day! Growing older, she realised, had taken away much of that passion. When she pointed at him in the classroom, he cringed down into his seat. She had given him a chance to react, to object to her accusation. She wasn't sure if he was the one who had made the scratch on the blackboard, but she thought he would point out the true culprit if he was innocent. Her anger had spilled over him, not so much because of what he had done, but because he was now doing what countless numbers of them had done before. He was not fighting back; he was simply giving up! She beat him wildly, over the legs and the body, even his head. The frustration of so many times exploded in her, spilled over this child who did not cry, who did not even wince. She wanted to beat some action into his bones, bring him to the point where he would say: "Enough! I will take no more!"

But he just clung to her, and when she dropped him, he scurried away, sobbing softly. She was exhausted; she felt she could die. Later in the afternoon, when her heartbeat had settled and the terrible sorrow just lay in her chest, she called him over. She saw the fear in his eyes, so she beckoned him to sit next to her. This time she let her words flow calmly over him, poured out to him all her confused thoughts and concerns about him and his people. She told him she was sorry for the pain; she told him never ever to lie down before anyone again, but to stand up for what he believed in.

It had been a turning point with the people in that village. She never knew what they had said to each other after the incident, but from then on she could sense they no longer feared her. Although she has been in D'Kar now for many years, these people do not know or understand her as well as that other little community, because she had fought it out with them. Although they did not all understand her language, the trust between them grew after that day.

It was ironic that between the people in D'Kar and herself there were enough languages, enough words, to communicate, but they did not hear what she was saying as well as those people she worked with before.

She was now approaching the Kgosi's house. Like her, the traditional leader and his wife had lived here for many years but had remained outsiders. The only difference was that he was posted here by the government, whereas she came of her own free will, out of a need to do something for the people.

The Kgosi's presence here was interpreted by the leaders of the Basarwa as a token of their oppression, a sign that they were not thought capable of producing or appointing their own leaders. They said they were not even asked if they wanted a Tswana Kgosi. They wanted their own leaders, their own representation. Yet, as always, when given the chance, they refused to play the system. She had often told them to act more cleverly. They did not attend elections, they didn't use the channels that were there for representation. They said they did not want this Kgosi who did not speak their language, but, she wondered, did they want a Kgosi of *any* kind? The irony was that they did run to the Kgosi to solve their marital conflicts, their labour problems, thefts, even debt settlements.

There were so many things she'd not been able to work out about them. They did not accept the Kgosi's leadership, yet they feared the powers traditionally ascribed to him by her own people, such as being able to control the lightning. And sometimes the poor man really tried his best. He was an educator in his own way, using opportunities such as the kgotla meetings or funerals to tell people what proper behaviour in the modern world meant. They considered it an intrusion. She knew he was also trying to give them some understanding of the ways of the Batswana, so they could adapt a little, work towards becoming accepted by the rest of society and earning respect from others. The difference between his approach and her own was that he had no doubts about the relevance of the traditional customs of the Batswana. He carried an unquestioning pride in his own culture, which she sometimes envied.

She noticed Debe was sitting with the Kgosi and his wife. He was one of the young leaders of the Basarwa in the village who had started to reach out to people of other cultures, because he had been around. Since he had started working for the Basarwa's own political organisation, he had accompanied their leader, John Battleman, all over the world. She liked Debe; he was fun to listen to and was a much stronger person in himself than most others in this village. She had admired his courage in kgotla meetings and political rallies. He spoke Setswana well; he also enjoyed the trust of his own people.

"*Dumelang!*" she greeted. Debe stood up and handed her his chair, while he moved over to sit on a small, dented paraffin tin. "So, Debe, where have you been lately?" she asked him.

"Debe was just telling us about his visit to Finland," the Kgosi said. "You must hear this." Debe then continued to describe how they were taken to a steaming, hot little room where everyone suddenly started taking off their clothes. The Kgosi sat up straight, mouth hanging open. "Yes!" Debe answered to their surprised expressions. "They all just started undressing, men and women alike. Everyone got a small white towel, and there we all sat on such hot, hot stones with our naked behinds."

"What for?" Mpho asked.

"They said it was good for you. After a while the sweat starts pouring from your body, into your eyes. You feel as if you can't breathe. Then they open a door, and one by one you have to jump into the sea, the icy, black water! Your heart does not beat for a long, long time, then your skin starts to feel as if thousands of needles are pricking you all over."

"*Au, Batho!*" the Kgosi said. "What would I have done? And all that water! With me who can't even swim!"

Mpho looked at Debe, amazed at how self-assured he had become of late. But, she thought to herself, she also knew that despite the confidence he tried to emanate, deep down he was fearful of his people's expectations. When he started taking a leadership role, he had spoken up so boldly at rallies that he soon became prominent, once even nominated as the candidate for the opposition party for D'Kar. The newspapers all wrote about it. He received a great deal of support from outside. A lot was expected of him. This was the first time a Mosarwa would be challenging the ruling party candidate! The Batswana in D'Kar, especially the MP who came from the very same village, went wild. The kgotla meetings turned into riotous sessions, broadcast to the whole village from loudspeakers mounted on the top of pick-ups. Were the Basarwa not thankful for what they had received? Did they not know how their lives depended on this government, its drought-relief jobs, its food packages for the destitute, its hospital services? For hours and hours the announcements would continue, punctuated with loud music and patriotic songs crackling over the loudspeakers.

Yet on the day of the elections Debe was nowhere to be seen. Queues formed at the primary school; the people received their purple stamp on their hands when they had cast their vote. Most did not know what to do. The politicians were at hand to explain about choosing the colour of your candidate by throwing out the colours of the other candidates. Some were shamelessly telling people which colour to choose, pretending that they were only trying to explain the technique. Very few Basarwa came to vote. Some obliged when they were collected from their homes; others bluntly refused. No one ever dared to ask him outright, but she was sure she knew where Debe had been that day. According to accounts, his house was locked and no one answered the door. But she was convinced that he was inside, simply waiting for the terrible day to pass so he could come out in the darkness.

They were all still laughing about Debe's story when they became aware of a distraction nearby. The Kgosi's hut was close to the drinking place. One could hear the noises of the revellers all through their conversation. Many people accused the Kgosi of having shares in the drinking place. Officially the place had no licence and was illegal, but few dared challenge the Kgosi. Tonight the din was louder than most evenings. Then usually there was throbbing music, and you could hear laughter and occasional shouts. Tonight it sounded as if there was a fight. Soon a scurrying group of people became visible, moving over from where they were gathered around a few large, plastic beer cans under a skimpy *moshu* tree, to the Kgosi's hut, about three huts away but in the same compound. The many shuffling feet were kicking up dust, so that it was difficult to see what was going on in the centre of the commotion. Some people were shouting, others tried to push through the circle to see.

"Oh, no," the Kgosi said, "They're coming our way. When will these people learn to behave?"

The procession was dragging along a woman, naked from her waist upwards. Blood was streaming over the side of her face. She let out a loud wail occasionally, and followed up by swinging a bleeding arm in the direction of her drunken partner, who had a vengeful expression on his sweaty face and was carrying a piece of wood. Both were finding it hard to stand, and most of their companions were unsteady on their feet as they loudly tried to tell the Kgosi what had happened. People pushed their fingers into each other's faces: the blame was being determined by whoever could shout the loudest. It was obvious that the woman had received a serious cut above her ear and had already lost a lot of blood. Her breasts and skirt were slowly being soaked by the mixture of blood and tears streaming down her face.

"Help me! Help me, he is going to kill me!" She wailed again, the sound trailing like a cloud around their heads. The woman tried to get closer to the Kgosi. He recoiled. Debe stood up and moved backwards. Mpho turned around and saw that he was approaching the vehicle of his organisation. It was parked just outside the front gate of the yard.

"Debe," she said to him. "Isn't this your chance to show your people that you can really help them? Why do you not put her in the vehicle and take her to the doctor?"

The woman had slumped to her knees; she looked as if she was going to faint.

Debe just looked at her, then got into the car and slammed the door. He started the ignition, then stuck his head out of the window and called to her, "You and your Kgosi, you help them!"

Dust and small stones flew out from under the wheels as he spun the vehicle and sped away, not looking back once.

FOURTEEN
# Shadow bird

"Kuru Project, good morning. Can I help you?" If only it is not the American. "It is coming, Chris. I am typing it now, but the phone keeps on ringing and it disturbs my work. You know, I also have other work to do here, but I promise to fax it to you soon."

She has to finish this report today. Not only has Stephen asked for it three times already, but this American keeps sending faxes about needing it. Now he's even phoning! They think she can do everything, at any time.

This business of being the "hope of the San people", as that one newspaper wrote after her speech in Oslo, sometimes it is just not worth it. All the people who envy her the trips she makes, what do they know about all the work they land in her lap? It just never stops.

She has to get up now and then, she finds it uncomfortable to sit for so long. She is too sore between her legs. It is burning and itching, and was bruised by Debe again last night. Sometimes he can be like a hungry hyena, but she has to give in for peace' sake. Why should he punish her, when he's the one who feels guilty? The drink on his breath tells its own story, she needs not even ask where he's been. Sometimes she doesn't care anymore, she just wishes Nqaba or someone else would satisfy him so that he would leave her alone.

The other day, at the Cultural Centre, they talked again about condoms, about why so many people seem to be dying these days. The lady from that women's organisation in Maun, she seemed to really believe what she was saying. "These things take a little trouble, but they might save you," she said. How could she, with her fancy, braided hair know anything about dealing with an impatient man who does not even mind the babies sleeping all over the floor! He sometimes does not even mind Qabo, who lies rolled in her blanket next to them on the floor. She is older and she must hear them, even if she pretends to be asleep.

Condoms! When he comes for her, how do they expect her to get up, find matches to light a candle, then find those things in the handbag hanging from the roof of the hut, without Debe getting angry and waking everyone up? Asking him to put one on will anyway cause arguments. She is so tired of the fighting. The last time they fought he carried her bite mark on his face for weeks! All that time he was furious with her because other people made fun of him. He even had to go to a conference in Gaborone with that bite mark on his face. Her own bruises mattered less that time. For once she felt that she had also marked him where it hurts.

What do they want her to put in this report anyway? The whites always want things orderly, in a proper structure. But they do not understand how difficult that is, things just do not hang together like that. One can only put down things in bits and pieces, in fits and starts, and afterwards you might be able to see what it had become. There were so many people in Oslo; she had to talk to so many after her speech. Now she can no longer remember what they had found most important. The American Indians, with their straight black hair and strong, bony faces, they liked it when she talked about the land that was lost. The same happened when she talked to those people with the wild hair, the Aborigines. They nodded, they shook her hand.

The whites seemed to want to hear more about the struggle of the red people in the schools. When she told them about discrimination against the children, they made notes, looked at her intensely. And she told them that the red people did not like the names that people call them by. The one then came to her and said people had called them the Lapps before, but now they were Sami, a name they had chosen themselves. This man also listened very closely when she talked about their culture that was dying, and especially about the dance. She mentioned the dance to him only because of the Joik, the traditional song of his people which he sang to open the meeting.

She can still see him in his red and blue coat, his pointed sealskin shoes and the red cap. She wondered then how it would feel to live in ice, like he said his people had done for ages. No wonder their traditional clothes looked like a winter outfit. It was his voice, but also his uplifted chin and his still body, there in the centre of the empty stage, which touched her heart. She can still hear his song. She can even still sing it for the others at the fire. Although she could not understand his words and did not know about his people or his place, she recognised it as music of the night, like theirs, when the dancers of her own people had been stamping around the fire for many hours. There is that moment when one, lone voice lifts itself above the others and finds its way into the stars. When the voices of the clapping women rise higher, and the lonely voice of the healer rolls with their notes, it is then that the sound takes off on a voyage of its own. That Joik, it brought back her father's song.

She was very little when he died, so she never understood fully what he did when he danced like that, but she still has clear images in her mind, flashes that remind her of his voice, how it started going up like that, and she would know that that special moment would be coming. Stunned in utter fascination at his collapsed, sweaty body, his jerky movements and glassy eyes, she sat tightly next to her mother in the clapping circle, gripped with fear that he would burn his muscled legs if he rolled over onto the coals next to him. Terrifying, it was, when she was so little, yet somehow so beautiful that she longs for him when she thinks of it.

"Q'ane, are you busy with something important? Can you please fax this form to the British High Commissioner's office? Please call the secretary first and tell her that we cannot open the e-mail document she sent. She should fax it. These people sometimes imagine we have all the facilities in the world. In any case, after the last virus we had, I also feel safer not downloading anything. If we catch anything from the Internet, we're again stuck for weeks."

"Yes," she answers. "They all think we live in a town. People from overseas are even angry because their faxes do not come through after five – as if we can run the generator all night."

Yet another thing to do. She can't admit that she is still busy with the report, Stephen will have a fit. Better phone first. She still hasn't done the cash reconciliation for her trip and these whites are so strict about such things. It's very annoying sometimes, this is supposed to be their own organisation, yet they are made to feel as if these whites and blacks are their bosses. Like with the study hour at night that they push them so hard to do. She has missed so many classes that they will throw her out if she does not go tonight. She wishes that this counterpart-training programme, which they brought in to upgrade the red people's qualifications, was over. The classes have their interesting moments, but sometimes it seems as if these things are just so never-ending. The worst is that their old people keep on pushing them to do it as well; all they are interested in is that their children take over the positions of the whites and blacks one day, not how they *feel*! Marcus, the trainer from Denmark, told her the other day that she had about six years of this kind of training ahead of her if she wanted to become a co-ordinator. So she'd better start getting serious, he said. Six years! God, she can only think about one day at a time.

She'll have to make time to go to the clinic this afternoon. She cannot stand this itching and burning any longer. She'll go mad, she'll have to scratch there, she tells herself, but then it gets even more painful. The problem of finishing this report is not as bad as having to face those nurses again, though. She already knows what they will say. She knows they have been waiting for her to come.

"Yes, look at the state you are in. We told you that you should have gone to the police. You people wander from one strange doctor to another, you drink your medicines in the wrong way and you do not listen to our warnings, but afterwards you run back to us and then we have to save you."

If only there was somewhere else left to go to instead of the clinic. After the episode with the doctor from Ngamiland she can no longer go to the village doctors. What made her believe that man! Actually, everyone started to trust these strange doctors from the north, ever since the case of Nxaedom's child. The clinic said it was diarrhoea and gave her the salt-water mix only, but the child got so weak that she got spasms and her eyes turned in her head.

That was when this doctor told them about the big, black bird that always flies above the people, looking to cast its shadow over someone. The reason the child's eyes turned in her head was to follow the shadow, he said. Eventually the child's soul would leave her, following the bird's shadow. When the eyes started to turn that moment was very near. The medicine he gave would turn the bird's direction, and the bird would find others who would follow it, he told the parents. It was a strange and frightening story, but the medicine helped, the little girl soon played again.

Xuse was actually the one who made her go to this doctor. She was so sure that he had cured her itching and her monthly pains. If only she had watched Xuse a little longer before she also visited him. In the broad light of day it now feels so strange to think of what he talked all the other girls into, herself included, but once you were inside his hut, it seemed like another reality and somehow you trusted him. There were so many strange and even scary things hanging from the walls of that hut, such strange smells, and his deep, grumbling voice with the accent of the people from the north so fascinated you that you did not really listen to what he was saying.

She took off all her clothes – he said that was the only way to find the disease. The ointment he rubbed over her body had a strange, putrid smell, but he kept on talking softly behind her where she was lying on her side on the rug, and she relaxed. It was only when he turned her over that she realised that he was already without his pants. He must have put a spell on her, she thought afterwards, trying to figure out why she had not panicked. He then pointed to his groin, to the area right above the big, black horn which was stiff and ready.

"This is where I carry my medicine," he said. "I have found your problem. It lies deep inside your body. Now, I cannot plant the medicine inside you without my arrow entering you, as I have to shoot the medicine right to where the disease lies. Other people feed medicine through your mouth, I send it up from underneath."

"Did he not even wear a condom?" The nurse's horrified face, her hand clasped over her mouth, made her realise the strangeness of her story for the first time and that the man had not cured her, but might instead have given her the most deadly of all diseases. A terrible fear gripped her body that time in the clinic, and she started to cry.

The sores on her genitals, the discharge, it had all come from this man, because the diseases Debe and his women had given her before had been different. In any case, there are so many diseases these days that their old people never knew of.

When she walked home from the clinic that day, with her few small bags of pills and the pain of the injection in her buttock, she decided to find Xuse. Why had they not talked to each other about this man and his strange cure before?

This was one of the things the social worker had said, when she had them together in the clinic. She would not phone the police before they had first talked and compared their experiences, so that they would have one story to tell.

"This is rape," the social worker said afterwards to them, in what she called a counselling session. "You have every right to take this man to court and you should do so before he infects more people. Rape is when a man has sex with you without your consent. This man has cheated you into consent."

Rape. If she thinks about it now, if consent is the issue, she wonders what the difference is between that man and her own husband.

> The representatives from different indigenous organisations all over the world came together and compared their histories as well as their present situations. Together they made a suggestion to the United Nations that the Decade of the Indigenous Peoples should be extended into the new millennium because of the many pressures these peoples are still facing.

Good. She's copied this paragraph from the invitation letter to the conference, but it will work as an introduction to her report. Maybe she should add another bit from the paper she and Marcus prepared for her to speak from, about the importance of culture and the dance. But there is so much disagreement within their group about that issue, she is sometimes confused about it herself. Debe, for one, would not agree with what she had said in Oslo.

> During the conference all the indigenous peoples' groups represented there discovered that they shared many similar problems. Such things were the language issue, the loss of dances and other cultural traditions. All people felt that their cultures were being killed and taken over by the stronger forces around them.

Sometimes she really wonders about what is becoming of their people. It seems to be the young men, mostly, who are against their traditions.

Some things are barbaric, they said in the last workshop in the Cultural Centre. Debe said it was now humiliating for them to undress and dance half-naked in front of other people. He said they were living in modern times and those dances had no meaning for today. Turu was very angry, said that she found those clothes beautiful and that she couldn't care less what the youngsters thought of them. She painted those things for them to learn about their culture, she said. She scolded them, accusing them that they had been to school but were only more ignorant for that.

She wouldn't want to come to work dressed like that herself, though, Q'ane thought, but she does not see what is wrong with putting on traditional dress to show people their music and their dancing skills. It certainly sets them apart from others. It's also fun, and it brings such good memories of her childhood. The other old women who dance with them are so pleased to do it. How she loves it when they are performing and their dance inspires some of the other women in the audience to join in, or even to start dancing and singing from where they are sitting.

She knows that Debe has these same memories of the dancing, but since he has been hanging out with that teacher from the primary school, he talks differently. "People are laughing at us," he said the other day. "They take photographs of our dances, not because they are interested in our culture, but because they want to take our pictures to their friends and show us as strange animals. My friend Nakedi says that it is not good for the children to see their elders in such a way, they will have no respect. He also said these dances are against the Bible."

She shrugs. All these churches and their many ideas. Moruti, in the catechism class, says they are the only ones who can analyse their own dances. He encourages them to try and interpret them, because maybe God had used these dances in the old days to talk to them. Some of the old people say that the dances are like praying. Moruti even wants them to use their own music in the church, but that is a ridiculous plan. Of course there is no way the words of the Bible can fit the rhythms and patterns of their music, they have told him. If he wanted it, *he* had to make it fit. In any case, they love the church music as it is, even if it was taken over from the Batswana.

Some people from other churches who have been visiting here told them that these dances were straight from the devil. They said Dxãwa was the same as their Satan and that the red people should denounce the old culture and burn their old clothes. One Moruti, the one who showed the videos about those naked white people and the big snake in the garden, even showed a big picture of Dxãwa in red clothes, a forked tail and black horns. He said they should pray to God to forgive their old people for practising the dance. One of the healers told her afterwards that he had once seen Dxãwa while in trance but that he definitely did not look like that man's picture.

Some of the black people's churches have even started to use the red people's dances now for their own ceremonies. She had once seen how some preachers from a church in Ghanzi came and simply joined one of her people's healing dances. They took over the role of the healer completely and the strange rituals they added were confusing and even scary. But afterwards, people talked about it and thought that these Baruti might have greater power than the red people's own healers. The worst is that they even ask money for their healing! She can add this to her report:

> We have not stopped dancing because we are embarrassed about our bodies, but because our culture has been taken over and our dances have been stolen.

Just like that doctor took her body and her health.

Her thoughts go back to the dances they used to have. When they were alone, dancing with their families at the fire, all joined in. At such times even Debe would take the cow's tail flywhisk and dance in the row of men. Now, when they have a performance at the kgotla or the Cultural Centre, he pretends not to be able to dance. For such events they can usually only convince some of the older men to join, and they often want to be paid. She sighs. How does she explain these things in her report if she cannot even understand them herself? The other day, when they had to perform for the Minister's visit, she did not dance because of her disease. That was not so long after her visit to the village doctor. Standing in the crowd, she listened to the school children behind her, shrieking with laughter at the dance. "Look at that one's flapping breasts! Ooh, have you seen the wrinkled stomach skin of the old woman?"

They did not understand a thing of what they saw, and it hurt her that they laughed at their own people. Have her people perhaps already lost their souls to the Shadow Bird, long before their bodies will follow?

It is almost lunch-time. She should hurry and go to the clinic. Most probably it was the nurses who asked the Cultural Centre people to invite those women from Maun to come again. What will happen now, after their last visit? Now that they know what has happened here they would want to do something about it. They talked to Xuse and herself for a long time about women's rights, told them that their case could be an example to others, that it could turn the history of oppression of women in this country. They took their statements and said they would support them in court if they would take up the case against this man. They even wanted them to take an AIDS test, but she refused. She will never be that crazy, and thinks: Like my mother says, we are dying of hunger, TB and malaria, and now they make such a big fuss about dying of AIDS. If it is like that, I would rather not want to know.

She really does not feel like going to the clinic today. She does not know what to tell the nurses, because they will definitely ask her if she and Xuse have done anything about the case. Xuse's mother came to them after that meeting, she was very upset. She was sure that this man had evil powers and that he could harm them. She said that he could even send lightning to strike them or that he could cause more disease in their families. The clinic people insisted that this was nonsense, he was just a fake.

Let me stop thinking about all this now and first try to finish this report!

She must start concentrating. Oh dear, what now, visitors! Wish she could run.

Just then Xuse enters, some men following her.

"Are you Miss Q'ane Dam? We are from the police. We have been informed about the practices of a certain traditional healer in this village and were told that you and the lady here might want to lay charges against him. Could we talk to you privately?"

She takes them into an empty office. Xuse and she sit on a bench, the policemen move in behind the desk, spreading their papers in front of them. Her heart beats so hard that she can hear it.

"Would you be willing to make a statement that a certain man had pretended to be a traditional healer and had used this as a cover for raping young women in this village? Would you like to say something about it?"

She looks at Xuse. What has she already told them? But Xuse looks down, winding a handkerchief round and round her fist. She speaks first: "Sir, we do not know anything about such a story. The people who have told this to you have either lied, or you have the wrong people here."

"Miss Dam?"

"What she says is true, Sir. We do not know anything about that. Now, I am sorry, but I can unfortunately not talk to you any longer. I have a really urgent report to finish."

FIFTEEN

# Dumbstruck

They had been trying for many days now, but she did not respond. She did see them, and she looked at them while they talked, but she clearly wished them away. It could not only be the language; these days so many of the Basarwa spoke Setswana. Most could at least understand a few words, and the place she came from was not that remote. All they knew was that her name was Qasa and that she came from the village of D'Kar near Ghanzi. Nobody was even sure how to pronounce her name. They had found someone – a male patient from her area who knew some of her language – to come and speak to her, but she only looked at him; she did not even try to talk. Maybe she was still in shock. That would not be surprising; it was a shock just to look at her. The burns on her body had made open sores; the blisters had dried, leaving thick pinkish crusts which in places had cracked to expose the burnt flesh beneath. The skin between the wounds was sooty and black. In patches where the pigment had burnt away there were large, white blotches. Her sheets were soiled with serum and detergent.

It was starting to get dark, and the clouds were rolling in fast from the east. The little hut was small, but they moved inside because of the strong winds that sifted dust all over the fire and their circle in unexpected gusts. She covered the water bucket in the corner with a cloth, and blew on the embers to rekindle the fire inside. The hut gave a little shelter, but not much since the walls were not yet completely plastered with cow dung and mud. It had been difficult to get hold of enough dung lately, there were so many people around. She had to wait at the kraal with other women, waiting for the cows to drop the greenish pats which they needed to plaster their homes.

The children snuggled in between the four adults; it was becoming chilly. It was definitely going to rain, if not here, somewhere else. She braced herself for another soaked night. If only it did not last too many hours; it was bearable if they all slept closely together. With a leaking roof like theirs, water kept splashing uncomfortably on your face, or your back, and you had to nudge the one next to you to get the whole lot to shift around in the tiny space. So they silently said to each other, Let's get warm while we can, the fire will be killed by the rain soon anyway.

She did not eat, but the intravenous drip gave her enough nourishment for the time being. Occasionally the nurses managed to help her swallow some water or cold tea, but it must have been very painful through those burst sores on her lips. The young Danish doctor, on a two-year contract in Gaborone, had the feeling that nobody was really trying very hard; it seemed as if they were even trying to avoid her, especially since it had become clear she was not going to talk. But the nurses did discuss her. Sometimes the doctor found them talking in little groups in the tearoom and realised they were discussing the case. But not with her. It was a fire, yes, but how? Was there something more to the story?

It was really dark now, but the embers were glowing brightly, a little flame here and there casting a glow on their faces inside the dark hut. They were in a happy mood, not talking about the cold night that lay ahead. But they knew that soon the rain would start falling and the chill would set in. It was rumbling in the distance already and from time to time a loud crack confirmed that the electric storm was getting closer. The wind still slapped at the hut, sending dust and plastic bags flying all over the place. Her aunt put the kettle on the fire; the two children moved closer in anticipation. There would not be enough tea for all, but it was nothing new, the children were used to getting the tea-leaves to suck on later. The adults always put in so much sugar to make the strong brew palatable that the leaves had a lovely sweet taste that softened the bitter tingling on your tongue.

What came first – the deafening crack, or the terrible blue-white flash that lit up everything inside the hut, even the whites of the eyes in everyone's horrified faces – before it turned into that awful crackling red? She never knew, only that they were suddenly all on top of each other. Was she screaming, or were the others? There were bodies in her way, arms grabbing her. Now the hut was burning so fast she just knew she had to get out. But the awful burning smell suffocated her. Which side was the door again? Suddenly there were arms pulling at her and she was outside. Lying on the sand in the open. She sucked on the fresh air but a terrible piercing pain struck her, made her cringe and squirm. Her husband was next to her; then they brought out her aunt's child. A terrible terror rose in her chest for she knew that they were dead.

A few days ago some other patients were brought in from Ghanzi, and in the tearoom the nurses had clustered eagerly around the one whom had accompanied the patients to Gaborone. On their rounds together, the doctor and the matron talked about the tragedy. The disaster had killed a man and a child almost instantly. But four people were apparently still alive. The villagers came running from all over, and the torrential rain unleashed by the storm soon killed the fire. The ambulance in D'Kar was out of order, so a young Kuru worker and his wife brought the survivors to the hospital in Ghanzi forty kilometres away. A second child, a baby boy, died shortly after arrival, and the other woman died the following day, just before the Flying Mission plane arrived to pick up the patient they were treating here now. The other woman who survived was not as badly burnt and was presently slowly recovering in Ghanzi. Their patient might still not know about the deaths of the others, as she was unconscious for most of the first two days.

After they learnt this, the matron was stricter with the nurses. She usually only supervised the nursing staff and took care of the general management of the hospital, but now she took this patient's well-being as a personal responsibility. Talk to her, try harder, she might start to eat, she urged the nurses.

The Danish doctor could not put the case out of her mind, not even at night. She had heard so much about these tiny people of the desert, with their click language and their nomadic lifestyle. She had seen other patients come and go and they'd always fascinated her; she warmed to them because of their easy smiles, the adult faces in the childlike, delicate bodies with the tiny feet and hands. They were sometimes so obviously out of place, miserable and scared. And they had the hardest time staying in the ward, which she discovered was because they were not allowed to smoke there, so you forever found them squatting outside. How well designed this hospital was for the needs of its rural patients! With each ward opening into the hospital grounds, patients were not trapped in a maze of corridors and flights of steps and elevators, like the hospitals back home.

She was fascinated by how they smoked. Inside the little leather bag decorated with glass beads, that usually hung on the bed post – and every single adult seemed to have one – there was a metal pipe, like a small cone, made of tin, usually with a copper mouthpiece. They crumbled the tobacco leaves in the palm of their hands and stuffed the mixture into the wide end before lighting up. She was told that when they were at home they used embers from the fire that was almost always smouldering. They would pick these embers up with their bare hands, rolling them around on their palms and holding the pipe close to ignite the tobacco. Once, the matron called her to observe the most ingenious lighter made from an old hollowed-out torch battery, blocked at both ends with pieces of wood. Inside was a flint stone and some fibres to catch the spark; the fibres, the matron said, were a mixture of spider webs and birds' nests.

Between the waves of excruciating pain that drowned out all other feelings and thoughts, clear images floated back to her. There was a car, but of the journey she recalled nothing, nor much of what had happened afterwards. There was a fly like the ones she had seen so often land at the airstrip in D'Kar. She was terrified of being loaded into its body, but the white man had a soft voice and gentle eyes. He had prepared a bed for her inside, on which they put her, but of what had happened after that, she remembered nothing.

They must have forgotten her little boy. Would somebody have noticed him in that shouting, burning chaos of people? What if he was left behind in the darkness? Did he also burn? If only she could speak, she could ask them, but she knows she will not utter a word. They kept trying to make her, but they didn't understand: they had not yet opened her mouth. If they did, they would see what she had seen in her dead husband's face. They would know then that it was no use even trying. She would never be able to speak again.

The matron talked agitatedly to the nurses. She was angry, impatient. It was their duty, they had to overcome their fear and forget what they had heard about the Kgosi himself visiting the burnt woman's house.

Later, after the two of them had been to the woman's bed again, the matron explained to the doctor why she had said that to the nurses. The Tswana Kgosi traditionally had the power of life and death, he was the direct link to the ancestors, so he could will the lightning to strike a person who did not respect him, or who was harming his tribe. As the Basarwa people were notorious for their disobedience and defiance of the Tswana laws, their refusal to vote or to participate in local politics, the nurses construed the survival of the woman to mean that she was bewitched. How else could one explain that she did not die from her terrible wounds. Now they were too scared of her to treat her.

Another wave of pain hit her. When the nausea subsided her husband was before her eyes. The image kept on coming back. It flooded her mind with its horrible truth. She clutched the mattress and closed her eyes. His body was so black, so stiff. He almost looked blue. There was a car; the headlights were on; she was lying in the full glare next to him. There were so many legs, hands, voices, and her pain was harrowing, but she knew the Kgosi was there as well. He had never come to her home before, but she now remembered him barking orders. They were all around her husband.

Then, just before they lifted her up, she saw his face. The dead eyes were staring, glazed blue in the headlights of the car. His whole body was black as soot, his skin burnt by the intense heat of the electric current. Then she, too, saw what others were talking about, their eyes big with horror. The tongue, they were pointing at his tongue. His mouth was open wide and she could see the tongue clearly. It was straight and stiff, an arrow point of pitch-black charcoal sticking out of a gaping hole.

One of the nurses noticed it first and came running, screaming into the office. When she had passed her bed, she noticed water on the floor, she said, so she turned around to look and realised the patient's waters had broken. Yes, she was having contractions, she was definitely in labour.

The doctor was in a state of shock, her hands trembled as she listened to the baby's heartbeat through her stethoscope. Was the patient aware of what was happening? She had to be in so much pain anyway, that she might not even have distinguished this pain from the other. How far advanced could the pregnancy be? She did not have an unusually large abdomen, but then again, her body was in such a state, and she was lying on her back in a deep bed. Some nurses stood around in frozen horror. She sent them away, anxious to protect the woman in this painful moment from their stares. The woman's eyes were locked on the ceiling, her hands clutching the sheets. You could not tell if she was aware of her surroundings, except for the writhing movements when the pain became too much.

To prepare her for the birth the matron tried to bring her knees up, bend her legs, but the skin burst as she and the doctor tried to do so, and pieces of blistered, pus-covered skin came off on their hands. They were both trembling, had tears in their eyes. For the doctor this was the worst thing she had ever experienced. She was torn between feelings of deep panic and terrible sorrow.

She was grateful to see that things were happening fast. She might have to use the suction pump to help the mother, she decided. There was no way they could manoeuvre her or touch her body any further. She could see she was dilating. The matron and a midwife whom they had called in had regained their composure. They were discussing how long it might take, when the matron caught sight of some nurses peeping round the corner. She barked them away angrily: "What do you expect her to give birth to, you stupid, backward girls!"

One face after the other swam into her mind. Were they all dead? Was her boy dead? She imagined him inside a huge fire, parts of him already burning embers, parts charcoal. Where were her mother, her aunt? Was she the only one alive? If that was so, she did not want to live. Yet she wanted her boy to live, and she wanted to see him grow. How much pain did she not have to endure when he was born, to keep him inside so that he could be born in a hospital, not in the vehicle in front of Moruti? Now she was the one in the hospital and she could not find him.

The pain blurred her thoughts, she closed her eyes. Maybe if she could go, if she could let go, let the pain take her along, if she could swim in it, she might find the others.

It was coming. The mother arched her back, she was almost fainting with pain. The little body slid onto the sheet, onto the doctor's open palms. It shone soft and pink next to the sooty skin of the mother's legs. It was a boy. The matron picked him up, lifted him high, for the mother to see. He started crying. He was tiny, premature, but he might live.

They stood at the mother's side while the midwife cut the cord and cleaned her up. The mother's eyes were fixed on the little body in the matron's arms. She now looked straight at the baby, and tears ran over the broken skin of her face. Through her own sobs, the matron held him upright and turned him round, so she could see that it was a boy. She turned to wrap a cloth around the baby. When she looked back, the mother's body had gone still, her unblinking eyes, turned towards the ceiling, were fixed in a glassy gaze into the unknown. The corners of her mouth had settled into something between a sob and a smile.

SIXTEEN

# The plastic wreaths

They were taking him back to lie with his own kind.

The sun was barely out, but the people on the backs of the pick-up trucks already had to squint their eyes against the sharp light as they held on to the railings and each other on the sandy trail winding through the huts. The second bakkie carried the coffin, with all the oldest women of the family huddled beside it in the back. People had come from all over the district. There were quite a few faces that Mmamoruti, who was cramped in among some women on the back of the third bakkie, did not know. In times like these, she usually had to give up her seat next to her husband who was driving the first bakkie, to make space for the church elders and closest relatives of the deceased.

They were taking a different route today, going north in the direction of old D'Kar, near to the old ruins. It was much harder to dig a grave there than at the regular burial site on the dune, south of the village, where everyone these days buried their dead. The gravediggers, mostly grandsons and nephews of the old man, had dug non-stop for two days and even through most of the previous night, to chisel down deep enough in the limestone formation beneath the top layer of sand.

Every single bakkie that could be commandeered for the occasion was crammed full. The Jimmy family was large and widespread, so there were more vehicles than usual, and no one had to follow the procession on foot. Some of the vehicles must have come from the farms surrounding D'Kar, others from Ghanzi. In some cases it was difficult to recognise the origin of these beat-up old vehicles, some held together with steel wire, some obviously composed of bits and pieces plundered from old wrecks so that a once-white body now sported red doors. The bakkies were rattling and grinding their gears, going as slowly as possible with their orange hazard lights blinking in unison, to show solidarity and demand respect from bystanders among the huts. But the noise of the engines and the creaking of the old springs could not drown out the sad singing of the packed mourners. The women held the highest notes in thin, almost metallic voices, their bodies swaying against each other as they moved to the rhythm or were thrown against the railings by the movement of wheels sliding in the thick sand. It was a beloved song, brought home by the school children:

> I'm going home, going home, 'ing home
> I'm going home, to die no more ...
> to die no more, die no more ...

The people had long stopped burying their dead at their homes, since they could no longer move away as they would once have done, leaving the body in a sitting position in the grave with some food and weapons to accompany it to the afterlife. Moving away was not only getting too complicated, but their old burial practices were frowned upon by other people and even their own young ones. One had to use at least a coffin these days, for it was important that someone's funeral showed that he was a worthy and equal citizen. The Kgalagadi, Tswana and Herero funerals in particular were grand, costly affairs, where Death was treated with the gravest respect, in an effort to control the power of the dead spirits on the lives of the living. Funeral practices were nowadays also affected by the "fridge" at the hospital in Ghanzi, which took away all excuses for a cheap and hasty burial, since it gave people more time to find family members all over the district and to collect donations.

Soon after the "fridge" was opened, there were more corpses in the little building than it could handle, and a special attendant had to be hired to rotate the bodies during the day. This meant that one could easily find a family member thawing outside on the porch, waiting to be exchanged with a frozen body inside.

That the person had been dead and frozen for quite a while, did not dampen the enthusiasm for big funerals. Even if it meant feeding everyone who attended, even those who only came for the sunset service each night of the week leading up to the funeral. Apart from the closest family members who usually moved in with the family and stayed for weeks before and after the event, the bereaved family had to contend with large crowds, for the first sign of death in a family usually was the huge carcass of a cow hanging from a branch in the yard, and four or five massive cast-iron pots on a fire.

Yes, if you were anybody at all, you had to have a big funeral, even if it meant that the costs put your poor relatives into debt for the rest of their lives.

The local district officials found the traditional Bushmen burial practices appalling, so the Welfare Department had started to help educate the Basarwa to bury their dead in a more acceptable way. They supplied coffins to the very poor and made sure that bereaved families received the proper white and black cloth for clothing the body. Often they would send one of the officials to join the family for a day and night before the funeral, to make sure no details were forgotten. Such as the big zinc baths with water where people were to wash Death from their hands after returning from the grave. Only after washing your hands could one start talking about the dead one, and that was when speeches about the life and the cause of death of the deceased, and the happenings around the death, were made at the home of the departed person.

At D'Kar a Bushman funeral offered the Kgosi another opportunity to educate: "Today I could see that the people of D'Kar are learning something, even if it is taking time. We had not been informed of the names of the bearers beforehand, but we have to praise this family that at least the body was laid out in the proper way ..." All this while the Bushman family under scrutiny sat completely expressionless and quiet, almost as if they were not aware that they were the ones under discussion.

This quietness and acceptance of death mystified the local Batswana and Baherero who could not understand at all the lack of outward emotion shown by the Bushmen. Surely there was something unnatural if even a small child could stand next to its mother's grave without shedding a tear? For this reason, Bushman funerals were often haunted by priests from all kinds of independent churches, clothed in white robes and holding sceptres and passionately demanding an "Amen, Amen!" after each sentence. Almost merciless, they would work on the emotions of their audience, not yielding until at least one or two women were moved to loud crying.

But the old man's family had even more preparation to do for this funeral than the normal family in D'Kar. They made sure they were attending to the smallest detail, because they knew they would be watched very closely. They didn't want to give anybody an excuse to accuse them afterwards of not knowing the proper way, or of being too poor and too backward to know how to conduct a funeral for a white person. Furthermore, even if Oom Jimmy's own family members in Ghanzi had long broken contact with him, one never knew if they might pitch up at his funeral.

So, they bought him a varnished coffin with chrome handles, unlike the simple pressed-wood coffins that were normally distributed by the council. They even ordered plastic wreaths for the grave, through the wife of the general dealer in Ghanzi. She made sure they were delivered on time from Gobabis, brought by the petrol tanker on its six-hour journey once a week between Gobabis and Ghanzi. The wreaths arrived two days before the funeral, and someone had specially driven to Ghanzi the day before yesterday to collect them; they were too precious to be sent by an ordinary lift.

Everything had to be just right. The first session of the funeral started this morning, at sunrise at Oom Jimmy's compound, and they were now on their way to continue the proceedings at the grave. Hereafter, everyone would go back to the house to take part in the final ceremony where the situation around his death would be discussed and the Kgosi would get his turn to speak.

During the early morning ceremony at the house, all the mourners entered the hut of Oom Jimmy and Ntcisa to pay their final respects. After the long line of people had shuffled in and out in a kind of loop, the coffin was brought outside and balanced on empty paraffin tins and chairs. Tshabu then screwed the lid on in front of everybody and all stood closer to the coffin for the first prayers and a short message by Moruti. All through the ceremony, the wreaths lay stacked on the one side, little plastic domes with purple, blue and white plastic flowers inside. Mmamoruti was secretly amused by how the children walked around the mound of colour in wonder and the dogs sniffed at the shiny surfaces with suspicion, while the adults were droning and singing in the background.

Most of the mourners had by now arrived, those who had not already been there since the previous evening and who had not stayed the night. Still none of his white relatives had arrived, but it was still early, they might come later, Mmamoruti had heard Esta and Kelebetse say to each other.

He must have been almost ninety when he died. Yet even he didn't know his exact age. But his age had never really been of any importance, and earlier, whenever anyone wanted to know how old he was, he would point out his age mates among the white farmers with whom he had grown up. Most of them, even Oom Fanus who had been eighty-two years old, had long since passed away, so there was now no way of knowing how old Oom Jimmy was when he had laid down his head seven days ago. Mmamoruti smiled when she remembered the last time she had asked him how many children he had had. Even that he could not always remember exactly. At least today would shed some light on that, she thought. In the course of his life, he had taken five Bushman wives. But already this morning Mmamoruti had her first surprise when the sixth place in the row of pallbearers was taken up by a very dark, tall and proud Herero son, as indicated by the funeral pamphlet Q'ane had typed and copied for the occasion. The other pallbearers, one son from each of the five official Bushman wives, ranged from about sixty to thirty years, but the resemblance among them was obvious. Everybody now moved towards the waiting vehicles, and the coffin was lifted onto the back of one, balanced on some old tyres to buffer it against the bumps in the road. Two of the sons cupped their hands together and bowed low, so that the old women could step on their hands to lift themselves into the open pick-up and sit around the coffin. The pallbearers then also got onto Moruti's vehicle that would go in front, so that they would be ready to take the coffin off again when they reached the grave.

When the procession left for the grave, Esta and some of the neighbouring women stayed behind to stir the pots and to keep the water boiling for the tea. Soon the whole procession would return, and after they had gone through the speeches, the collection for contributions towards the cost of the funeral and the introduction of the family members of the deceased, everybody would be served with a heaped plate of *seswaa* and samp. Yes, Esta thought, the ceremony at the house was also the moment most people were waiting for, the moment of truth. All children from present as well as former relationships that the deceased had had, would be called forward and put on display, and introduced by names and history by an uncle or close relative. This was sometimes a time of revelation, but also of reconciliation. Those who didn't want to be associated with each other before, found it hard to openly deny their connectedness, especially after they had been facing each other across an open grave. That was also why she was hoping that some of her white cousins or other relatives would come. Not only had they worked hard to prepare everything, but maybe her father's death would bring them closer to each other?

The children, who did not go along to the grave, were enjoying the sudden freedom and were releasing their pent-up energy among the chairs and cold heaps of ash from last night's fires. They had to be told off by the women each time they ran too close to the fire and kicked up sand around the pots of food. But they let them play on. Up till now, for the whole, long week, they were expected to watch from a distance, dead quiet.

"Don't make yourselves dirty! Stay away from the ash!" Esta suddenly remembered about their role in the ceremony afterwards and shouted towards the riotous bundle of children. Once the people had come back from the grave, the children of the deceased were called forward and gathered in a little group among the adults, to be admired, praised and even touched. Their mothers would be pointed out too, and a short history of the relationship to the deceased would be given by a relative.

But even though the children had to be quiet all week, they had been watching, and observing. Sometimes all one could see of them were pairs of large, questioning eyes peeping through the sticks of the cooking shelter or from around a corner. Last night, when all the adults were doing the night wake around the fires, they were huddled in between their mothers, or lying a little distance away in their blankets, waking up all through the night, startled by a new song or passionate prayer coming from the group of adults. At first light some of them were still lying in their blankets, when the first grown-ups started to shuffle towards the hut of the deceased. One by one the grown-ups had disappeared from the children's sight as they bent down and stepped into the dark hut. The grown-ups were mostly also still wrapped in their blankets. They had been singing all night around the fires outside, which were specially made to keep the mourners warm. From time to time one would rest briefly, by toppling over right where they were sitting for a few minutes' sleep on the cold sand. Nobody dreamed of going home. The fires consumed more firewood than a single family would do in many months. But the glow on the many faces, the cold on their backs and the weary singing in the dead of night, when all the world was silent and only the stars' stark white light reminded them of the depth of the darkness surrounding them, brought a companionship and comfort beyond words. Once or twice in the night, sweet cups of tea were passed around to warm up the cold bodies and oil the voices.

Mmamoruti, too, had fallen asleep while singing around the fire, taking comfort from the shape and feeling of the bodies next to her. In the morning, after they had shaken out their blankets and once again were given a cup of tea, she joined the procession entering the hut, wrapped in a blanket against the chill, her head respectfully covered for the occasion.

Inside the hut, Ntcisa, the old man's young wife, had sat next to the corpse on the floor right through the night, supported by her mother and an elderly aunt. Ntcisa's face looked drawn and tired. The three were accompanied only by a small candle, still burning on a heap of wax on the sand floor of the hut. A sheet fastened by clothes pegs was hung over a piece of string spanning the room to form a curtain which separated them from the body.

Mmamoruti slowly moved past Oom Jimmy's tiny brown wife and her old companions, and extended a hand of comfort to the three quiet women. Someone moved the sheet curtain away. At her feet lay an old, white man in his coffin, with only the face left uncovered among layers of cloth. The old, white face among the typical contents of the Bushman hut – a pile of clothes, a bag of mealie meal, tattered old shoes and a beaded skin bag hanging from the mud and stick wall, moved her beyond words. To her left a flattened mound of moist earth, still covered with pepper-tree leaves to keep the flies away and prevent smell, indicated where the body had been kept cool since it was brought from the "fridge" until it was put into the coffin last night.

She looked at how the grey-streaked scraps of reddish beard had been lovingly combed and lay in thin strands on top of the cloths wrapped around his neck. His thin hair, which he had always worn long in his neck, was folded around his face and ears, a few wisps neatly combed onto his forehead. The lines around his eyes and thin mouth and on his forehead had settled into little furrows in the waxen, cold face. In the flickering candlelight the eyes were sunken, dark patches, the skin a light purple, already turning black in places.

Mmamoruti left the hut disturbed by feelings of immense sorrow mixed with pride and admiration for this old man.

The funeral procession had now reached the graveyard. The row of bakkies fanned out and each one tried to find a parking space among the thorny scrub. Women were readjusting their skirts and headscarves, men were off-loading the shovels and two of Oom Jimmy's teenage daughters carried the wreaths. The pallbearers first helped the old women to get off the back, then lifted the coffin off and led the procession slowly into the small encampment. The women followed, humming a familiar funeral tune "Hmm hmmmmm, hmm hmmmmm ..." Not far from the place two tall palm trees indicated the presence of an old ruin and the remains of an old dam built with chiselled limestone. Close to the graveyard the elevated edges of an old well were still visible.

Eventually more than a hundred people squeezed into the small fenced paddock where the grave had been prepared. They were careful not to step on or disturb the few other graves, several of them of small children, already there. The well-worn handmade cement headstones with their roughly chiselled edges were cracked by many years of sun and rain. While waiting for the people to settle, Moruti stood reading the names on the other tombstones. They carried only names, no other details – *Ferdinand du Preez, born 1855, died 1912*, and *Anna Catherina Botha, born De Witt, 15 January 1870 – 12 June 1905*.

Some of the children buried in the small graves had lived only a few months. *Davina Elizabeth Coetzee, born 12 December 1911, died 4 January 1912*. Another baby shared the date of death with what must have been his mother. *Petrus Johannes Botha, born and died 12 June 1905*. The graves were overgrown with tall weeds and the letters were worn and difficult to read.

The family members now crowded around the open grave, holding

179

on to each other. Oom Jimmy's grave had been dug in a corner of the fenced-off piece of land, a little removed from the other graves. Debe and Tshabu jumped into the open grave, holding their hands up to receive the coffin which was lowered down onto their outstretched palms. The coffin was balanced on two ropes by the bearers and many hands were extended to steady it at the top and bottom ends. Once they had put the coffin down, the two men were pulled out of the grave by Moruti and Kelebetse. The final jerk to lift them out of the grave created a shuffle and the crowd was pushed backwards as the men struggled to regain their balance. This caused muffled laughs from a few youngsters.

The women had already burst into loud song and were lining up, each to toss her handful of sand onto the coffin. The sombre row passed the edge of the grave to where one of the gravediggers was holding out a shovel full of sand, so that all who passed could take a fistful to toss over the coffin down below. The small children who came to the graveyard were also brought closer to grab a handful, and then gently prodded to release that sand onto the coffin, listening to the hollow resonance from within the grave. Ntcisa took her baby's hand, filled it with sand and emptied the little hand above the coffin. It landed with a soft thud. She kept her eyes lowered all the time. Ncaoka then moved closer with her baby on her hip. She pulled out her breast, squeezed some milk from it and, half hanging over the open grave, let it drip on the lid of the coffin. Almost as if she was trying to re-establish the ties that were cut off by Death, Moruti thought, as if she wanted to say, "No matter who you will be now where you are going, you too were once somebody's child ..."

Nqaba started to cry hysterically by the sight of this and collapsed. She wailed loudly and kicked in the sand. She was sharply reprimanded by one of the older sons. "How can Moruti go on if you make such a noise? Behave now!"

So distracted was everybody with this disturbance, that they never heard the vehicle approaching. It took a while for anyone to notice the two white women who had arrived from the opposite direction. They had stopped their bakkie behind the last vehicles and had quietly walked towards the group at the grave. It was Martha Vermaak and her daughter. The old woman was supported by the arm of the younger. A small shiver ran through the group of people as they nudged each other and pointed out the newcomers. Both wore floral dresses and sandals and their heads were bare. The old woman, though wrinkled and stooped, was still strong and her red hair, like Oom Jimmy's, showed grey only here and there. For a moment the women almost forgot to sing, the men with the shovels to fill the grave. Reluctantly the people tore their eyes from the two women when Moruti started reading from the Bible: "Let us read from Psalm 91 ... I will say of the Lord ... Surely He will save you from the fowler's snare, and from the deadly pestilence. He will cover you with His feathers, and under His wings you will find refuge ... you will not fear the terror of night; nor the arrow that flies by day ..."

The men fetched the shovels and took turns to fill the grave. A row of volunteers waited behind each shovelling man to take their turn. Now and then they wiped the sweat from their brows. All the while the women raised their shrill voices with renewed energy. Everyone was singing vigorously now, turning their heads away to avoid the dust blowing from the grave. Some women held their doeks in front of their faces.

The two white women remained outside the fence, and Martha lightly held on to the top strand of the barbed wire fence. Their faces were expressionless. Only a few children occasionally still peered at them. Song followed song, growing stronger as the hollow sound of the spadefuls of sand hitting the coffin grew duller.

> Rest in peace, beloved, rest in peace
> Even the shadow of death we shall not fear.

Nobody noticed that the two white women had turned and were slowly walking back to their vehicle. They left without a word to anyone. The plastic wreaths, still covered in their plastic wrapping, were waiting unseen at the side to be put on top of the mound when it was all over.

SEVENTEEN

# Someone's war

The Kombi's headlights fall on the ox-wagons parked in the yard, next to the tall aloe that guards the gate. Braam leans over to me and whispers, "Are you sure this is the place? Did they really say we could all stay here? Just look at the ox-wagons!"

I feel nervous. Maybe I should have told them. We had stopped at a road-house about an hour ago, and bought food for everyone. It was already almost midnight and we were all feeling tired. "It's getting too late to continue," Braam had said as we approached a filling station on the road. "Can't we find a place to phone a guest-house so that we can break the journey in the next town, in Vanrhynsdorp?"

We are on our way back from Cape Town, where we attended an exhibition in the South African National Gallery. Quite a few people from D'Kar had gone with us, and we met several other Bushmen from Namibia as well as from elsewhere in South Africa. We had gone to see an exhibition about the history of the Bushmen which was causing quite a stir. We had travelled non-stop for two days, to be in time for the opening, where the different Bushmen groups were given a chance to make statements about their situation today. The D'Kar Bushmen were eager to learn more about their past, especially about the extermination of their ancestors on South African soil. Then we had spent two days at the exhibition, listening to speeches, attending meetings and discussions, and now we are all heading home. It has been an immensely packed, emotional but rewarding experience.

"We are a group of twelve people from Botswana. Do you perhaps have accommodation for us for tonight?" I had picked the first name and number from the list of guest-houses.

"Sure we do! You may come from Botswana, but you're not a stranger.

I can hear that lovely Afrikaans accent. You are most welcome." The voice was very friendly.

When I hung up, I felt a little uncomfortable. Should I have explained that we were not all Afrikaners? Don't be silly, I argued with myself. This is the new South Africa. A business like that must surely be open for all? And besides, we've just seen in the exhibition how this whole area used to be the Bushmen's land before the white settlers moved in. The least people can do now is give accommodation to a few of them. In my thoughts I was quite brave: If these people are not ready for that, I decided, it's high time they looked facts in the face.

The little voice inside me was smothered by the sight of the waiting hamburger and chips. We had to push on.

Now, there's no turning back. Braam parks the Kombi in the yard and we are ready to get out. But a white man rushes out and indicates that we must remain where we are. He's hanging onto two snarling black Dobermanns on a leash. They bark ferociously, straining the chain.

"I'm not getting out here," Xuse announces. "Those dogs want to eat us!"

The guest-house owner beckons to Braam and me, who are sitting in the front, that we can now get out. Mmapula lies on my lap and I wake her up.

"Let the other people just stay in the Kombi a little longer," the man says, looking in through the open window.

We slowly lower ourselves out of the vehicle, but I can feel my knees become jelly at the sight of the two sets of vicious dogs' teeth. The man's wife has joined him.

"You are the Afrikaans woman I talked to," she says. "I can see that. Look at the lovely blue eyes both you and your husband have. No wonder she has such beautiful eyes too and look at the blond hair!" The wife smiles and pats Mmapula's sleepy face.

The husband remains reserved, though, and sternly says, "We need to be honest with you. We are a bit upset that you didn't tell us that you had coloured people with you. You've tricked us into a situation where we were forced to make certain decisions. We've given you our word, so we won't go back on that, and we'll not send you away, but we needed to change our plans a little."

"I did not think it was necessary to say, honestly ..." I start explaining meekly. A slight sigh escapes his mouth.

"Now if you would let your group out of the Kombi one by one and have them walk in single file, I'll lock the dogs in and we can discuss the situation over a cup of coffee. Please go past the first building and go around to the house at the back."

"Let's just go," I whisper to Braam.

"Wait," he answers. "The next place is two hours away. The group won't be able to hold out that long. Let's see what solutions they offer."

Inside the main house, the Bushmen scurry around excitedly with their mugs of coffee and biscuits. The house is full of antique furniture and old farming appliances, the kitchen shelves are lined with colourful bottles of home-made preserves. Some of them recognise things they saw on farms in Ghanzi when they were young.

"Come here, Mmapula, look! This is what they used to churn the butter with," Turu says. "When everyone still made cream to take to Gobabis, before it became so dry in Ghanzi."

"Have you seen the rooms we've got?" Xuse was bright-eyed. "Each one has his own soap and there's a little chocolate on the pillow for everyone!"

While our hosts pass the coffee around, Braam talks to Debe, softly, on the side. He is the only one in the group who has travelled in the world enough to be able to judge this situation. Ever since Q'ane's death especially, he has taken on more and more responsibility and has become a strong leader.

"Debe, what do you think? I do not feel good about this place. Shall we not just drink our coffee and move on? It might be a little tiring, but ..."

"No, man, what's wrong? Let's just stay. We are tired and this place is perfect."

Debe turns around and starts talking to Kelebetse next to him, showing him some photographs on the wall of a historic hunting expedition in this area.

We are stuck. We'll have to see this thing through.

The woman and her husband have started to question Turu and the others about the work they are doing in D'Kar. They tell them about the church, the projects, the pre-school and the art exhibitions. Turu happily chants the names of the overseas countries she has been to. Behind us there is excited chatter coming from the bathroom where three girls have entered the shower together and are splashing away. Nervous about the reaction of our hosts, I walk over to ask them to be a bit quieter and remind them to dry the floor.

"Mamma, can't I go to sleep now, please?"

The man leads me and Mmapula to our room. Unlike the others, our room is outside the house, in a building at the other end of the garden.

When I return to the house, I notice that most of the Bushmen have already disappeared into their rooms. The last ones are in the shower. It is well past midnight now. Our hosts have prepared a second cup of coffee for the four of us. "We phoned the road-house after you had left," the woman suddenly says. "They told us you were not all white. So we decided to put the Bushmen in our own home and not in the guestrooms. It will be bad for our business if people knew your group had stayed here." She looks me straight in the eye: "You should really have been honest."

She talks to me like a mother disappointed in her teenager's behaviour. Her husband seems to feels a bit more in control now. "Your people say you are a minister doing development work," he says to Braam. "I admire you for working so hard for the purpose you have obviously chosen," he says in a firm voice. "It is just a pity that all your work will be in vain. The souls of these people can't be saved. They're not chosen; they are not even truly human. Why do you waste your time and energy on them while there are so many of the true children of God, your own people, who need you? You shouldn't turn your back on your own, you know."

We are both dying to go to our room, but Braam tries to argue from the Bible, that all people are equal before God. But it is an argument that goes nowhere. It soon becomes clear that this man has created his own Bible; he admits that he has even thrown out certain chapters. Braam gives up. "Can we please pay now?" he asks. "We'd like to leave very early tomorrow morning."

As he signs the cheque, the man leans forward eagerly and looks at his signature. "I knew it! I have been trying to place you all evening! You were a chaplain in the army in the north of Namibia! We were in the same battalion!"

Braam looks cornered. "Yes, I was there," he says weakly. "But it is a time I would rather forget."

"Yes, me too. Pity we lost that war, isn't it? Such a humiliation, and a victory for Satan! We were defending the last bastion of Christianity on this continent. Now the forces of evil will spill over us unless we rid ourselves of the unpure."

Braam and I hurry to our room. I am anxious. How can we trust this man? What if he attacks us all in our sleep? Who does he consider to be the "unpure"?

We lie in the dark, whispering not to wake Mmapula. I think about the sign I had seen behind the door, when I had hung my clothes on the hook: *All labour used to maintain and clean this guest-house is done by members of the Volk.* Some of Oom Jimmy's grandchildren also have blue eyes, I think and smile.

"If only he hadn't been with me in the army. That really adds insult to injury," Braam says after a while. "And the bitter irony that he thinks I was helping him fight his miserable war! And to think how many Bushmen helped him fight that stupid war and now they cannot even enter his heaven!"

He turns on his side, resting on his elbow. "Do you remember what that Bushman had told us in that little community near Tsintsabis, the one we visited together when I was in the army?"

I remember. We had visited a sickly and impoverished group of Bushmen in northern Namibia, who lived near the army base where Braam was stationed for most of the week. I had been given a house in the nearest town, granted permission, as the wife of an officer, to live among the families of members of the Permanent Force. Every Friday evening till Sunday morning early, Braam was granted permission to visit me and the two children we had then, one a baby, one a toddler. He had just finished his studies and had to do his two-year military service, like every other white male in the country. We had been married for four years. As chaplain they gave him the freedom to serve whoever he thought needed him, including the local communities outside the army. The people he had taken me to visit that one Saturday were the families of the famous Bushman trackers employed by the South African army in the seventies and early eighties to hunt down SWAPO insurgents.

"The army doctor refused to work with this little community," Braam told me at the time. "He said they were too dirty and he wasn't going so risk going out of base camp to be blown up by land-mines to serve people who weren't officially under his jurisdiction."

We drove out on the gravel road, fringed by thorny bush and clusters of palm trees, signs of flood plains and abundant water in earlier times. Now the area was dusty and there were no signs of surface water. It was the traditional territory of the Haix'om Bushmen, Braam explained. I thought about how it could be possible for anyone to penetrate the dense bush around us, let alone follow the tracks of people on foot. The gravel road showed marks of the mine-sweeper that had gone ahead of us that morning.

I went with Braam to see what medical services were needed so that we might try to find help somewhere else. The plan was that I would approach the wives of the Permanent Force for help. It was around midday when we arrived. People were lying under the shade of a big camelthorn. One or two army tents were erected inside an area protected with sand-bags, the rest of the houses, loosely scattered around the centre, were shabby grass huts and shelters of plastic and cardboard. Garbage was strewn all over the place and children were playing with tin cans and shattered glass. The sound of cicadas pierced the air and flies crawled over my children's faces. Little did I know at that time how similar the scene was to the one I would some years later call my home, D'Kar.

One of the people lying on the sand in the shade was a man missing a leg. He had a piece of soiled cloth tied around the end of the stump, just above the knee. He had more wounds on his arms and chest which might have been caused by shrapnel. His sunken eyes told us he had been suffering a lot of pain, probably for quite a while already, caused by his badly infected wounds.

"You were a soldier when this happened," Braam said, "therefore, surely the army should take responsibility for you? Let me help you file a complaint. I assure you these officers will get into big trouble for neglecting you like this."

For a moment the man's dull eyes opened wide. "I cannot do that," he said. "They did take me to hospital. How can I now turn against those who have come to help my people fight the war against the black people? Our land has been taken from us, and the only way we can get it back is to fight with the Boers. They have come to help us fight our war."

Braam has already fallen asleep next to me. I let myself drift into sleep, exhausted, not only from the long journey, but also from the many thoughts and memories and images that battle each other for space in my head.

Turu and I are walking among strangers from many different countries – tourists, journalists, holiday-makers. We enter a large hall in the National Gallery. Inside, we come across the rest of our group.

To the one side of the room, a group of Bushmen from South Africa is looking at the exhibition, wearing their traditional dress. They look bewildered and cold in their scanty skin clothes. A white woman sits next to one of the adults on a bench, holding his hand possessively.

"Are they crazy?" I had heard Debe say to Kelebetse when we came in. "This is not the place for such clothes. They look ridiculous."

"Yes," Kelebetse said. "They make us all look like fools."

There were many expectations before we came to Cape Town. "Where else can we learn about the things that happened to our people," Debe had said. "Nowhere in books can we find our history."

Now we are here and the exhibition is a bewildering, whirling mass of images. We are all silent. We huddle together, milling around in our little group.

In the first hall there's a replica of the Dutch fort built by the first settlers in the Cape. Guns point outwards from all five of its corners. All around the fort fibreglass casts of bodies – Bushmen bodies – are strewn in grotesque piles, genitals exposed, faces distorted, museum code numbers visible. From the walls Bushmen faces peer – images of people of yesterday and today. There are enlargements of photographs of body parts of Bushman used as ornaments: breasts made into tobacco pouches; shrunken, dried heads used as paperweights.

The next wall sports rows of pictures of faces of living people. "Look, there is old Sophie!" Turu gasps. "Where did they get her photograph? Her people don't even know that they have her in here!"

We move into the next hall. It is bare, except for the framed photographs on the wall: pictures of Bushmen drinking, dancing to the music of cheap radios, some just sitting, staring, others fighting. Some in army uniforms.

Turu pulls at my arm and points to the floor. The entire space is covered with enlarged newspaper and other clippings. They had printed the images onto the linoleum tiles to cover the floor. We recognise the photos of the prisoners the Bleeks had studied. These books, published in the early 1900s in Cape Town, are also in our own library at the Cultural Centre in D'Kar. We recognise the faces of the informants of these late-nineteenth-century researchers. A different part of the floor shows photographs of chained, naked Bushmen with questioning, desperate eyes. Another shows a strong, stout Bushman standing next to a white hunter with his one leg on the carcass of an elephant, proudly holding the rifle which caused the animal's end. On the one side of the carcass a heap of tusks are displayed.

Turu gasps. Right under our feet are pictures of Saartjie Baartman from 1810, one displaying her wide, protruding buttocks, another offering a full frontal of the naked woman. We are just about standing on close-ups of her genitals. *The Bushman Venus*, the caption says, *who captivated audiences all over Europe.*

Suddenly, Turu throws her arms around me, clings to me, hangs from my shoulder, her knees clasped around my hips. I hold her frail body and I look down in her anxious eyes.

Her headscarf has disappeared, so has her dress. She is clothed in her traditional skin apron and shoulder bag only, her chest naked, except for the beads around her neck.

"Help me!" she winces, her fingernails digging into my shoulders, my arms. "I cannot walk over the shame of my people!"

As I hold her, lifting her feet off the ground, the images on the walls around us begin to swirl and they become the faces of people I recognise. Some accuse, some plead. There is Q'ane, her youthful face now age-old, her cheeks hollow and her eyes sunken, as she looked in the last days before she died. Her eyes are turned over backwards, as if they are following something. There is X'aga and Cao. They now both have bald heads and swollen faces. They point their fingers in my direction. I see John Battleman, who died last year of cancer, leaving his organisation leaderless and confused. He holds a microphone in his hand, his face pleads passionately.

Then I see him: the guy with the dreadlocks His eyes are red and his mouth is wide open as he shouts, his face is lifted up and distorted and he shakes his fist in rage. It is as if I can see him shaking our fence.

I am still holding Turu. Her hot breath is in my neck and I notice that she is sobbing. Warm tears drip on my chest. She bends her neck to look down at something. Beneath us I notice red blotches on the floor. Blood splashed over the black and white letters on the tiles, over Saartjie's humiliated body. There's blood on my shoes. Then I see footsteps all over the floor, all over the room. Over the newspaper articles are footprints of blood, wherever I and everyone else have stepped.

## NOTE TO MY NCQAKHOE
## AND OTHER FRIENDS IN GHANZI

My life with you inspired the writing of this book. However, apart from where I was given permission by a person to use his or her story in a direct and recognisable way, or in the case of people who have since passed away, the names and events have been changed in such a way that the characters and stories no longer depict real people or true events. The stories are based on a combination of insights and experience garnered during our time together in D'Kar; they should not be read with the purpose of trying to match them to the daily reality of D'Kar or Ghanzi. By transforming everyday reality into a multi-faceted metaphor, I have tried to depict the complex layers of your and our lives together in this tumbling, bewildering transition process – I hope that by opening up these realities to more people, their hearts will be touched as much as mine was.

To give the stories authenticity and to situate them in a local context, I have used the orthography we all helped develop for the Naro language, based on the Setswana/Nguni symbols which are used generally to write your language in Botswana. I have chosen to use the words *Bushmen* and *Basarwa**) when talking about your wider group, not as a statement of my personal preference, but again to be true to the idiom of the place and the people around you.

With this book I want to honour you and thank all of you for allowing me and Braam and our children to share intimately your joys and pain. By doing that you have greatly enriched our lives and our understanding of humanity.

WILLEMIEN LE ROUX
*Shakawe, May 2000*

---

\* The words Bushmen, San or Basarwa refer to the about 100,000 remaining first peoples of southern Africa. However, these people themselves have not yet decided on one name for all of them; and the more or less ten groups prefer to be called by their own names, e.g. Ncqakhoe, Ju/'hoan, !Xõo etc. During a consultative meeting of the Working Group of Indigenous Minorities of Southern Africa (WIMSA) in 1997, however, an agreement to accept the term San as an interim collective name was reached by representatives from several groups.

The Tswana prefix Ba- is used wherever language groups in the plural are indicated, and Mo- whenever a single person is indicated. The prefix Ma- has always been used for indicating groups who are non-Tswana and fall outside the human class. The use of this prefix for indicating the Bushmen has now been banned in Botswana.

## ABOUT THE AUTHOR

Willemien le Roux was born in South Africa. At the age of fourteen, she first settled at D'Kar in Botswana's Ghanzi district with her farmer-turned-missionary father, her mother and four younger siblings. She completed her schooling in Gobabis in Namibia, and studied Communication at the University of Potchefstroom in South Africa before working as a journalist and later in the Potchefstroom Museum. Her pastor husband's work eventually took them back to D'Kar. Here they became involved in relief and development work, and later in the establishment of the Kuru Development Trust,  the creation of a San representative organisation – The First People of the Kalahari – and the regional Working Group of Indigenous Minorities of Southern Africa (WIMSA). Since 1993, the United Nations' Year of Indigenous Peoples, Willemien has helped organise several overseas exhibitions of San art. She currently co-ordinates a community-based oral testimony project involving the documentation of the Ju/'hoan, Khwe, Hai//om and !Xôo peoples' history.

In 1998, after seventeen years at D'Kar, Willemien's husband started a new programme for Kuru in Ngamiland. They now live in Shakawe, on the banks of the Okavango river, in a safari tent under a huge wild fig tree.